A Novel Solution

Sue Clark

SRL PUBLISHING

SRL Publishing Ltd
London
www.srlpublishing.co.uk

First published worldwide by SRL Publishing in 2024

ISBN: 978-1915-073-28-0

1 3 5 7 9 10 8 6 4 2

A CIP catalogue record for this book is available from the
British Library

SRL Publishing is a Climate Positive publisher offsetting more
carbon emissions than it emits.

To my family, with love

One

I had no business being on a bike. Not really. Not with all the Bordeaux I'd been putting away. I was trying to do the right thing, you see, by leaving the Mini on the drive. This was before I twigged trying to do the right thing was exactly where I'd been going so wrong.

Not hungover. Just a bit fuzzy headed. And I had to go shopping or face yet another banquet of peanut butter from the spoon. My shopping list wasn't long. White bread and cheap, Day-Glo lemon curd – in tribute to remembered Sunday teatimes round the fire – seven ready meals, seven family-size packets of posh crisps, a slab of Cheddar and a double pack of cream crackers. As an afterthought, I threw a bag of easy peelers in the trolly. No sense in going down with scurvy on top of everything else.

Shopping done and scary robot voice on the checkout braved, I set off for home, carrier bags swinging merrily on the handlebars. I don't remember hitting the pothole but I do remember flying through space and seconds later looking up at two strangers, a salty liquid dribbling from my mouth.

In A&E, it wasn't exactly *Code red. Adult female,* like it

is on the telly. More like, *Take a seat for a few hours over by the machine that, despite its impressive light display, can dispense only a cup with no drink, or a drink with no cup, never the two together, until someone shouts a name that approximates to yours.*

I sat, shopping bags round my feet, blotting my mouth with toilet paper. And I sat. Next to me, a woman was holding a paper cup of warm tea, or maybe coffee, to the side of her face, every so often letting out a low moan. Opposite, a boy of about nine in full footie kit, was waiting with his mum, his knees one part blood to three parts mud.

After an eon or two, they sent me to X-ray. After that, I waited some more, now promoted to a cubicle. I was thinking of bunking off to lick my wounds at home, when a cheerful Ozzie doctor, who couldn't have been more of a cliché if he'd had a didgeridoo under one arm and a wallaby under the other, whooshed back the curtains.

'G'day,' he said, voice too loud, teeth too white. 'Had a shufti at your piccies, Pat …'

'Trith,' I lisped.

'Come again? Whatever – upshot is, looks a lot worse than it is. No fractures. Superficial cuts and bruises only. You've got off lightly. Except for this.' He dug into the pocket of his scrubs and dropped something into my palm. 'Pressie for you. Got shook loose when you face-planted the old tarmac, I reckon. Don't thank me. Thank Sally in the Rad Department. She found it kicking about on the floor. You're lucky.'

I looked at the little yellow dental crown. It was tiny. Yet, as I poked around in my mouth with my tongue, the gap felt enormous.

'Thankth,' I said, feeling the blood trickling down my chin.

2

Don't she make you wanna shake her till her fillings pop like champagne corks? Timid Trish, that was her playground nickname and nothing much has changed since schooldays. About as assertive as a wet flannel. Five hours! Five hours she sits in A&E without a word of complaint alongside the muddy schoolboy and the groaning woman. From time to time she tries to catch the eye of someone in uniform scooting past, but it seems she's wearing her invisibility cloak today.

What was that Ozzie doc thinking? Broken arm, mangled collar bone or mashed-up nose: no charge, thank you very much, NHS. Loose dental crown, only wants bunging back in with a squirt of superglue: a hundred smackers, if you please. Don't call that lucky, lucky, lucky! Still, as mentioned before, Trish ain't one to kick up a fuss.

I got home and went straight into hibernation, waiting for the swelling and bruising to go down, and scabs to form on the grazes. I've never been what you'd call a beauty. Best I've ever been able to manage is curvy. But I figured going out in public, looking more battered than a cod fillet, would cost innocent kids years of future therapy. I stamped about the house, crunching on ibuprofen, black half-moons under both eyes, lips thick and purple, smile gappy.

Not that I did much smiling.

As the days went on, that gap in my teeth bothered me more and more. My tongue wouldn't leave the flipping thing alone and salty ready meals made it sore. Got an emergency appointment at the dental surgery. Replacing the crown took a matter of minutes, though it cost an arm and a leg. I joked to the dentist she didn't need to bother with an anaesthetic, because one glance at the bill and I'd be out cold. She looked at me like I was off my chump.

Perhaps I was. Who could blame me?

In spite of the damage to my bank account, it was good to be out of the house at last. There was a fresh, new-cut grass smell in the air. Spring was well on its way and, for the first time since my world had begun to crumble, I felt more like myself. What, after all, was there for me to stay at home for? Exactly. Time to stop moping and fill the rest of my day with stimulating and meaningful activity. The only question was, what?

All of a sudden, I had a flashback to what I'd said to Stephen on that last day. Though I'd said it without thinking, now I did come to think of it, the idea might actually have legs. It'd give me a purpose, maybe even some dosh: two things I desperately needed.

I performed a sharp U-turn, causing a minor pedestrian pile-up outside the Kwikimart, and headed towards a place I hoped would have some of the answers to my problems. Unfortunately for me, it was Tiny Tots Time at the library. Not what I had in mind. Instead of a place of calm and literary mindfulness, I found myself in a carpeted pit among a group of squirming toddlers.

If they weren't running in circles making aeroplane noises, they were laying on the floor screaming, or squatting suspiciously quiet in a corner. Doing anything, in fact, other than listening to the librarian read them the story of Deirdre, the baby dinosaur, and her friend, Terence, the pterodactyl chick. I could only admire the way she soldiered on, as junior Armageddon raged around her. At last the mayhem ended and the families began to wend their ways home. The librarian came over.

'Wish more grannies would set a good example like you,' she said, pushing reddish pre-Raphaelite – is that the word? – curls behind her ears, cheeks going pink. 'I'm sure if the adults would sit quietly, the children wouldn't get so hyper.'

A granny! Me! I was shocked. I was wearing my Fat Face denim jacket for flip's sake!

'You got that wrong,' I said. 'Probably I look older than I am because of this.' I pointed to my beat-up face. 'I never learned to ride a bike proper, you see. Bride of Frankenstein isn't my normal look.'

'Anywhoo,' the librarian said, backing away, looking like she wished she was anywhere but chatting to this mad woman. 'You'll have to excuse me. I have some urgent indexing to attend to.'

'I'm not a granny. I'm a writer,' I blurted out.

You should have seen the transformation in the librarian! She halted, all smiles. 'A real-life author. How exciting. If there's anything I can do to help, please ask. Anything. There's nothing I like better than talking books and writers.'

Did she ever! Though a shy person, the librarian – Felicity she said her name was – came to life talking about books.

'How long have you been an author, if you don't mind my asking?' she asked, shadowing me as I wandered the shelves.

I glanced up at the library clock. 'Coming up for … thirty-five minutes.'

'Oh!' she said, disappointed. 'And what kind of books are you going to write?'

Realising how little thought I'd given to what I'd actually write about, I said the first thing that came into my head. 'Hopefully the sort that make loads of money.'

I could tell from Felicity's face, this was not the right answer. Nevertheless, she was helpful. Almost too helpful, giving me a guided tour of what was 'in' in the world of fiction. I went along with it, flicking through

5

several thick novels, wondering if literary success might be like chicken pox: catching.

When she had to leave to do some actual librarian-ing, I drifted over to the 'How To' section. This was more like it! The books there had encouraging titles like *Six Simple Steps to Publishing Success* and *Write That Bestseller in 21 Days*. As I skimmed through the pages, I thought about all the other hopefuls who had leafed through them, and wondered how many had become bestsellers.

'What are you doing?' Felicity hissed, prising a copy of *Write What Sells and Make Your Fortune* from my fingers. 'All this,' she waved an arm, 'is what's called displacement activity. If you want to be a writer, you have to write. Non-stop until your head pounds, your fingers bleed, and you can't feel your buttocks. Look at Charles Dickens. Thirty novels to his name, not to mention short stories and journalism. He didn't waste time reading books on creative writing; he created writing,' she finished, cheeks blazing.

'Can't stand Dickens. Too many words. Don't even like that musical.'

'That's not the point. The point is, Dickens put in the work.'

'And my point is, how do I start? Because, quite frankly, I don't have a Scooby.'

Felicity's eyes narrowed. 'Wait here. I have an idea.'

When she came back she was holding a flyer. As I glanced at it, I felt a surge of hope.

'Felicity, you're a genius. I could kiss you.'

I didn't, of course, for fear her cheeks would spontaneously combust.

***

In bed that night, I read the flyer again:

**Meet the author. Local celebrity writer
Amanda Turner will read from her
bestselling romslasher, *Love You to Bits*,
and sign copies.
Central Library. From 2.30pm.
Light refreshments provided.**

Was this Amanda Turner woman the person I needed to get my life back on track? It was worth a try. And if it didn't pan out, well, free nibbles were not to be sniffed at.

Two

Whoah there! We're getting ahead of ourselves here. Let's back up a bit. Do one of them 'previously in Trish's disaster of a life' thingies, like they do at the top of telly dramas.

It's fair to say, even before she come off her bike, Trish's life weren't exactly going gangbusters. First off, there was The Meeting with Stephen then, like shit after the Lord Mayor's Show, The Email from Gregory. She ain't mentioned either of them yet has she? That's Stephen, her boss, and Gregory, her partner, in case you was wondering. Knowing Trish as well as I do, she'll have to psych herself up.

Someone more clued-up would've foreseen them both. Taken steps. Not Trish. She's never been one to pick up the ball and run with it. Fumble it into the hands of the opposition, more like. A follower, not a leader, our Trish. That's how come she's ended up with Gregory. He's what they call a natural leader. Another bossiboots, like Amanda Turner, in other words.

When she does get off her considerable arse and do summat, Trish usually gets it wrong. I mean, Trish,

Trish! What in the name of the sainted Michael Palin was you thinking? You can't go around blabbing to complete strangers that you're writing a book. Not unless you wanna come over as a dork of the first order. You only got away with it this time, cos it's Felicity you was talking to. Felicity, the shy librarian's shy librarian, whose dork-o-meter is seriously busted, due to lack of use.

While we're at it, where did this thing about writing come from? Cos it didn't just pop into her head, like she said, as a way of passing the time, or — 'scuse me while I snigger — earning big bucks. It's been lurking in the background for quite a while. I have a theory, if you're interested. Or even if you're not. It's down to all them years of holding back, pushing her feelings down, not saying anything, accepting second place. But they don't melt away, do they, them blocked emotions. They pile up, like dirty snow on the side of the road. And what do you need to smash through dirty snowdrifts? A sodding great snowplough, that's what.

Some people go out into the countryside and scream at the sky when life gets too much. Not our Trish. She's not the screaming sort. Writing is gonna be her snowplough. For her, meeting up with the great Amanda Turner is like climbing up into the cab and having a first fiddle with the controls: the beginning of a long journey.

That, even though she don't yet understand it herself, is why Trish decides she wants to be a writer. Not a spur-of-the-moment, rash decision but summat that's been fermenting inside her for decades. A way to let out what she's been keeping hidden inside practically all her life.

Please Gawd she makes an effort, though. Amanda Turner ain't gonna take her serious if she rocks up in a T-shirt her girls used to wear for netball and leggings so tight they could double as compression stockings.

9

Who am I? Sorry. Deepest apols, me ducks. Rude of me. Should've introduced meself. I'm Trish's bolder, bitchier, rougher, ruder Inner Voice. I.V. You can call me Ivy.

Three

I was late getting to the library, due to a last-minute wobble of confidence that triggered a hormonal mutiny which then meant a frantic change of shirt. Amanda Turner had already started reading from her novel. I slipped into the front row, under her nose – well, I didn't want to miss my chance. She frowned at the interruption. I mouthed, 'Sorry'. She made a big show of clearing her throat, before going back to reading out loud in a bored voice.

I had a good look around. Though a dozen chairs were grouped in front of the little table, only two other seats were occupied. An old man in a coat, much too heavy for the spring weather, sat at the back, and a young woman with a nose-ring, hanging onto an enormous pushchair – presumably with a baby inside, though I could see no sign of it – was at the end of my row.

'Right,' Amanda suddenly announced, slapping the book shut. 'That's quite enough of that.' She peered over her audience of three – four if you count the invisible baby. 'I think one will end the reading here and proceed to the signing. Who's first?'

11

Trish's first glimpse is from across the library. Could hardly miss her. Sea-green eyes laser out from a face the colour and smoothness of a peach. The mouth, set in a chin, large and firm but not manly, is like a rosebud on the point of doing its thing. The blonde hair, thick and shiny like in them ads, falls poker-straight to her shoulders. The fringe looks like it's been precision cut with a spirit level.

Am I overdoing the arty-farty description? Better to simply say, Amanda Turner is an absolute stunner, despite having a huge head, at least three times normal size.

Not the real one, you understand. The Amanda Turner I'm on about is printed, head and shoulders, on a roller banner six feet tall. Flesh-and-blood Amanda Turner, sitting beside it at a wonky card table, reading aloud and looking as if a yawn might be on the cards, is of standard proportions and less of a knockout. Hair a bit more disobedient, wrinkles a bit more conspicuous, green eyes a lot more steely grey. Smartly turned out, mind, in a well-cut pale blue trouser suit. Looks expensive.

True to form, Trish models the very latest in washed-up netball shirts and skin-tight black leggings. Will she never learn?

Giant, airbrushed Amanda Turner looks about twenty-five, thirty at most. The actual author, slim legs tucked under a local authority plastic chair, is about Trish's age. That's all good. With the author showing the same signs of menopausal fraying as our Trish, the two of them can perhaps bond over cosy chats about unruly hormones, facial sproutings, and thread veins.

I hung back, nervously biding my time, as the old man,

with much grunting, shuffled forward and, totally ignoring the author and the stack of books in front of her, grabbed a handful of the advertised light refreshments – Rich Tea biscuits on a paper plate – and scurried off, still grunting to himself.

Next it was the turn of the woman with the nose-ring. Abandoning pushchair and unseen offspring, she made her way to the table, took something out of her pocket and whispered in the author's ear.

'No, I will not sign your scruffy scrap of paper,' Amanda said loudly. 'Buy a copy of my book and I will happily write my name in it. Otherwise – next!'

That was me. By now, Amanda was clearly miffed.

I approached the table. 'Miss Turner. I wonder if …?'

'Didn't buy a copy of the book,' she cut in, eyes on the young mother wrangling the pushchair through the swing doors. 'Hasn't ever bought a book in her entire life, I'd wager, apart perhaps from light S&M erotica and volumes one to three of some juvenile celebs' enthralling autobiog. One signs, next thing one knows, one's autograph is up on eBay for five pounds ninety-nine, including postage, totally cheapening the brand.' She switched her gaze to me. 'What about you? Are you going to buy one? Or are you only here for the snacks like The Hundred-Year-Old Man?'

'No. That is, yes. I'd like a copy. A book. That is, your book,' I replied, scrabbling for my wallet and handing over a twenty. She took it and stuffed it into a cashbox. I waited for change but she didn't offer. It felt rude to ask.

Then she did a marvellous thing. For me, nothing less than a life-changer. Or do I mean 'more than'? I get those confused. Anyhow, it blew my mind. She took one of her paperbacks from the pile, opened it at the title page and, with a flourish, a double underlining and a solid full stop, signed it with a fine black felt-tip. A thrill went through me. If this was what it was like to be a real writer, count me in!

Caught up in the moment, again I inserted trotter in gob.

'I'm an author like you,' I said, as my sleeve brushed across the page, smudging the ink. 'A novelist. Leastways, I want to be. I wonder if ...?'

'No.' She put up a hand, like she was stopping traffic. 'No unsolicited scripts. One simply doesn't have the spare moments. Even if one did, one wouldn't. Ask yourself, why give succour to potential competition? Get yourself a *Writers' and Artists' Yearbook*, and pester the life out of the agents. That's my advice.' She looked me up and down. 'Can't say I hold out much hope but that's the best I can do. Good luck.' Then she looked away, dismissing me.

It wasn't going well. I searched for back-up: Felicity. It had been her idea after all. Catching her eye, I shot her a silent 'Help!' and she came over, cheeks already a-glow.

'Miss Turner,' she said without hesitation. 'Do forgive me for not being here to make a proper introduction. Please allow me to present one of our most promising local authors, Trish ... erm?' She left a space. We hadn't known each other long enough to get around to surnames.

I was amazed. Here was Felicity, skydiving out of her comfort zone to big me up. *One of our most promising local authors.* I liked the sound of that.

'Lightowler. Patricia Lightowler, Miss Turner. Honoured to meet you.'

Beaming, Amanda rose and took my hand. 'What an extraordinary moniker. What in heaven's name *is* a lightowler?'

I thought I was on a roll. That grin had convinced me

14

Amanda was interested. I started to tell her what I'd found out on *Find Your Forebears* about Gregory's unusual surname. I'd found it fascinating. She let me go on for a few seconds, then cocked her head and said, 'Do you understand the meaning of the word 'rhetorical'?'

'I think so. Does it mean, when you ask a question ... oh! I get it,' I said, the penny and my face dropping at the same moment. 'I'll shut up.'

'Good girl,' she said. 'Hmmm. Patricia Lightowler. It's certainly memorable. A big advantage. Look at that actor, Thingie Cumber-Whatsit. No-one ever forgets his name.'

Was this meant to be a joke? I smiled, to be on the safe side.

'Step closer,' she commanded.

This was unexpected, but surely a good sign. I did as instructed. Then, with a glint in her eye, Amanda leaned forward until our brows practically touched and stage-whispered, 'If I were you, I'd sue that plastic surgeon.'

Out of the corner of my eye, I saw Felicity's eyes bulge.

'No, my face isn't ...' I spluttered. 'I haven't ... This is ...'

Amanda rested a hand gently on my arm. 'Don't bother explaining. My version's bound to be much more amusing than yours.'

'What Trish meant to say,' Felicity said, stepping in smoothly once more, 'is do you do private tutoring? You know, taking a raw talent and guiding them to publication. That type of thing.'

Raw talent. That sounded good, too.

'I can pay. I mean, I have money,' I stammered, clumsily re-entering the conversation, thinking *Thank goodness I didn't say it was redundancy money.* Then immediately spoiled it by adding, 'Redundancy money from when I got the boot from my job.'

I saw Amanda's lips twitch. 'I'll give your proposal some serious consideration,' she said, rising and glancing at her watch, 'over tea and cake. A hoard of sticky-fingered little oiks and their potentially book-buying yummy mummies will be invading quite soon. I'll need fortification if I'm to survive. Would you mind?'

I panicked. A writer, a real writer, was inviting me to join her for tea! Where should we go? What would we talk about? Should I offer to pick up the bill?

'It comes to something,' she went on, 'when one can't safely leave one's things in a municipal library without worrying someone will nick them. Since you're apparently hanging about here anyway, Patricia Lightowler, if you would be so kind. I'll be back in fifteen minutes. Twenty at most. I'll furnish you with my answer then.'

Nearly an hour she was gone. In that time, I gave in to curiosity and lifted the velvet cloth covering her little table. Underneath I found: a cardboard box of *Love You to Bits* paperbacks, the brown cashbox, locked, two packs of black Sharpies, one opened, two bottles of mineral water, both tepid, a pack of wet wipes, dried out, and a copy of a novel by Lee Child, well thumbed.

I made a mental note. Inside knowledge on the little things, like what pens to bring to a signing, might come in useful when I was an author myself, I thought.

Spotting me, Felicity came over, all a-fluster. 'What are you doing? That's private.'

'Essential research,' I dropped the velvet cloth. 'Thanks for saving my bacon earlier, by the way. Magnificent, you were. I blew it. Turned into a wittering goldfish.' I did the mime.

Felicity's cheeks flushed. 'That's what you get when

16

you go to a second-rate girls' boarding school like I did. Top notch public social skills, zero personal self-esteem.'

'Fifty pounds an hour,' Amanda informed me when she did return. 'Cheap at half the price. For a course of weekly, two-hour, one-to-ones.'

I gulped. Blimey. A hundred pounds a week! That'd make a good-size dent in my lump sum. And if she wanted to go on after the summer …

'Thursday mornings. Starting next week. Ten o'clock. On the dot. My address.' She handed me a business card.

Woodview, Dark Lane, Oaker Wood Country Park, and a post code.

'It's a bit tricky to find,' she said. I didn't even know there were houses in the Country Park. I thought it was only for ramblers, dog walkers and, well, dogging. 'Just down the lane from the old ochre pit.'

'The what?'

'You know, the disused ochre workings. But don't get any ideas. I'm only taking you on because your name tickles me.'

Four

She was right. It wasn't easy to find, Amanda's place. Spent ages lost in the lanes, three-point turning, and panicking, straining to look over hedges. There's a surprising number of houses tucked in and around the edges of the Park. A few modern ones, constructed as far as I could see, mostly of huge bifold doors joined together. The rest older, some Edwardian or even Victorian I shouldn't wonder. Buildings that an estate agent would probably describe as 'superbly well-proportioned'.

At last I happened upon the green tunnel that was Dark Lane and at the end of it – praise be! – her house. Woodview, let me tell you, is *not* superbly well proportioned.

Me and Gregory have a nice house. *Had* a nice house. Well, I still have. In a road called Walnut Grove that's notable for being totally lacking in walnut trees. Four bedrooms. Four bathrooms, if you count the cloakroom, and I do. Travertine tiles in all four. Twin sinks in the main *en suite*. Real granite in the kitchen. Enormous American fridge/freezer in the corner. Little office for

Gregory to juggle figures in. Walk-in wardrobe for me, containing my extensive collection of baggy T-shirts, bum-hugging leggings, and boring navy business suits. Garden on the small side but professionally landscaped, with an arbour and a water feature that Gregory puts away every winter. *Used* to put away. Double garage with automatic up-and-over electric doors.

All very nice but even I know that, in the property game, older houses – even ugly 1930s specimens like Amanda's – beat shiny, ten-year-old executive homes any day of the week, no matter how many Travertine bathrooms they've got.

Truth is, Trish is shitting herself. What's she let herself in for? What business has she got, a failed P.A, getting lessons from a published writer who, quite frankly, scares the bejeebers out of her?

She sets out good and early, stomach in knots. She's been to the Country Park before, course she has, many times. Her and Gregory used to walk there when the girls were little, a lifetime ago. She always loved it. The way you drive over the flyover, and up the steep lane, and without warning you're in another world, far away from the noise and dust of the city, in the cool, green peace of the woods with only birds and squirrels for company. Like you've time-travelled back into history.

Here, hark at me!

I drove up to Woodview's double gates. Oh yes. The gates. Gregory was always incredibly, you could say pathetically, proud of our remote-controlled garage doors. He'd be eaten up with jealousy if he could see the black and gold wrought-iron monsters that stand guard over Amanda's gravel drive.

The house I saw through the gates, as I think I've

already stated, was quite a let-down. Dating from a time when houses were built to live in, not to look at, it was mostly red-brick with some random grey pebble-dash. Bay windows bulged each side of the front door, and flat-roofed extensions clung to its sides.

It seemed sad. The house. No, more than that. Call me crazy but it seemed resentful, if that's possible. It glared out through peeling window frames, tears of lime running down where gutters had overflowed. Weeds sprouted through the gravel drive. Gangly shrubs straggled up to the light and twisted trees stooped over. The only cheerful thing about the whole scene was a Virginia creeper scrambling over the frontage in its spring jacket of lime green.

I announced myself over the intercom and the metal gates swung open with a screeching like a pig having its throat cut. Not that I ... well, you get the idea. I drove through and they pig-screamed shut behind me and I thought, *too late to change my mind now.*

Even before I could ring the bell, the front door creaked open – clearly no-one had ever heard of WD40 in that house – reminding me of one of them schlocky old horror films. On the doorstep stood waiting to greet me, not a hunch-back servant, a leering vampire, or a decomposing mummy, but an extremely well put together Amanda Turner, celebrity writer. I pulled my shoulders back and stretched out my hand.

Ignoring it, she said, 'Come in. You'll have to excuse the smell.'

Woodview was as gloomy on the inside as the outside. Faded, over-stuffed and over-decorated. Dark antiques hid in the shadows, and plump, green sofas – glimpsed through a half open door – crouched like toads in what I suspect Amanda calls her 'drawing room'. But worst of all, over it all hung the most appalling pong.

I tried to breathe through my mouth as she marched me through to the kitchen, a large space at the back, dominated by a rectangular scrubbed pine table, bearing the scars of many a carelessly wielded knife.

The day was warm for early May and Amanda was wearing a summer dress in red and white, with a full skirt and a narrow belt, 'fifties style. Suited her. She's slim, as I said before, though not particularly tall. Not as tall as me. Few women are. Or men, for that matter. A long-term bone of contention between Gregory and me. He even made me take off my kitten heels for the first dance at our wedding. Spent the rest of the reception barefoot, and the rest of my married life in flats. Should have realised.

Amanda seemed more approachable on home ground. I, on the other hand, was a bag of jitters. She pointed to a straight-backed chair and settled herself at the head of the table, a thick, hairy blanket in shades of lavender and purple – National Trust I bet – draped over the back of her chair.

'Hope you don't mind,' Amanda said. 'I've decamped.'

'Decamped?' Two minutes in and already she had me confused.

'We'll be operating in here.'

'Operating?' I questioned, eyeing up the table and imagining some kind of gory, Sweeney Todd-type set-up.

'Yes. While Pavel goes about his business.'

'Pavel?'

'Yes. Pavel. My handyman,' she said, as if to an extremely thick child. 'He's painting the study. I thought I'd conduct the class in here. If, that is, that arrangement meets with your approval?'

I wasn't sure but I think she was being sarcastic.

'Oh, is that what that terrible stench is? Paint? I did wonder,' I said. 'Though it doesn't smell like any emulsion I've ever used. Smell's more like …' Was going to say 'stale piss' but I thought better of it.

'Yes, well, one trusts the disagreeable odour will fade once the paint dries. Shall we begin?'

She started to outline what she planned to teach me. Instantly there I was, back at school. And like back then, I tuned out. All I caught was the bit at the end when she told me – commanded me, more like – to keep a journal.

'Explore what – if anything – lies in here.' Amanda tapped her temple. 'Let your words flow uncensored. Be honest. Make the journal a repository for your darkest fears, your pithiest observations, your most fanciful fancies. Make it your best friend, your confidante, the holder of your most intimate secrets, your lover.' This last word she all but growled out.

I wasn't at all sure I wanted my darkest fears and intimate secrets exposed to anyone's scrutiny, let alone a sarcastic madam like her. Somehow, she read my thoughts.

'No need to look so scared,' she grinned. 'You won't have to show me your scribblings. One has absolutely no interest in your suburban neuroses. This is for you and you alone. Write it by hand. It'll make it more organic.'

Not even sure what that meant, I protested anyway. 'But I never write anything by hand. Not even shopping lists.'

'Excuses. Excuses. What is it with you? Nevertheless, that is what you will do. Keep a journal. Write it by hand. Carry it with you at all times. That is, if you want to pursue the matter. Do you?'

That put me on the spot. Did I? Or was the whole thing too stupid for words? Then I thought, *might as well give it a shot. What else did I have going for me?*

22

'Yes. Sure.' I said. 'Why not?'

'I'm bowled over by your infectious enthusiasm,' she said, at it with the sarcasm again. 'In that case,' she planted her hands flat on the table, 'what did you think of it? My book?'

She'd asked me to read *Love You to Bits,* you see. As preparation for this first lesson. Read it and give her my view. A 'critique', she called it. She sat back, arms folded, awaiting the verdict. 'Go on. Don't spare me.'

'I found it … interesting,' I answered.

'Is that it? From the gorgeous gallimaufry of English adjectives, acquired and absorbed down the centuries, you pluck the word 'interesting'?'

'Well, no. That is …' Again, she had me flustered.

'Come on. I'm a big girl. I can take it. Did you or did you not like it?'

'Erm …'

I didn't, you see. Like it. Her book. It was far-fetched and overcooked. It mixed romance with bloodthirsty goings-on in a way that didn't work for me. And the plot! So complicated and full of coincidences. I put it down several times, thinking *Come on, Amanda! You surely can't expect me to swallow that?*

Yet, I read on. And on. Lost two nights' sleep finishing it. Over the top and not even especially well written though it was, I *had* to know how it ended.

This is the start. See what you think.

I was twenty-three the first time. I didn't especially enjoy it. It was messy and unsatisfying. No wonder, I hadn't a clue what I was doing and the object of my attentions was disobligingly uncooperative. Adam's first was when he was fourteen, a fact he took great pleasure in reminding

me of. I was a late developer, he would tease, even when it came to cold-blooded murder.

See? It's definitely got something, though it's not perfect. Far be it for the likes of me to nit-pick but there's that clumsy 'of' hanging off the last-but-one sentence and that clichéd 'cold-blooded'. I liked 'disobligingly uncooperative,' though. That sounded proper writerly. But, more important, the whole thing hooked me in. Hooked me in, dragged me from bank to bank, and reeled me into the shallows, before finally dropping me, flapping helplessly, into its keep net. No masterpiece but I was gripped.

I didn't say any of this to Amanda. 'I think it might sell,' is what I said. 'The main characters are quite good. Could even stretch to a series.'

'Thank you so very much,' she mocked. 'You think it *might* sell. My characters are *quite* good. It *could* stretch to a series. That's not what one yearns to hear, Trish Lightowler. What one yearns to hear is: it will *definitely* sell, your characters are *irresistible*, and it will spawn a whole slew of bestsellers that Netflix and Amazon will scrap over, culminating in three six-episode series, with an option on a further four, and a move to a mansion in the Hollywood Hills, where you will be fawned upon for the rest of your natural.'

'That's what I meant.'

'Self-belief is the key, you see, Trish. Total and shameless self-belief. You'll never make it as a writer if you don't believe in yourself, heart and soul. If one believes in oneself and one's work, others will too. I believe in all my books, even those no-one reads. Congratulations, by the way. You passed.'

'Passed? Passed what?'

'My little initiation test. You didn't drone on about

narrative arc and plot twists. You didn't admire my syntax or praise my transferred epithets. In short, you abandoned anything you might have been taught about the analysis of literary form and technique. You did what the average person would do and cut to the chase: does it or does it not have reader appeal? Which college were you up at, by the way?'

I blinked at the sudden conversational swerve. 'Erm. Camden.'

She chortled. 'No, no, Trish. I was referring to Oxbridge colleges. Never mind. You weren't to know. One is a Girton girl oneself. BA and MA Cantab. Not that you have any cause to feel intimidated by that. None at all.' Though, as I was sure she intended, I was.

'Know what my best ever review was?' she went on. 'Four words. *Brilliant book. Buy it.* And you don't need a first-class degree from an ancient seat of learning to write that.' Her face clouded. 'Sadly, I no longer attract such five-star notices. It's all post-apocalyptic wastelands, jolly geriatric amateur detectives, or witches and wizards having it off with vampires and werewolves these days. Still, one day I'll be back in fashion, if I live that long.' She gave me a searching look. 'You all right?'

'Actually,' I fidgeted in my seat. 'Can I use your facilities?'

On my way back from the downstairs loo – poky, full of cobwebs, with one of them old-time pull chains – I passed the so-called study. I knew it was the study because that was where the whiff was the strongest. Hearing faint music, I pushed open the door. Sure enough, there he was, the handyman, up a step ladder, rollering away, humming along to Radio 2. Younger than I'd expected with flecks of cream paint in his dark blond hair. He looked across and I nodded. We didn't speak.

'Stress incontinence,' Amanda said, as I sat back down, 'How women of our age suffer.'

'It's got worse, since ...' I stopped myself. The conversation had got way too personal, way too quickly. I wasn't ready to discuss my inner workings quite yet.

'Since you started the menopause?' she offered. 'One can only sympathise. Although I myself have yet to experience its ravages.'

I suspect my eyebrows shot up. She was at least as old as me.

'Industrial quantities of HRT,' she whispered from behind her hand. 'That's the secret of a merry peri. Keep the horrors at bay.'

'Sorry about this.' I bobbed up in my seat and headed for the loo again. 'Have to pay another visit. Talking about it always makes it worse.'

When I got back, she waved a finger vaguely in the general direction of my crotch, 'Can't you have them put a stitch in it, or something?'

Clearly, she was a woman who didn't believe in holding back on personal comments.

'I'm used to it. Ever since I had the girls, my pelvic floor swings in the breeze like a garden hammock.'

Amanda broke into a throaty guffaw. 'That's more like it, Trish Lightowler. You have something of a gift for dry humour, you know. Use that. Tell me, your daughters, how old are they?'

'Nineteen. Twins. Flo and Nell. At separate universities in Southampton.'

'And their father?'

My heart sank. *Why bring him into it?*

'In America,' I said, thinking *Change the subject! Change the subject!* 'Do you have kids, Miss Turner?'

'Please, before we go any further, can we stop with the 'Miss Turners'? We're equals here, both pilgrims in

26

search of true creative expression. Call me Amanda. I've got one son,' she went on. 'Twenty-two next birthday, would you believe? Louis. The product of a short-lived disaster of a marriage. Ah, the folly of youth! He lives with his father in Cardiff.' She fell silent, no more willing to share than me. 'Right. Let us begin the metamorphosis. So. Genres.'

Five

Lesson 1: Genres

I've always been a bit ropey when it comes to genres and stuff. Never been entirely sure what they are, if I'm honest, and if they matter. Far as I'm concerned, a book is either fiction or non-fiction, good or bad. The rest is white noise. Trish is hoping Amanda will shed some light. Some hope.

Amanda spoke about hybrid genres for quite some time, though not long enough for me to grasp what they were.

'So *Love You to Bits* is a crossbreed?' I said, trying to fathom it out. 'Like a labradoodle or a shitpoo?'

Amanda gave me a side-eye. 'What are you on about? I'm simply stating there are no rules in fiction. Novels may blend the elements of various genres. One has essayed more than one on one's literary journey. I started with heart-warming family sagas, moving on more recently to thrillers which, I have to admit, are great fun. The research particularly.

'I've learnt so much. How many deadly plants would you think there are in your average garden, for instance? Actually, I forget how many, but it's a lot. And where precisely do you need to stick the blade if you want to ensure the death of your victim?' she asked. 'Not in the left chest, you may be surprised to learn, because that it *not* where the heart resides. My latest, a bestseller by the way, is listed under 'romslasher', a most satisfying sub-category. What is your siren call?' She caught my puzzled look. 'In which genre will you dip your literary toe?'

Caught on the hop, I snatched at the first idea that surfaced. 'Something like that one that got made into that film with that woman, *Behind the Eyes of the Girl Gone on a Train*. What breed was that?'

What had I said wrong now? Something, obviously, judging by the snidey look on Amanda's face. 'A little *passé*, if you ask me. A word of warning. The publishing world is a hungry, fickle monster. It gorges greedily on the latest fad until it is satiated, then moves on without so much as a backward glance. One week it's cosy crime, the next it could be humorous sci-fi or, I don't know, AI romance. There's no telling. But it's your book. You write what you want.'

Without realising it, Amanda had put her finger on the button. I had no idea what I did want to write.

'They say, write what you know,' I said. 'Trouble is, I feel I don't know nothing much about anything.'

'Don't *ever* say that – not even grammatically. You're alive, aren't you? A living, breathing, feeling human being? Of course you know things. Everyone does, by being someone's daughter, mother, sister, aunt, neighbour, employee, boss, lover, friend, or enemy.

'I'll let you into a secret. People – non-writers I mean – are always asking, from whence comes an author's inspiration? They almost never get a straight answer. I'll give you one: inspiration comes from existing. From living and learning to read people, including oneself and those one encounters. Take you, for instance, Patricia Lightowler. Here's what I know you know.

'You know about unhappy marriages, unsuccessful careers and ungrateful children. Am I striking a chord? And you know a whole lot about feeling unwanted, overlooked, and unappreciated. Don't look so gobsmacked. I recognise a woman at rock bottom when I see one. Look at your hair.' I pushed back my greasy fringe. 'And your clothes.' I smoothed the creases out of the T-shirt I'd grabbed out of the tumble drier that morning.

'As for the rest, your expression when I brought up your husband spoke volumes. You were tight-lipped about your daughters, too, when most parents never shut up about how beautiful and brainy their offspring are. And almost the first thing you let slip when first we met was that you'd been given the old heave-ho from your job.'

'I was nervous,' I admitted glumly.

'Chin up. Being pissed off isn't necessarily a bad thing in a writer. Despair and bitterness underlie many a great tale.' She stood. 'Well, that's about it for today. Except ... I'd prefer cash but I'll take a cheque if you don't have it on you. Five sessions, we said. Five hundred pounds. In advance.'

I glanced at the clock on the kitchen wall. 'It's never two hours.'

'As good as,' Amanda said, heading for the door.

I opened my mouth to protest but she got in first. 'Another important lesson. I'll throw this one in for free. Always get cash upfront if you can. The life of the self-employed is precarious enough without unpaid invoices piling up.'

Feeling like an accomplice at my own mugging, I rummaged in my faithful old leather bag and, stuck in the torn lining, found an old cheque book, curled with age.

'Thank you *so* much.' She made a great show of accepting the cheque from me, as if it was a gift willingly given. 'I'll show you out. Next time, use the code. I don't want to have to keep buzzing you in and out every week. It's 1234.' The woman clearly has no clue about security!

I was almost at my car when Amanda called me back to share the worrying news that she expected me to do homework.

'Homework! Haven't done homework since I was at the comp. Even then, I didn't always get around to it.'

But Amanda was firm. 'Write a synopsis. One page. Beginning, middle, and end. The essence of a story you are passionate about. Thrill me with your ideas, Patricia Lightowler. Don't overthink. Write. And don't forget to start that journal.'

Synopsis? Journal? As the gates pig-squealed shut behind me, I was troubled. Had I bitten off more than I could chew?

That's how come Trish starts writing the journal. The ramblings you've just been reading. Amanda tells her to do it and Trish, being a biddable sort of a bunny, does what she's told. Buys the best notebook WHSmith can provide: a fat thing with ruled lines and a dark rose-pink cover. Made to look like one of them pricey classic novels you buy by the yard, to show off but never read. She carries it around in her bag. It's on the heavy side but exactly the right size. The notebook, that is. Not the handbag. The bag is way too big, has seen better days and sags in the middle, exactly like its owner. She loves it, nonetheless.

Verba volant, scripta manent *it says on the*

front. I'm back to the notebook again now. Trish looks it up. Google detects Latin. Spoken words fly away, written words remain. That's the clunky translation.

Daunting. Daunting enough, at any rate, to give Trish a touch of the syndromus imposterus. *But she don't give up. She sticks at it. This is more like it, my girl!*

***

What do I know? Tonight I took a long, hard look at myself and came up with this.

I know draping a scarf round your neck doesn't take off two stone.

I know when you're size 14 or bigger and you wear torn jeans, your legs look like burst sausages.

I know the older you get, the more your breasts spread sideways. Eventually I expect they'll meet round the back.

I know not to scoff cream crackers in bed because, like the actor David Tennant, they get flaming everywhere.

I know the number of working pens in a house is in inverse proportion – is that the right phrase? – to the total number of pens.

I know your friendly local radio station always cuts in on the car radio at the very moment in the *Afternoon Play* when the detective is saying, 'Of course, it's obvious who's the killer. It's … '

I know, when your friendly local radio station cuts in to ruin the drama, it's to inform you that 'Traffic throughout our region is running normally.'

I know, with very few exceptions, men come in two varieties: bastards and bores. If you are very unlucky – or have poor taste, like me – you end up with a boring bastard or a bastardly bore. I'm still working out which one I got.

And I know, while in theory life comes at you in a series of ups and downs, sometimes the downs follow cruelly one after the other until you can hardly bear it. Bam, bam, bam.

***

It was like Sunday evenings back home with Mum and Dad all over again. Only this feeling stretched out over a whole seven days. The dread in the pit of the stomach. The dark cloud hanging over everything I did. But I wasn't a nervy schoolgirl, struggling with trigonometry. I was a middle-aged woman with a synopsis I had no idea how to tackle.

I told myself the only answer was to phone Amanda and tell her I'd decided to pack it in. Novel writing wasn't for me after all. I mean, five hundred pounds! Yep, I would call her and tell her I was packing it in. Only that would mean ... calling her and telling her I was packing it in, which gave me more heebies than writing the flaming summary. Nothing for it but to apply backside to chair and thrash out something.

I tried. I really did. Googled loads of websites, stayed up practically the whole of Wednesday night, for all the good it did me. Panic shrivelled up what little creativity I might have had. I did write a synopsis, a few in fact. All pants. Every thought I came up with dissolved into nothingness when I tried to pin it down on the screen. By four in the morning, my laptop trash bin was overflowing with rejects and my eyes drooping like an insomniac bloodhound's, but at last I felt I had something. It wasn't great but it was better than zilch. And it had a twist I was quietly pleased with.

Six

Typical Trish. Going on about a sodding synopsis when she still ain't got round to filling you in yet on the juicier subject of how come her life has been knocked to cock. By that, I don't mean by coming a cropper off her bike. I mean by The Meeting and The Email. In denial, the soft cow. Still, she's getting round to it now. Better late than never, me ducks.

The Meeting. There had been mutterings for weeks. I didn't pay them any attention because, well, there were always rumours and I knew I wouldn't be on the list. I'd been with the agency since forever, and me and Stephen were good mates. Sort of.

'We're getting rid of that whole tranche of admin,' he said, pacing. 'Surplus to requirements in this digital age.'

I was sat at the boardroom table with only one thought in my head: *Don't cry. For flip's sake, don't cry.*

I swallowed hard. 'I'm not surplus,' I said, voice a-wobble. 'I know I'm only three days a week but Frank and George rely on me.'

'Ah.' Stephen stopped pacing. 'I'm seeing Frank and

34

George after you and I are done here. Along with one or two others.' He waved a sheet of paper at me. As the light shone through it, I could see there were a lot more than one or two names on the list. 'All strictly in accordance with redundancy law. If you'd care to check.'

He pointed at the folder in front of me. I didn't move. Annoyingly, though I'd won the battle of the tears, now I felt a drip form on the end of my nose. I sniffed. Stephen was onto it like a lurcher who's missed dinner.

'I'm not unsympathetic. You're upset, Trish. It's been … what? … three years?'

'Nearly five.' I sniffed again. 'Since you started up in that rented rabbit hutch above the betting shop and took me on.'

'That long?' He leaned over and pushed a box of tissues towards me. 'Help yourself.'

'I'm fine,' I said, rubbing snot onto the back of my hand like a two-year-old.

Bit of context. What happens is Stephen texts her over the weekend, asking for an urgent meeting, in the process ruining her Sunday evening wallow in Call the Midwife. *When Monday morning comes around, he shows her into the boardroom. That gets her all of a dooh-dah for a kick-off. Normally the boardroom is strictly 'clients only', especially since he's had new Scandi blonde-wood flooring put down. Room reeks of latex.*

I examined Stephen through the fumes. When I first worked for him, back when we were friends more than colleagues, he wore M&S suits and pale blue shirts. Now he was running an agency big enough to be nominated for last year's *Marketing Monthly* regional awards – longlisted; didn't make the shortlist – he went in for distressed jeans, black graphic T-shirts and ankle-high converse trainers that squeaked as he walked. Not a great look on a shortish bloke in his mid-forties with a thickening waistline and thinning hair.

'… as set out in the terms of your employment contract. You know, PILON.' Stephen, who I realised had been going on for some time, ground to a halt.

'Pylon?' I said, distracted. Why hadn't I noticed before how his eyes flicked from side to side at he talked, like a lizard's?

'Payment in lieu of notice. PILON. It was all explained in the email the new CPO sent out.'

'CPO? Wasn't that *Star Wars*?'

Stephen sighed and rolled his eyes. 'Chief. People. Officer. You probably know her better as Tracy in HR.' His reptile eyes widened. 'Christ's sake Trish, you did read Tracy's email about the changes?'

'Of course.'

I hadn't.

'Right. Questions?'

I had questions all right. Like, how could he do this to me? Like, what about loyalty? Like, what about friendship? They buzzed around in my head like wasps in a jam jar.

'No. No questions. Thank you for explaining so clearly.'

'Great.' Stephen moved to the door, plainly thankful he'd got to the end of this awkward conversation. 'Violet will get your things. Violet! Where is that girl? Violet!'

'You can't mean …?'

'No sense dragging things out. I'll walk you to the door.'

Whatever a tether is, I was approaching the end of mine. I had an uncontrollable urge to lash out and it was Stephen's fancy flooring that took the brunt. As I stood, I scraped the chair legs hard as I could into the wood, and glanced down. Two satisfyingly deep parallel lines were scored into the floor's perfect surface.

Petty, I know, but a tiny payback for the humiliation that followed: the lonely walk past the down-turned heads of the child-employees whose jobs were, unlike mine, *not* surplus to requirements, clutching my little box of photos and knick-knacks, the only sound, the squeak of Stephen's trainers.

Stephen stopped at the front entrance. 'What will you do with all this free time?' he said, eyes flicking. That stumped me. What *was* I going to do? I took a breath to stop my head from spinning, opened my mouth and surprised myself by saying, 'I'll write. A book. A novel. The only subject I was halfway decent at in school was English. Might as well give it a go. How hard can it be?'

'That old chestnut, eh?' Stephen heaved open the glass door. 'Remember you banging on about wanting to write in the pub years ago.'

Time was, I'd have let that pass, but he'd got me riled. I said, surprising myself for a second time, 'Yes, well, I've always felt I was a frustrated writer at heart.'

Stephen made a little noise in his throat that could have been a sneer. 'Good luck with whatever you do, Trish. For what it's worth, you're a good sort.' He let the door go.

'And you, Stephen,' I threw back, 'are a cold-blooded reptile in stupid trainers no-one over sixteen would be seen dead in.'

Alas, timing ain't Trish's strong point. She launches her hairdryer treatment as the heavy door closes, blocking out her voice. Stephen don't hear a word of her tirade. He saunters off, lips pursed, whistling, though Trish can't make out the tune.

I sat hyperventilating in my car, the box of trinkets on my lap, waiting for my heart to stop trying to power-drill its way out of my chest. Then drove home, not slowing down for the speed cameras.

It was still early, not even midday. Nevertheless, I crawled into bed in my crackling polyester suit, and fell into a heavy sleep. I woke, sweaty and confused, sometime in the late afternoon, to the ping of the laptop.

***

The Email. Gregory was away in America on business. Course he was! He was always away. In the old days, he used to phone me every day – hang the cost, hang the time difference – but lately we'd been keeping in touch by email. So an email from Gregory didn't ring any alarm bells. Not till I read it, that is.

Here it is. Copied out in full in this journal. The extra comments, by the way, are what I added later. Scratched out in green biro. Thought about blood but I was too squeamish.

Pats, (Is a pet name appropriate in the circs?)

You've no idea how long I have agonised over writing this. (A week? A day? Two minutes?) **It's so hard to write but I know it has to be done for everyone's sake.** (Such self-sacrifice.)

As you know, I've been spending more and more time Stateside. (That explains the overflowing bins and the empty ironing basket.) **What you don't know is, it hasn't only been work that's kept me here.** (The plot thickens.)

There is no easy way to say this (Pompous cliché.) **and, you must believe me, the very last thing I want to do is hurt you.** (Funny. I have the opposite reaction.)

You are truly a wonderful human being. (Gee. Coming from you that means … less than diddly squat.) **But I can't go on living a lie.** (Cliché upon cliché.)

The truth is, Pats, (See above.) **I've met someone.** (Uh-uh!) **Her name is Madison-Rose** (One name not enough?) **and she's funny and beautiful and from the moment I met her a few short, wonderful weeks ago** (Purlease!) **I knew I couldn't live without her.** (She's good in the sack then.)

She's a business analyst (American for bookkeeper?). **We have so much in common.** (Unlike me and you, with only the two kids and nigh on twenty-one years.) **I know it will sound strange to you now, but I think if you met Maddy-Rose, you'd like her.** (A joke, surely?)

It's a lot to take in, I know, (Seems straightforward enough. You're walking out on me and the girls, you rat.) **so I'll leave it at that for now.**

Suffice to say, (More pomposity!) **I won't be back at the end of the week. Maddy-Rose and I are buying an apartment in Bushwick. She tells me it's an up-and-coming area of NY. Very hipster – whatever that means!** (1. Do you have any idea how old that makes you sound? 2. Don't go for pally jokes. And 3. Your domestic arrangements are of zero interest.)

Inevitably, there will be some legal stuff. (You betcha!) **I hope we can keep things civil.** (Don't bank on it.) **I'll leave it to you to talk to the girls. You were always better at that sort of thing.** (I *was* good at something then.)

I want you to know, you will always be special to me. And I sincerely mean that. (Hope you rot in hell. And I sincerely mean *that*.)

Best wishes.

Gregs

There you have it. Nearly twenty-one years of marriage down the toilet in less than 270 words. That's around 11 words for every year, if you're interested. I worked it out. I've been short-changed.

> *Fuck's sake, Trish! I mean, what sort of nutjob gets dumped and the first thing they do is reach for a calculator. Makes no sense. Any case, 270 divided by 21 comes to nearer 13.*
>
> *I ask you, what hope is there for a woman who can't even do revenge maths?*

40

Seven

What does Trish do next? Sweet Fanny Adams, that's what. For days. Speaks to no-one. Goes nowhere. Too traumatised, outraged, embarrassed, hurt, depressed — take your pick — to do anything but drag herself through each twenty-four hours. The double whammy of The Meeting and The Email has floored her.

She don't eat, not properly at least. Mind you, the size of her, that's no bad thing. She exists on a giant tub of peanut butter excavated out of the back of the store cupboard and two loaves of frost-burnt bread from the magic bottom drawer of the freezer, her Tardis. The peanut butter is so old it has separated into a solid slab of nut concrete with a slick of oil on the top. When the bread runs out, she chisels off chunks of peanut hardcore and gnaws on them straight from the spoon.

In short, she falls apart. Not a grown-up way to deal with her troubles but that's how Trish rolls. Spends her days basically staring into space through puffy eyes, chin smeared with peanut butter, and her nights semi-conscious. Oh yes, that reminds me. She does do summat. She drinks. Quite a lot of a quite decent Bordeaux left

41

over from Christmas. Pauillac, what Gregory usually keeps for hisself. 'Wasted on you,' he says.

She lays propped on the sofa, glass in hand, monster bucket of nutty concrete perched on her chest, curtains drawn, telly on in the background like a fake fire. Her only goal: to kill time till she can sway upstairs and collapse on the bed or, on a bad day, the bathroom floor.

What would've happened to her and her poor liver if Amanda Turner hadn't come along that day, I dread to think.

I try not to dwell on them. Those days. Though I did write about them. Amanda reckoned I needed to practice. This was me getting in some practice. The next voice you hear will be that of debut womensfic author, Trixie Owlighter.

The house is silent, save for the creaking of the stairs. Grace, her mother, is wont – is that an actual word? **– to say it is haunted. Absolute codswallop. We're talking an almost new, high-end, executive home, not a gothic pile fully kitted out with ghouls from a Tim Burton film.**

'Built over a graveyard or a Druids' gathering place. Or blocking a ley line. Sure as eggs is eggs,' Grace says.

Her daughter only laughs. Now she is spending so much time there, however, she's beginning to wonder if her mother isn't onto something. Perhaps the place is cursed.

Fighting against a constantly knackered feeling, the daughter totters across to the mirror over the mantelpiece. Who is that woman? What is the point of her? And where the heck did them ... those wrinkles come from? She leans in. Is this what she

has to look forward to, a face that's slowly falling into folds, like a … like a … why the flip is the only folding thing I can think of, a flaming ironing board?

She lurches sofa-wards. A carrier bag winds itself round her ankle and she almost takes a tumble. She surveys her surroundings. Not a pretty sight. A towel leaves a damp stain on the sofa. Plates crusted with dried food lay on every surface. The cushions are in dire need of a plump. There are wine stains down her shirt and breadcrumbs stuck to her leggings. They are both in a mess, her and her house. It never used to be like this.

That's not entirely true. There were messes before but they were different, the sort that come from leading a hectic life, not the sort that come from not being arsed.

She stretches and feels the bones in her neck grind against each other. Mid-grind, the sunlight reflects off a photo on the bookshelf. She reaches for it and her eyes sting. If only the girls still let her take their photos without insisting on a final veto. If only they still slipped their hot hands into hers, as they walked to the shops. If only they didn't roll their teenage eyes, when she asks what exactly a social media influencer does.

When did this Grand Canyon open up between us, she wonders? Certainly it was already there by the time her and her husband dropped them off in Southampton.

Ah yes, her husband! She can't help herself. Her gaze moves to the man in the picture, dark and slim, looking down into the girls' sweet faces. She sighs again. Doesn't want to think the thought, but it comes anyhow, unbidden and unwelcome. Even now, even after everything, when she wakes, she misses seeing his head denting the pillow beside her, his balding, snoring, dandruffy, two-timing head.

She's blowing her nose on a tea-towel, when it happens. Her anger boils over. Damn them all! The traitorous husband, the patronising daughters, the ungrateful boss. She draws back her arm and chucks the photo at the fireplace, not caring one jot that it falls short, and shards – is that the word? – skid across the floor. That'll show them, she thinks, though she knows full well it will do nothing of the kind. In the end, it's just another mess.

Aaaargh! Stop with the snivelling, woman. Trish needs to buck up. Fight back. Give them boiled sprats of daughters a two-fingered salute, not worrying about hurting their feelings, cos they it seems couldn't give a stuff about hers. As for wanting Gregory's head on her pillow. Ye gods! Only on one condition, I'd say, and that's if it's detached from the rest of his body. Does she really wanna stand by a man who's lost his hair, his flat belly and all sense of common decency?

Woman up, for Gawd's sake!

Eight

Surprise, surprise! Trish ain't told the girls. Not about her job. Not about her and their dad. She knows she'll have to. But not yet. She's too brittle. Liable to shatter, like the photo that gives her so much grief, which by the way, she still ain't got round to sweeping up.

Tried phoning Gregory. I know! Somewhere deep inside me I suppose I must still have had hope. Perhaps it was a passing crush, like middle-aged politicians are prone to. He'd hear my voice, realise what a mistake he was making and beg forgiveness. I'd use some choice words, hang up, sulk for a good long time, and gradually, grudgingly, allow him back in favour and, after an even longer time, my bed. Not before I'd made him suffer, mind. Boy, would I make him suffer! In the end, though, everything would go back to how it used to be, with the added bonus now I'd be appreciated.

Trouble was the more I considered that scenario, the less I liked the sound of it.

It didn't matter one way or the other in the end. Gregory never picked up. I left several long, rambling

45

messages. Then deleted the lot and texted this instead,

Dumped from job and marriage on same day. Must be a record. Thanks a bunch. Patricia.

Thought a bit and deleted 'dumped' and put 'bum's rush' instead. To let him know how pissed off I was.

Awake in the small hours, worrying if people still said 'bum's rush' or if that wasn't horribly untrendy, when in pinged a text.

Pats. We must talk. Please!

Oh, we must, must we? I thought, feeling strangely soothed. I switched off my phone, rolled over and fell into a deep, dreamless sleep. Gregory had missed his moment.

***

Friday came around, as Fridays do. My day for phoning the girls. They'd know something was up if I didn't. I tried Nell first, thinking she'd be easier.

'How are you, Mum?' she asked, sounding bright as a button. 'And Dad? Still coining it in the Big Apple? He's such a big shot these days.'

Before I could draw breath, she charged on. 'Guess what? There's this boy. I know you'll say I'm too young and my degree comes first but I think this is it. *He* is it. His name's Johnny and he's the same age as me. Well, technically younger, but only by a few months. He loves everything I love, Mum. It's uncanny. Sia, Stormzy, roller coasters, penguins, the scent of bluebells. Not rice pudding. Hates the stuff. Makes him want to puke. Exactly like me. Isn't that great? He's completely perfect.'

As you might have gathered, Nell – the oldest by sixteen minutes – is the talkative one.

Nell has hazel eyes. Flo grey. As a tiny baby, Nell had

a cowlick of dark hair. Flo was bald as a Buddhist until the age of two, when white-blond curls sprang from her crown. From day one, Nell had us pacing the floor every night. Flo slept so soundly, we kept a hand mirror by the cot for her first few weeks. In the sixth form, Nell played rhythm guitar in a punk band. Flo sang in a madrigal choir.

Get the picture? Non identical doesn't even touch the sides. From their earliest days, grabbing each other's dummies, jabbing at each other's eyes, pulling each other's ponytails, my girls were the least fraternal of fraternal twins.

That's why I was astounded when they chose universities in the same city, though the degrees they picked couldn't have been more different. Nell is stomping about the University of Southampton in black patent Doc Martens, reading Mechanical Engineering (including Aeronautics, Astronautics and Acoustics and other things beginning with A beyond my understanding), while Flo is getting to grips with Psychology down the road at Southampton Solent. And they are not, repeat not, they told me – separately and together – ever going to share a house. Ever.

It's always been, 'the girls'. Never 'the twins'. They hate that. 'We are not some sort of multi-person amoeba,' Nell yelled at me once, outraged as only a thirteen-year-old can be.

Giving birth to babies with the combined weight of almost five kilos was no picnic, I'm telling you. Plays havoc with your waterworks. That's why I'm obsessed with loos. They are the bane of my life. Wherever I am, whatever I'm doing, I have to know where the nearest toilet is and not stray far from it. It makes new places a nightmare.

Is there any worse torture than knowing, no matter

how hard you bite your lip and recite the alphabet backwards, you won't be able to stop that tablespoonful of wee soaking your knickers? Now I'm passing through that zone known as the Perimenopause, my bladder is rebelling even more.

Not that I'm moaning. Well, I am, but … what I want to say is, in spite of the peeing thing and the constant bickering thing, Eleanor and Florence are … well … my everything. Gregory chose the names. He made all the big decisions: where we'd live, where we'd go on holiday, whether we'd get Sky Sports or Atlantic. And while he was busy being masterful, I was doing my impression of a doormat. Keeping the peace. Holding my tongue. Getting by.

The girls' names was another thing I said nothing about, though secretly I felt Eleanor and Florence a bit knobby. Can't tell you how chuffed I was when people started calling them Nell and Flo. Gregory never shortens their names.

Nell was still talking. 'Won't be home at the end of term by the way. Johnny's got this friend with a houseboat in Amsterdam. Isn't that cray-cray? He's invited us. We'll stay there for a bit and then head off, who knows where? You won't have to worry about me until I pitch up at the end of summer with an enormous bag of dirty washing and an Insta account of the coolest pictures. Mum? You still there?'

'Yes. Yes, I heard. You've met this boy. Name of Johnny. Fan of Sia. Can't abide rice pudding. You'll be spending the summer with him. Go, my pretty, spread your wings and fly. Go with my blessing.'

'You OK, Mum? You sound weird. How's work? Is that wanker Stephen still pissing you about? Never mind. Dad's home soon, isn't he? That'll be nice.'

That was my cue to tell her. I opened my mouth but

a lump stopped my throat. Then I thought, how can I dump this bucket of cold water over her when she's planning a summer adventure with the current love of her life? Could I do that to my Nell? Of course I couldn't.

Youngest-by-sixteen-minutes-Flo was always the more level-headed. I phoned her next, determined not to bottle it this time. I started off fine but early in the conversation took a wrong turning and found myself up a blind alley discussing Gregory's new flat in New York. I may even have let the word 'hipster' pass my lips.

'Wow! How about that, Dad buying an apartment in New York!' Flo said. 'Way to go, Dad! You should defo go over, Mum, and give it the once-over. Get stingy Stephen to give you a few weeks off. Light a joss stick over the John Lennon memorial. Take in some Broadway shows. Learn the rules of American football. Have a ball. You deserve it.'

How could I tell her I wasn't invited to the party? That the New York love-nest wasn't for me, but for their dad and his thinner, younger lover with her perfect skin, plumped up lips, beautifully defined eyebrows, and bunion-inducing Manolo Blahniks. Not that I had any idea what the woman looked like, but I had guilt-watched enough episodes of *Love Island* to know the type. Could I do that to my Flo? Well … maybe I could.

'Actually Flo, I've got news,' I said, taking a breath. 'And it's not good.'

Nine

Lesson 2: A Bikini Or A Balaclava

The second lesson. Another couple of hours I won't ever get back. Somehow, I survived. We tried to work in the study, a cramped room with overflowing bookcases and a view of the bins, but the stench was unbearable. The paint must be dry by now, surely? We couldn't stick it, even with the windows open and a through-draught. Had to move to what Amanda, as I predicted, calls her drawing room. Still and all, the hum found us.

I shall attempt a description of the drawing room.

The next voice you hear will be that of junior feature writer on the interior design magazine, *Chic It Up!* Flavia Golightly.

How to ruin a room. Take a basically decent, high-ceilinged space and fill it with junk. Be sure to include a huuuge six-piece suite in a shade of heavy Leylandii green and hang these chairs and sofas with ridiculous gold tassels that unravel to trip the

unwary. **Dump this muddle of once-good, now dated, furniture against wallpaper in a shade that is, or should be, called 'custard yellow'. As finishing touches, add several small brown tables at exactly the right height to skin your shins, and floor lamps with fringes that shake themselves ominously at you as you pass. Scatter the whole lot any old how on a swirly carpet, supposed to be dark blue, but pale with dust where no hoover has ever reached, designed not so much to pull the room together as to blast it apart.**

There you go. Job, as they say, done!

Trish don't like her living ... sorry, drawing room. Can you tell? Don't like any of the house, come to that. And strange though it may sound, I don't think it likes her.

Amanda arranged herself on the Leylandii sofa and indicated one of the armchairs for me. I lowered myself slowly down. It was big enough to swallow me up.

'Right, Syn-op-ses,' Amanda said, drawing out the word. 'Your fabulous tale condensed into one sensational single page.'

The day hadn't started well. I'd overslept. It was half past by the time I got to Amanda's, unwashed, unmade-up and in yesterday's creased T-shirt. Holding the bit of paper I'd given up almost the whole night to, I raised my hand to ring the bell, then froze. It wasn't good enough, my synopsis. I knew that. She would know it, too. Spot it straight away and use it as an excuse for some more put downs. Wasn't sure I was up to that, so I shoved the paper into the lower reaches of my bag and did up the zip.

'What do you mean, you haven't done one?' She crossed her legs, encased today in immaculate linen trousers in a shade she probably calls *chartreuse*. 'I thought I made it clear. For today's session, you had to write a synopsis.'

'I did,' I explained, pulling at the sweaty crotch of my too-tight cut off denims. 'Several. None of them were fit to be seen. The truth is, I don't feel ready to write a synopsis. Not until I've got an idea of what the story is about.'

'Bravo.'

'Bravo?'

'Your face!' Amanda chortled. 'Trish, one should never write one's synopsis until one has completed at least the first draft. It's like …' She paused. 'It's like packing one's bag before one has booked one's flight. With no destination in mind, how does one know if one will be requiring a tube of factor 40 or a pair of snow boots?'

'A bikini or a balaclava,' I suggested.

'What?' For one foolish moment, I wondered if she might be about to praise my neat turn of phrase. But no. I should have known. 'Yes, well, one could say that, I suppose, if anyone ever actually wore a balaclava outside of a bank raid. But do you get my drift?'

I sighed. Yes. I got it. All too well. It was another of her annoying little tests.

'You never meant for me to write a synopsis?'

'Precisely. I wanted to see if you could demonstrate independence of thought. I'm glad to see you did. Synopses are universally boring in any case.' She gazed up at the ceiling and recited, voice sing-songing, 'A loves B but their families hate each other, so they marry in secret. B is then careless enough to bump off A's cousin C and has to flee. A, meanwhile, is told she has to marry D.

Well-meaning friar E comes up with a solution to their problems. A pretends to kill herself, but stupidly omits to forewarn B. B, discovering A and thinking she's dead, kills himself. A wakes up and, finding B dead, kills herself. Absolutely no-one lives happily ever after. The end.'

'Shakespeare?' I hazarded.

'Spot on. Rom and Jules. Who, in their right mind, would commission that load of old cobblers?'

'You don't reckon William S went in for synopses?'

'Too busy writing plays and swiving his Dark Lady. Right, that's synopses done and dusted,' she said, though I was far from sure it was. 'Let's move onto secondary characters.'

At that moment, I heard a muffled banging.

'Take no notice,' Amanda said, a funny look in her eye. 'I've got a man in the garage.'

Immediately, I had the vision of a man, gagged and bound with tape to a chair, eyes popping with terror.

'It's only Pavel' she went on, 'On the hunt for the source of that smell. He thinks it could be the drains.'

'The handyman? He's still here?'

'He's whipped off my manhole cover and is having a good old root around in my nether regions.'

Was it me with the mucky mind, or her?

On cue, the man himself marched past the bay window, a wrench in his hand. Amanda gave him a wave. He stopped in his tracks and, unsmiling, lifted his hand in greeting.

'All praise to whydoityourself.com. A wonder of a website.' She tugged at the window. 'Pavel,' she shouted. 'Come and meet Trish Lightowler, wannabe writer.' He crossed the lawn and approached the window. 'Trish this is Pavel … what's your last name again?'

'Kuznetsov,' he said.

Amanda giggled. 'I call him Pavel Unpronounceable. Easier to get your tongue round. Pavel here is my jack of all trades.'

There was an awkward moment when me and Pavel tried and failed to shake hands through the half-open window. Giving up, Pavel stepped back and gave the tiniest of bows. 'I am please to meet you, Treesh,' he said, before continuing on his way.

'See what I mean?' Amanda's eyes were fixed on his departing back. 'An absolute wonder.'

I'll attempt a description of Pavel. The next voice you hear will be that of greenhorn crime writer, P.G. Lightning.

He was not a tall man but his posture was good and he was strong. Biceps strained at the sleeves of his shirt. His hair was dark blonde, cut short and brushed forward in that style favoured by the Slavic nations. His eyes were pale blue but a bit disturbing. His lips were shapely but a bit fleshy. Deep frown lines furrowed between blond eyebrows. Good cheekbones, mind. You could have sliced ham on them. I mistrusted him on sight.

If only she'd kept her trap shut. But she don't. The class goes OK, so Trish, encouraged, thinks it'd be cool after all to tell Amanda about her synopsis. The one she'd chickened out of showing her before.

Amanda listened as I outlined the plot of my story. The action took place, I said, all in one day with the main character – the MC, Amanda told me to call him – getting into all sorts of bother: he got locked in a shed, tore a hole in his coat, and was chased by black and white monsters.

'I could leave it with you, if you like. I printed it off,' I began, digging into my bag. 'And the big reveal I'm kind of pleased with is – '

'It's a dog. Or a cat,' she said wearily. 'Or some other creature.'

'A fox,' I said, the air sucked out of me. 'You've heard it before?'

'"A tale told by an idiot. Signifying nothing," to quote the Bard.' Amanda patted my hand. 'Best leave it where it belongs, well out of sight.'

My hot flush of humiliation lasted all the way to the bypass.

Ten

OK. Full disclosure. Trish don't tell Flo about her and Gregory. Only about losing her job. Flo is upbeat at the news.

'So Stephen stabbed you in the back? Not to worry, Mum. You're a brilliant admin. You'll get another job easy, somewhere where they'll appreciate you.'

Then, in the way of young people, she moved on to talk about herself.

'Anyway, I'll be home soon so you'll have no time to get bored.'

'Lovely. How long can you stay?'

'Actually, Mum, I'll be with you the whole summer, if that's OK. Why?'

That was unexpected.

'Nothing,' I said. 'It's … nothing.'

The truth is, I was panicking. I'd got used to my weird, solitary life. The idea of someone else being around, having to clean and tidy things away, cook proper meals and get dressed whether I was going out or not … well, it seemed like a load of faff.

56

'You're not off travelling like Nell?' I said hopefully. 'Or seeing friends?'

'What is this, Mum? You trying to palm me off?'

'Course not. It's fantastic news,' I said, wondering where I'd left the vacuum cleaner and when I'd last defrosted the freezer.

***

Holy Moly, how I hate video calls! But Nell and Flo insisted.

'Heaven's sake! Click on the icon,' Nell shouted, as if I was deaf as well as technically challenged. 'At the top. On the right.'

I could see the row of icons but worried about clicking on the wrong one in case, I don't know, I blew up GCHQ or something.

'It looks like a little video camera,' Flo said. Just then – lo and behold! – I spotted the little devil. I clicked and there I was, on the screen in my own little box. At least, some of me was.

'What's your laptop resting on?' Nell asked, craning her neck. 'All I can see is the top of your head. Your roots need doing by the way.'

I bent down to check. 'Roget's Thesaurus, the Dictionary of Quotations, and the Shorter Oxford. Both volumes.'

These mighty tomes were the result of a late-night online shopping spree at Bookrazee, at a time when I was unrealistically chipper about my future as a writer. A shopping spree that, incidentally, almost resulted in the poor courier having a hernia. This was the first, and possibly last, time the books had served any useful purpose.

'Too high?' I asked. 'I'll get rid.'

That only made things worse. Now all they could see was my belly, not my finest feature.

'I'll scrunch down.' This tested my flexibility and found it wanting. 'Hold on. I think a couple of Alan Titchmarshes might do the trick,' I made to shoot off in search.

'Christ, Mum,' Nell said, clutching her head. 'It's a simple video call, not a SpaceX rocket launch. Just sit still.'

'We'll make do with talking to your midriff, ' Flo said, ever the voice of reason. 'Otherwise we could be here all night.'

I tried to jolly the girls along. It was, after all, rather a hilarious situation, me with my head out of view, them talking to my spare tyre. At least it tickled me. Flo and Nell stayed decidedly untickled. Gradually it dawned on me it was more than my lack of IT skills that was souring the mood.

'So Mum, when were you thinking of telling us?' Nell said, when my titters died away.

'Ah. You've spoken to your dad.'

Trish should've known. Gregory was always gonna blab, get his angle in first. She's as much to blame as him, mind. She should've spoke up. She kept putting it off. Truth is, she couldn't bring herself to say them fateful five words: 'Your dad's left me.'
   Or would that count as four words?

'How could you, Mum?' they said. 'What were you thinking?'

How could *I*? What was *I* thinking? Words, literally, failed me. No sympathy for me. No anger with him. Flo and Nell were livid with me, if you please, the innocent victim of this family RTA! I was stunned. Why weren't they raging at their dad for driving a ten-tonne truck through our perfectly happy family? OK, let's not get carried away. For driving a ten-tonne truck through our *reasonably* happy family.

Why weren't they slagging off his American bit on the side for 'taking up', as my properly-bonkers mother would say, with a married man? Why was I, purer-than-the-driven-snow Trish, getting it in the neck? Why? Because I hadn't come clean straightaway.

'How could you keep such a big thing secret from us?' Nell demanded, the tinny speaker exaggerating the harshness of her words. 'That's no way to behave.'

I found my tongue at last. 'What about *him*? What about the way *he's* behaving? Breaking up the family. Messing up your lives. Messing up mine.'

'Seems to me you've done a pretty good job of that yourself,' Nell barked into the camera, her lovely mouth distorted. 'Honestly, Mum. Getting yourself sacked like that.'

'I was not sacked. I was let go. There's a difference. I'm a casualty of restructuring. And I got a generous pay off. Well, fairly generous.'

'But why, Mum? Why are you splitting up, after all these years?' Flo said, so plaintively I felt I had to provide an answer. Not *the* answer, obviously. I wasn't ready for that. But something plausible. Casting about frantically, the only thing I came up with was, well, not that plausible.

'He makes noises,' I said. 'All the time. Your dad. When he's watching telly. When he's driving. Or shopping. Anytime really. Grunts of approval or disapproval. Tuts of irritation. And don't get me started on the whole getting-into-and-out-of an armchair thing. What a performance! The 'oofs' and 'aahs' I have to put up with! In fact his whole life is a series of …'

Looking up, I saw I'd lost my audience.

'Noises?' Nell said into the silence that followed. 'Dad makes old man noises? And that's it? That's what finished off your marriage?'

'I'm not explaining very well.'

'I'll say.'

Flo chipped in. 'You and Dad can't break up. You're a team. You have to stay together. You love each other.'

Did we? Do we? We did once. I was almost sure of that. But somewhere along the way, I don't know when, we seemed to have lost the knack. One thing *was* clear, as my conversation with the girls stumbled along, when Gregory broke his promise and told them about the split, he hadn't given them the full skinny. Hadn't mentioned one crucial factor: the girlfriend. I could have filled them in, there and then. Dropped Gregory right in it. But I decided, no. Why should I do his dirty work for him? Let him do it. Let him tell them and watch their shock become anger, their sadness, hurt. Let him hear the heartbreak in their voices. Until then, I'd bite my tongue.

'Have you tried talking to Dad?' Nell meant well but she was properly getting on my bits. 'I get it's not easy. What with him being so busy with work and on the other side of the Atlantic and everything, but you've got to put the effort in.'

'A marriage as long as yours is worth fighting for,' Flo added. Even on the small screen, I could see the tear-shine in her eyes.

I took a breath. 'Look, I've had plenty of time to think and I've come to the conclusion I don't need your dad, or the poxy job for that matter. I'm capable of making a life on my own. I'm going to reinvent myself.' Irritation made me reckless. 'Like Madonna.'

After a silence, Nell said, 'Sorry. Did you say Madonna?'

'Perhaps not quite like Madonna,' I said, backtracking. 'She's a singer and I'm … not. But of course you know that. I'm going to be … well, I hope to be … a novelist.'

Twin mouths dropped open.

'What? Nell said. '*You*, Mum?'

'What will you write about?' Flo asked.

'Life,' I answered, recalling Amanda's rallying cry. 'I'll write about being a mother, a daughter, a wife … an ex-wife. Inspiration, after all, comes from existing.' Didn't sound so impressive when I said it. It's fair to say, the girls were duly unimpressed.

'Who'd want to read that?' Nell scoffed.

'Hate to say it, Mum, but she's right,' Flo said. 'People want escapism, excitement, fantasy. Not dull, everyday life.'

'I'm taking lessons,' I went on regardless, 'from a famous author.'

'Mum,' Flo said, 'Don't mean to be unkind but you can't *teach* someone to write. It's not like making a white sauce or crocheting a coaster.'

'You've either got it or you haven't,' Nell chimed in. 'Writing's a gift.'

'I have a gift. Amanda Turner told me so.'

Well, she had. Sort of. She'd said I had a gift for dry humour.

'Amanda who?' the girls chorused.

Eleven

Lesson 3: Breathing Life Into It

'Details,' Amanda lectured, 'are crucial if you want to bring a scene or a character to life. Don't write, *His eyes were blue.* Spend some time staring deep into someone's eyes and write…' Amanda closed her own eyes and breathed in and out through her nose. In and out. In and out. In and out.

How could she do that? Without choking on the stench, that is. I was almost retching, even though I'd taken the precaution of soaking a hanky in Ghost. Despite dabbing it under my nose like a dainty damsel out of *Bridgerton*, the smell still cut through to the back of my throat.

I'd taken trouble with my appearance this time. Even to the extent of brushing the cobwebs off my grubby make-up bag and having a go at the old smokey eyes. You know, layer upon layer of shadow and at least five coats of *Black is the new black* mascara. You pile it on till your eyelids are so loaded, you can hardly lift them. Used to be quite good at it back in the days when anyone, including me, cared what I looked like.

'Got your party eyes on, Pats?' Gregory would say, with a grin.

My phone pinged. It was as if the mere thought had summoned up the man himself. I'd been doing fine until Gregory's message came through.

Important letter in mail, it read. *Special Delivery. FFS stop fannying about. OPEN THIS ONE!!!!*

Complete with shouty caps and multi exclams.

I lost interest in the make-over after that. Right put me off.

Eyes shut, showily puffing in and out like a shaman in a trance, Amanda launched into her description.

'Persephone couldn't help herself,' she began. 'She was lost in his eyes, drawn like a fallen leaf into the eddies of azure and jade, steel and sapphire that swirled around the black whirlpool of his iris. There!' She opened her eyes. 'Not bad for an *ex tempore* effort, though one says so oneself.'

She beamed, pleased with her performance. Out of politeness, I patted my hands together.

'Thank you,' she said with a gracious dip of the head. 'Now you.'

'Off the top of my head? No. I couldn't.'

'Don't worry, I'm not expecting prose as polished as mine. Relax, close your eyes, open your mind, and let your imagination roam where it will.'

I did as I was told but my imagination didn't seem to fancy going for a wander. I opened one eye. *How long,* I thought, *should I sit there, pretending to be lost in thought?* Then, to my amazement, I had an idea.

'The coloured part of the eye is called the iris,' I launched in. 'The black hole in the middle, where light enters, is called the pupil. By widening and narrowing the muscles of the iris, the size of the pupil is altered, controlling the amount of light that reaches the back of the eye. Eye colour on the other hand is ...'

'Stop! Stop! That's quite enough of that,' Amanda said. 'I asked for a flight of fancy, not a TED talk on the anatomy of the eye.'

'Ophthalmology, it's called, the study of the eye. My dad worked in a spectacle factory in Leicester, grinding lenses. All done by computer now, of course. He taught me. It stuck with me, you know how some things do when you're a kid, the parts of the eye.'

Amanda glared but I was enjoying the feeling of being one up for once. 'It's the pupil, Amanda, the hole in the middle. That's the black whirlpool in your mate Persephone's blue-eyed man's eye, not the iris. You got that wrong.'

It was only a sniff, albeit loud and drawn out, but the sound Amanda made left me in no doubt what she thought of my cheek. 'Moving on,' she said after a tense few seconds.

She was grumpy for the rest of the lesson, which concerned the senses. All six of them. Six? I put up a wary hand.

'Yes, I know. Scientists say there are only five. They forget the most important, the *umami* of senses: intuition. My own intuitive instinct, you won't be surprised to learn, is extraordinarily finely tuned but even I would find it hard to put my finger on what it actually is. Gut feeling or hunch come somewhere near I suppose. All I know is, if one has it, one knows.'

'Are you saying, Amanda, you're psychic?'

'One could make a case. I am good at reading people. You, for instance, let me see now. You started your morning with the best of intentions, determined to pull yourself together. However, between the thought and the execution something upset you, and it all went horribly wrong. How am I doing?'

My flabber was duly gasted. How *does* she do that?

Trish, you plank! If she was to look in the mirror, she'd see Amanda's not blessed with the gift of ESP. ABS, more like. Absolute Bull Shit. One of Trish's eyes is smoked up like the Winkle-woman's, the other, where she was interrupted, is bare as a baby's bum. And she went round the whole day looking like that! Blimey O'Riley!

That ain't all. If she'd been paying proper attention, she'd have cottoned on to the real issue. If Amanda is Persephone — and my gut tells me she is — whose blue eyes is it she's been losing herself in?

Twelve

*More practice, that's what Trish needs, Amanda says.
Get them writerly muscles all pumped up, raring to go.
Still a slave to the whims of the bossy author, Trish
knuckles down and has a go at a memoir.*

The next voice you hear will be that of emerging
memoirist, Patsy Lightbody.

It was a phony, the village I came from. True, it had
a patchy village green where the men knocked a
cricket ball about in the summer months while the
women buttered bread, and around it there was a
group of pretty, black and white cottages, mostly
owned by people who worked in Leicester during
the week. But it wasn't a real village.

Stray more than a few streets from the centre,
and you would see it for what it really was: suburbia.
Rows of mean houses packed too close together, an
industrial estate of MOT testing centres and car
repairers, one church, three pubs, a betting shop, a

hairdresser's, a decent-sized supermarket and an open-all-day chippy. And on almost every street, bar the one round the village green, cars parked at all angles, their tyres digging deep ruts into the verges. Not exactly *The Darling Buds of May!*

Our pad was on the outskirts of the outskirts, a boxy, ex-council house down a cul-de-sac, well out of sight of the people with views over the village green. It had strange concrete cladding you don't see any more, and metal windows that streamed in the winter, so we never needed net curtains for privacy. The walls were so thin my properly bonkers mother used to joke when the people next door turned over, she could hear their bedsprings creak.

Village or not, people used to say our neck of the woods had that thing that people are supposed to crave: a sense of community. The drama group did a panto every other year, when people got to boo the chairman of the parish council and cheer our neighbour, a taxi driver, whose comic turn poking fun at local bigwigs always brought the house down. One of the pubs put on a quiz every Sunday night, with a box of meat as the prize. And a campaign to raise money to build a public toilet in the church vestry reached its target in less than four months.

All very community minded. All very warm and cuddly. And how I flipping hated it!

I ached for anonymity. For no-one knowing where I lived, what my dad's job was and, quite probably, how much he earned. For there to be no nosy parkers sticking their beaks in, judging me and reporting back. 'I see Patricia was at the rec last night. Well after nine. On a school night too.' Couldn't wait to grow up and move to somewhere where there weren't dozens of eyes on me, where I could stay out as late as I liked on any day of the week, and the possibilities were limitless.

But I botched it. It started promisingly enough with a move to North London and the comparative excitement of Camden College. In my final year I met Gregory – dashing, flat-stomached Gregory with his thick quiff of back hair, posh accent, and degree in accountancy. Gregory who, unlikely as it seems now, swept me off my feet. Nothing else mattered but being with him and having a good time. Not my career. Not my future. I took on any old temp jobs and concentrated on him. What a fool! Then, one day, he announced he'd landed a job in Oxfordshire and would be moving. Oh, and perhaps it was about time we got married, if that is, I wanted to go along too. I was ecstatic. Marriage, mortgage, and the move can swiftly after. And a few years later, motherhood.

Stymied by the four Ms! No breathing space to get going on a career, though Gregory seemed to manage all right. No opportunity to explore all the possibilities I'd dreamed of back in the phony village. The years whizzed by. Gregory landed the big job with Vanstone and I found myself in a much bigger house living a much smaller life.

Don't get me wrong. I like where we live now. It's quiet. No nosy parkers, interfering. Except now, with no husband, no job, and the girls in a permanent huff, I am a bit lonely.

I don't have any friends. Not real friends, like I had before we moved to Walnut Grove. People you can have a giggle with. Or a cry. I used to be friendly with some of the people at work but I can't face them since I got the boot. The rest of our social circle were people who knew me as half – the lesser half – of the Gregory and Trish double act, to be seen, looking lost and out of place, at golf club dinners or rotary dances. Obviously I don't see *them* anymore.

The truth is, I married up and have been just about hanging on to the rungs of the ladder ever since. Lately my grip has been slipping and I find myself nostalgic for the village life of my childhood, for a nosy parker to meddle. The woman across the road, for instance.

She's younger than me with two kids at secondary school. Moved in about a year ago. Could be two. Anyhow, on the day they arrived, soon as the removal men were gone, I went round with a lopsided chocolate cake. Not Mary Berry standard but I expect it tasted all right. Never found out. After thanking me, she told me her name was Virginia … or Vanessa, or Valerie – I forget – took the wonky cake from me and shut the door. Haven't spoken since. She's nodded in the street a few times if we happen to coincide on our respective drives, and that's it. Never bothered going round to get my plate back.

Bet she's a dab hand at baking. Bet her cakes rise evenly.

A cheery greeting from Vicky or Veronica and an invitation to coffee or, better still, a glass of 'seccy, would go down a treat right now.

'You look down in the dumps,' I imagine her calling out. 'Got time for a quick …?' She'd waggle her hand, making the international sign for a cheeky little drinkie. I'd give her the thumbs up and spend the afternoon in her *Furniture Village* living room, knocking back the wine, complimenting her on her cushions, and spilling out my troubles. Perhaps under her gentle coaxing, I'd shed a few tears.

She'd listen, without butting in or taking the mickey. She might even put a comforting arm round me. When I'd finished, she'd break out the vegan beetroot brownies and say a wise and wonderful thing that would make me feel less crushed. But Vivienne or Vera doesn't do any of that.

I know it's stalker-y but I got into the habit of tuning into her daily routines. In term time, she 'for God's sakes,' every morning as her teens pile into their Vauxhall Zafira, squabbling over who's turn it is to sit in the front. The school run done, I see her come back and shut herself indoors. What does she do all day? Sew novelty coats for pampered pooches? Write software for NASA? Binge watch *Schitt's Creek*, tears of disillusion running down her cheeks?

In the afternoon, she 'for God's sakes' again as the kids pile out of the Zafira, squabbling over who has first dibs on the PS27, or whatever. She never notices me staring round the curtains, like some saddo out of *Jane Eyre*.

Can't even do that now. There's been no sign of her or her kids since the schools broke up. Off to their second home in Brittany or poolside villa in North Cyprus, I shouldn't wonder. Probably as well. I doubt we'd get on. Not with all that off-putting swearing in the street. Thank God I've got Felicity and Amanda to talk to. Neither are exactly besties but, for now, they'll have to do.

Jeez, that was quite a download! Trish is in a bad way, hence the gloom-fest. Like many of the things wrong in her life, it's down to that shit Gregory. He – or rather his London lawyers – have been bombarding her with letters, you see. Trish, in the grown-up way she has, piles the letters, unopened, into a mini-Jenga stack on what used to be Gregory's desk, and ignores them.

Until today. When today's delivery landed on her mat, for some reason best known to herself, she made the mistake of opening it. Ain't been herself since.

The letter was addressed to, 'Mrs. Patricia Gertrude Lightowler, neé Murphy, on behalf of representatives of the applicant, Mr. Gregory Alan Lightowler, concerning …' The rest of the words floated past my eyes in a blur, without conveying any meaning. Something about a Conditional Order. Something about a Final Order. Then I came to the last bit, the bit that brought me up short: 'If this is granted, the two parties will be divorced, and the marriage legally ended.'

No possible misunderstanding there. There it is. The D word.

I hadn't expected it to hit me so hard. I thought I was prepared. But it was like I was sleepwalking. I went upstairs, undressed and stepped into the shower, turned the hot water up as high as I could bear and stood there for a long time, the water washing away my tears. I went outside in dressing gown and slippers, got in the car and drove aimlessly round town, at first in a trance-like state, then banging my fist on the steering wheel and screaming, while satnav woman – Hattie's her name – issued pointless directions in her newsreader voice. Then I drove home and took another shower, hotter and longer than the first one.

Didn't make it to Woodview this week. Feel like death, I croaked down the phone to Amanda. Bawled so long I burst a blood vessel in my eye and yelled so loud I lost my voice.

Thirteen

Lesson 4: Ride The Rollercoaster

I give up. You can't help some people. What is she doing, going back to Woodview, the stupid cow? Her head's all over the shop and her eye looks like an exploded tomato.

I know what she'd say if you asked her. She'd say she has her reasons. She'd say she misses the company. She'd say she worries if she don't get out of her house, she'll turn into one of them losers who has to be dragged out, clinging to the brickwork by their fingernails.

She'd say that but we know the truth, don't we? She's too chicken to tell Amanda to fuck right off.

Two weeks! I'd only been away two weeks but what a difference in Amanda. She was on sparkling form, chattering ten to the dozen, hair fabulous with new, expensive caramel highlights. Expect they call that colour *Fiona Bruce Brown*. Or should do.

Today, Amanda was in a pale lilac jumpsuit that made her legs look endless. A jumpsuit! I haven't worn a

72

jumpsuit since I was a teenager. Even then, I suspect, I looked like a sack of spuds. Nothing spud-like about Amanda Turner. With her neat figure and non-existent hips, she could carry it off.

The only clothes I have are weekend 'cazh', gardening scruff or machine-washable work suits. Never going to wear *them* static electric monstrosities again. Going to burn them, melt them more like. Or donate them to The Home for Distressed Admin Assistants, if there is such a charity. If there isn't, I shall use the first thousand of my book advance to start one. We are a neglected minority.

Joking, by the way. There's still no book, let alone an advance.

Jump-suited Amanda met me at the door. 'You sure you're up for this?' she asked, stretching up to inspect my eye. 'I'm not medically qualified but I'd say you look like shit.'

'Cheers. That makes me feel a whole lot better,' I said. 'And before you ask, I've done no writing. Or reading. Haven't done nothing of anything much. So please, go easy on me. I'm not up to it.'

'You poor thing. You *are* feeling sorry for yourself.' At these out-of-character kind words – insincere though I assumed them to be – my sore eyes filled with tears. 'There, there,' Amanda said, a hand on my shoulder. 'Don't upset yourself. As for the lesson, we've already established we're not into meaningless exercises, like, say, give me three synonyms for green.'

I dried my tears. 'Erm … emerald, olive, and erm …'

'No, no, no,' Amanda said, normal tetchiness re-emerging.

'Grassy!' I bellowed in panic.

'What I meant was, that was an example of what I *don't* want you to do.' She stopped and arched an eyebrow. '*Grassy*, Trish? Seriously?'

'I told you, I've been poorly.'

We set up at the kitchen table and got stuck in. At least, we tried. Pavel, the handyman, was still loitering, banging about, somewhere in the house, out of sight but still distracting. He knows a good thing when he's onto it. He'd given up on the drains, Amanda explained, and was bleaching the life out of anything that didn't move. The result was, to the whiff of wee was now added the unmistakable bouquet of bleach. Reminds me of the toilets at the old municipal swimming pool, before they had to close it down for health and safety reasons.

'Write,' Amanda commanded, pointing a stern finger at me, as soon as I'd parked my rear-end. 'Starting now.'

'What? I thought we'd said, no exercises.'

'No *meaningless* exercises. This is very much meaningful. How are you going to meet deadlines, if you can't write under pressure? Real writers write even when they don't feel like it. So stop whining and get writing. Trust me. I know what I'm doing. Come on, let me see if you have a spark. You've got fifteen minutes, starting … twenty seconds ago.'

The back of my neck prickled. This was it. The moment to prove myself. Or not. I opened up the laptop without a single idea in my head. Amanda left me to it and went outside to talk to Pavel. She'd instructed him to give the bleach a rest and do something about that 'mess of a garden.' I wandered over to the window. Pavel was poking the dry ground at the top of the garden with a spade, not putting much effort in. When Amanda appeared, he stopped altogether. They chatted, heads bobbing companionably. I watched for a while, then sat down at the kitchen table and began tapping.

I wrote the stuff about the Zafira woman, except I

didn't make it personal. Didn't say it was about me. Didn't say it was about my neighbour. I was struggling with a last sentence about Jane Eyre and – spoiler alert! – the mad wife in the attic, when Amanda re-entered and, behind her – my heart sank! – that blasted man.

'Hello again, Treesh,' he said, almost cheerful. For Pavel, that is. 'Remember me? I am the handy man of Amanda.'

Maybe I was being over-sensitive but something about the way he said it, with a slight emphasis on the word *handy,* gave me the creeps. I looked across at Amanda but she didn't appear to have picked up on anything. He helped himself to a glass of water and Amanda gazed at him as he drank, leaning back for a better view.

Pavel went outside and I slid my laptop across to Amanda. She took an awfully long time reading.

'Hmmm,' she said, when she'd finished. 'Well, well, well. I'll be honest, I wasn't expecting that. Who'd have thought it? From you of all people. A lesbian fantasy.'

'No. No. It isn't … It's … She's a woman on the edge. Lonely. Desperate. Not me. Well, a little bit of me … possibly.'

'Gracious, Trish. So defensive! You need to lighten up. You'll need to grow a thicker skin if you're going to be a writer. A thick skin to take the knocks. A thin skin to write with sensitivity. Quite a dichotomy.'

Normally I'd have asked what *dichotomy* meant but today I latched onto a less poncey word.

'You said *if* Amanda. Do you think I *could* make it as a writer?'

Amanda glanced down at the screen. 'Not entirely hopeless. Overwritten and self-indulgent but, yes, one could detect a spark of something. Whether, between us, we can fan that into a big, blazing bonfire that will set the whole of Waterstone's alight.' She looked into my eyes. 'That's up to you. How much do you want it, Trish Lightowler?'

My thoughts went back to the night before. Giving up on pushing a mushy ready-meal around my plate – cottage pie, lasagne or moussaka. They're pretty much indistinguishable – I looked over at the calendar stuck on the kitchen pinboard. I hadn't changed the month since that day at the end of April when the crap had collided with the ventilation. I took the calendar down from the board. The April page was full of scribbled notes: along with birthday and bin day reminders, there was a continuously flushing toilet to be persuaded to stop, a council tip to be gifted the contents of a shed, and a bikini line to be waxed. Oh, the glamorous life of a middle-aged woman!

I flipped over to the May page. Nothing. Not so much as a chiropodist appointment or a smear test. I flipped forward a few more pages. The following months, completely blank. I had literally nothing to look forward to, not even having my verruca scraped or my legs stuck up in stirrups.

'Yes,' I told Amanda. 'I do want it. I really do.'

Fourteen

'Not a facelift, Mum,' Flo said. 'Please tell me you haven't had work done.'

'Is this why you were acting so unbelievably dumb when we did the video call?' Nell said, grabbing my chin and roughly twisting my head. 'So we wouldn't see you'd gone under the knife?'

They had turned up together, the girls, unannounced, and once again I had to go through the rigmarole of explaining that the marks on my face – now fading into pink scars and yellow bruises – were not the result of cosmetic surgery. I am, quite frankly, getting thoroughly pee-ed off that everyone jumps to that conclusion.

'My bike hit a pothole, all right? And I nose-dived into the tarmac,' I told them, hoping for – but not expecting – sympathy. 'It was quite painful, actually.'

'What were you thinking?' Flo asked. 'You haven't ridden a bike since we were in the juniors.'

'And you were always coming off it, then,' Nell added. 'And you were much younger.'

I let that one pass. Though I love my girls so much it hurts, they can usually be relied upon – like my ancient pushbike – to bring me crashing down to earth.

'And the house? What's going on with that?' Nell strode past me into the living room. 'Well,' she declared, hands on hips like a fussy maiden aunt. 'What a shit hole.' A potty-mouthed maiden aunt. I bit my lip.

Gawd's sake, Trish. It's a wonder she's got any lips left, the way she chews on them. Why's she still letting them get away with it? This is Nell, the Nell whose bedroom was a biohazard throughout her childhood. What right has she to get a cob on about the state of Trish's house? Ask her if she cleans her room in halls. Or even makes the bed. Go on! I dare you, Trish. Ask her.

'I've had too many things on my mind to bother about housework,' I told the girls. 'What with your Dad. And the novel.'

'Ah, the novel.' Even gentle Flo couldn't keep the cynicism from her voice.

Nell was more direct. Moving the remains of last night's TV dinner out of the way, she flung herself down on the sofa, one leg hooked over the armrest. 'Come on. Sock it to us. Let's see it.'

'Can't.'

'Why not?'

'We don't mind if it's work in progress. We only want a sneak peek.'

'That is, I would, only ...'

Only what? Only I don't have anything to show them, even if I wanted to. The only writing I've managed is this load of old tosh you're reading now. And I'm certainly not going to show them this. Honestly, I've had a more creative time tweezering my eyebrows.

'It's only a rough first draft,' I said, thinking fast. 'Not much more than a concept. And as Earnest Hemingway

78

– or someone – once remarked, "All first drafts are shit."'
Amanda had told me the story. 'The magic comes in the
rewriting.' That was Amanda, too. The girls looked at me
as if I'd grown a second head.

'If you're going to quote Hemingway at us,' Nell said,
'I for one will need a sugar top-up. What ice-creams have
you got hidden away in that magic drawer of yours?
Better be some cookie dough.'

At short notice, the nearest I could come up with for
a snack was fish paté, a couple of days past its 'use by'. So
it was that, a few minutes later, we sat, three abreast on
the sofa, risking all kinds of stomach problems, a tub of
smoked mackerel paté balanced between us.

'Isn't this cosy?' I dipped in a stale nacho. 'Reminds
me of Sunday nights ages ago when we'd cuddle up in
front of a DVD after your dad had left for the airport.'

'I'd prefer ice-cream,' Nell said, grumpily.

Flo sniffed the tub. 'How many days past did you say
this was?'

I didn't care. I had my girls beside me. It was a return
to the closeness I worried we'd lost forever, and I
wallowed in it. The grazes and bruises on my face were
fading fast but my invisible wounds would take longer. I
needed my girls to help me heal.

'Can you stay over?' I pleaded, stretching out my
arms to enfold them both. 'Please say you will.' I gave
their shoulders a squeeze. 'You can spare your old Mum
one night, surely?'

'I could, I suppose,' Flo said. 'Don't have any lectures
tomorrow.'

'I have three,' Nell laughed. 'But they're skippable.'

Good. That would give us time to talk. Time for me
to finally give them the full story.

'Come on, girls,' I encouraged. 'Don't hang back. Dig
in.'

'How much has your dad told you?' I was at the kitchen sink, washing out the mackerel tub for recycling. Behind my back, I sensed a drop in the temperature. 'It's all right. You can tell me. I'm not going to go off on one.'

Nell did most of the talking. I made camomile tea. She talked some more. I made more tea. As Nell filled me in on what their dad had told them in their transatlantic conversations – and there had been a lot – she kept repeating, 'Dad said, it's no-one's fault. No-one's to blame.'

Each time she said it, I felt my stomach muscles tighten. And it wasn't the paté. Gregory was playing them, I could see that. Obviously they couldn't. By repeating that no-one was to blame, he was planting the seed that someone *was* to blame. And that someone was me.

I tried to explain.

Flo dunked her teabag. 'So, you're telling us that when Dad says no-one's to blame, what he means is the opposite?'

I was relieved. They were onto him at last. So I thought.

'That's plain paranoid, Mum,' Nell said. 'Verging on bonkers.'

That word! I took a moment. When I spoke again, I sounded calm, though the stomach cramps were worse than ever.

'Remember that summer,' I began. 'You were seven or eight, when we couldn't afford to go on holiday? We had days out instead. The wildlife park. Changing of the guard in London. The maize maze at that Pick Your Own place.'

For the love of Bake Off, Trish! Nell's tapping her

fingers. Flo's picking at her nail varnish. I'm rapidly sinking into a coma. Just come out with it! Tell them!

'The reason was,' I took a deep breath, 'your dad had spent our holiday money. On a course. In Sweden. On a boat. Very expensive. He needed it for his career, he said. For us. For the family. I went along with it. Another time, he bought himself a little two-seater without telling me. Totally impractical for a family of four.'

'Don't remember that,' Nell said.

'You wouldn't,' I replied. 'He sold it after a few weeks. Lost a packet. I could go on but I won't. The thing is, your Dad's one of them … one of those people who go through life doing what suits them. Whatever he wants, he gets.'

'Dad likes to treat himself,' Nell said. 'And he can be a bit of a selfish prat sometimes. So what? He's always been the same. Why, all of a sudden, does it bug you so much?'

'Is it money?' Flo asked. 'Is that what's behind the bust-up?'

'You misunderstand.' I massaged my cheeks. 'He acted like that because I let him. Not anymore. This time he's gone too far. This time I won't be going along with it. Because this time, what he wants is a woman by the name of Madison-Rose. Don't imagine he thought to mention *her* in any of your cosy transatlantic chats?'

'Madison-Rose?' Flo frowned.

'And she is …?' Nell asked.

'She's your dad's …' I'd promised myself I wouldn't slag off their dad or his girlfriend and, up till that moment, I'd done a pretty good job of sticking to that. But now wasn't the time for mincing my words. Now was the time for straight talking.

'She's your dad's American shag,' I said.

81

Bravo, girll! She got there in the end.

Fifteen

What's that phrase? *Once you pop, you can't stop.* Forget where I heard it, but that was me. The floodgates had opened and I couldn't stop. I told Flo and Nell at some length about The Email and The Letter, then, feeling guilty, doled out a shedload of cheesiness to soften the blow. Though, you know, cheesy can be sincere.

'Your dad still loves you,' I said, piling it on. 'Nothing will ever change that. He'll always be your father. Always be there for you. The last thing I want is for you to hate him.'

That's my job, I thought, but didn't say.

I waited, willing the girls to speak. As soon as they did, I wanted nothing more than for them to flipping well shut back up.

'There must be more to it,' Flo said.

'Did *you* have an affair?' Nell asked. 'Has he done this to get back at you?'

I sighed and tried again. 'I did not put it about. I did not get addicted to poker. Nor did I join a swingers' club, become a pagan, and dance naked in the woods at full moon, or get Gareth Malone's face tattooed on my left buttock. I didn't do anything out of the ordinary. Just did my best to be a normal, devoted wife and mother.'

'That's it.' Nell slapped the chair arm. 'You bored him into it.'

Even I can only take so much. I let rip.

'I am the wronged party here!' I said, jabbing myself in the chest. 'Me! Since when does the love-rat get all the sympathy? Since when does he get to be let off the hook? Whatever happened to female solidarity?'

There was more. I can't remember what now. I raved on, all restraint gone, exploding with the resentment I'd been storing up since Gregory sent me the break-up email. When I ran out of rant, I stormed out, slamming the door, and sat alone in the sitting room, hugging a huge glass of Sauvignon. A while later I heard the girls go up to bed. No kisses. No hugs. No Waltons-style good nights.

I'm back in the kitchen, alone but for what's left of the bottle, wondering if I should have had more self-control. Been more considerate. Then I've been self-controlled and considerate all my life and I'm sick to death of it.

I could have had affairs, like Gregory. It's not like I haven't had opportunities. Well, one. A few years back when me and Gregory were going through a stale phase.

I was at a tedious business conference in Brighton. At the end of the final session, I was gathering up my papers when Paul from IT Support – early thirties, good sense of humour, full head of brown curly hair – sidled up and asked if I wanted to go for a drink. I assumed there would be a crowd of us but when I got to the wine bar, it was only me and him. Being friendly, I supposed. He wouldn't be interested in me. Not in *that* way. After a couple of drinks, to my amazement, he sidled closer and it became clear he *was* interested in me and very much in *that* way. Couldn't get out of that bar fast enough.

The fool! She must see it weren't conscience or an outdated idea of right and wrong that held her back. It was fear. Only hope she's learnt her lesson and the next time she bumps into a 'Paul from IT', she won't be so quick with the Usain Bolt impersonation.

The girls have always hated sharing a room, even when they were little. The twins thing again. Too bad. This time they'll have to lump it. With the Dutch courage of the Sauvignon, I have made up the two singles in the spare room. I have a plan, you see.

Oh God! It's all gone pear-shaped. It started off OK. After leaving it a while, I tiptoed along the landing, glass in hand, and knelt outside their door. At first all I could hear was murmurs. Couldn't make out actual words. Then voices were raised and I caught the odd phrase.

'... hard to know what to think.'

'... lost the plot.'

'... so unlike him.'

Then '... two sides to every break-up.'

Two sides! There were *not* two sides to this break-up. There was only one: mine. In my agitation, my head bumped against the door. Only a gentle nudge but it was enough. The murmuring stopped. I froze.

'Mum!' Flo flung open the door. 'What do you think you're doing?'

Caught in the act, I dropped my glass.

'Oops. Spilled my wine,' I slurred, rubbing at the carpet with the cuff of my fleece, all too aware what a sorry sight I must have looked. 'Good job it was the white.'

'Were you eavesdropping?' Flo demanded.

I hung my head.

'You are so out of order,' Nell said.

In the past I would probably have apologised. Not now. This Trish doesn't say sorry, even when she's in the wrong.

I struggled to my feet. 'I'll tell you what's out of order, shall I? You two defending him. I don't get it. I told you what he's gone and done. How he's treated me.'

'We're not defending him,' Nell said.

'We're staying neutral,' Flo added.

'Neutral!' I clutched my head. 'May I remind you, your dad's been having an affair with some woman in New York, not much older than you, I expect. He's destroyed this family.' I flailed my arms in exasperation. 'How can you see all that, and stay *neutral*?'

'Mum,' Flo said quietly, 'don't you see? You can't only blame one person when a marriage falls apart. It takes two to make a relationship, and two to break it.'

'Oh, please! Spare me!' I cried. 'This isn't *Made in Chelsea* or *Dear Deirdre*. You can't mend this by watching a YouTube video. This is real life. Real life in all its untidy messiness. And, for the record, when I want counselling from someone not long out of Pampers, I'll ask for it.'

'In that case,' Nell spun on her heel, 'you won't mind if Flo and I leave you to it and go back to bed.'

Mouthing, 'Sorry, Mum,' over her shoulder, Flo shut the door on me.

'Don't think this is the end,' I shouted into the woodwork. 'We'll talk this through properly in the morning.'

I stared at the bedroom door for some seconds before shuffling to my room.

Next morning was grim. It felt like major roadworks were

going on inside my head and neither girl would speak to me. They left early, tight-lipped and refusing my offer of coffee. I've been in my dressing gown all day, nauseous and full of regret.

I had my chance and I bollocksed it up. I'm more wretched than ever.

Sixteen

Lesson 5: Sir Simon Or Jamie?

Dear-oh-dear! Five hundred quid she handed over, and for what? After five weeks, she's no nearer writing a novel than winning Only Connect. *Further away if anything, as week by week Amanda chips off more chunks of her confidence. Now, she's after yet more dosh.*

Five classes is what we agreed. What I paid for. Today was number five and I know what I should do. I'm only hesitating as giving up would add another failure to my list.

But I will. I'll tell her today. *Thanks very much, Amanda, but I've spent enough. No more, thanks.*

OK, so I didn't. I signed up for more of the same. But only because, on the drive over, I realised I'd miss my weekly jaunt to the Park. Anyway, I think Amanda might be right. I am starting to get somewhere with the writing.

Not that today went well. Amanda's approach is full-on at the best of times, and today, after the business with the girls and the Sauvignon, I was feeling especially fragile. She was bright and breezy. Looked the part, too, in a navy tailored dress. Navy washes me out but on her it looked sharp. What does she have to be so bouncy about, I wondered? Then I remembered: my five hundred.

He was there again. Pavel. Doesn't he have any other customers? She's got him tiling the upstairs bathroom now. Meanwhile, the house still stinks like a scrofulous – an Amanda word I had to look up – khazi.

We sat in the drawing room, *eau-de-wee* wafting in every time that man opened the door to ask another of his stupid questions, which was often. Amanda doesn't mind. Me and my bank balance do. The man cost me at least twenty quid today with his interruptions, I reckon.

It was another bewildering session.

'Index cards, photos, cuttings from newspapers, whiteboards, blackboards, mood boards, mind maps, tree diagrams, spreadsheets,' she began. 'All aids writers swear by.'

'Hold on, while I get that down,' I said, scribbling furiously.

Amanda didn't hold on or even slow down. 'They make a fetish of them, spending as much time drawing time-lines and writing CVs for even their minor characters, as they do composing the actual manuscript.' She fluttered a hand. 'Most of it a total waste of time.'

'Oh.' I paused, pen aloft. 'You don't believe in planning and stuff?'

'What does it say on my passport?' Amanda asked. 'Not *mood board builder* or *card indexer.* It says *writer.* I am a writer. Therefore, what I do is write.'

'I should launch in,' I queried, 'without a clue where I'm going with it?'

'Up to you. Personally, I find any kind of diagram or graph off-putting. No. I write. I write the first draft, beginning, middle, and end, warts and all, bad spelling, bad grammar, plot holes, inconsistencies, repetitions, *non sequiturs*, however it falls from my fingers. Then I polish. And polish. And polish. And ...'

'OK. I get it,' I said impatiently.

But Amanda was only just getting started. 'As in music, some of us are improvisers, others like to follow a written score. What one has to ask oneself, Trish, is: am I a Sir Simon Rattle, sticking to what's down on the sheet music, or a Jamie Cullum who wings it?' She looked me up and down. 'If I had to put money on it, I'd say you were a Sir Simon. Am I right?'

I smiled in what I hoped was an enigmatic manner. Amanda wasn't to know, I'm not an anything. My journey to publication hadn't yet begun. The folder on my laptop labelled *The Novel* was empty.

She didn't press it. Ever restless, she moved on to the importance of staying flexible. 'Remember, nothing is set in stone. You're the dictator of the world you have created. Nothing happens without you. And if you, the great dictator, feel something's not working, change it.'

She bounded to her feet and, to my astonishment, began hopping from foot to foot, shadow boxing. 'Be quick on your feet. Duck and dive. Roll with the punches. God I feel good!' she gasped. 'Be radical. Be ruthless. Above all, be adept at adapting.

'Even if you've written a hundred thousand words and triumphantly typed *The End*,' she wheezed. 'If that little voice inside you tells you it's not right, listen to it. Your first idea isn't necessarily your best. Plan B might be better. Or C or D ... or Z, for that matter. Many of my best ideas have come about after hasty last-minute rethinks. Keeps you and the reader on your toes. Keeps it fresh.' Amanda collapsed into a chair, breathless.

'What if …?' I was about to ask, *what if you haven't got a Plan A?* when the door opened and, for the umpteenth time, Pavel entered.

'Have no more of the tiles,' he said. 'I go to The Fire-red Earth. You give me banking card?'

Amanda sighed, but it was the kind of sigh a parent might give a favourite child. While she searched out her wallet, Pavel stood waiting, scratching his chin.

'Is not correct what you say about passport,' he announced to no-one in particular. 'I hear your talkings from up the stairs. No *writer*. No nothing on passport. I know. I show passport many, many times. It does not say nothing about job.'

Amanda pursed her lips. I knew she didn't like being contradicted, even on small matters. 'Let's see it, your passport,' she challenged, flicking her fingers at him.

He took a step back. 'I… I not have. Is at home.'

'You have to show it all the time, yet you don't carry it with you?'

'Is more safer at home.'

Amanda's eyes narrowed, then she smiled. 'Only teasing,' she said, handing over her bank card. She turned to me. 'Now we've disposed of boring old planning, let's get down to the fun stuff: foreshadowing.'

Then to Pavel, still hesitating in the background, 'Go on if you're going. Off to The Fire-Red Earth with you.'

You total meringue, Trish! So much for telling Amanda where to get off. Of course she has no trouble batting away Trish's feeble bleats.

'Cheques are so old-fashioned,' she says boldly the minute Trish agrees to continue. 'This arrangement is more business-like.' After she presses her bank details into Trish's hand, the upshot is inevitable. Another five

hundred is soon winging its way from Trish's account into
hers. Not cos Trish wants it, but cos she doesn't have the
sheer Gordon Ramsey to tell Amanda where to shove her
useless lessons.

It's not only the wasted dosh, though Gawd knows
that's bad enough. It's the way Amanda behaves. Ogling
that man, muttering about his 'tight little cheeks'. She
don't actually wink and go 'Nudge, nudge,' but she may
as well of done.

Can you be that blind, Trish? Don't you see what's
going on under your nose? Or don't you wanna see?

Seventeen

The voice was husky but she recognised it at once. Of course she did. She'd lived with it for more than two decades. And who else would call her at two in the morning? He couldn't know she was still awake. Of course, like a fool, she answered.

What's up with your throat?'

'I don't want *her* to hear,' Gregory whispered. 'Maddy-Rose. She's in the next room.'

Call me spiteful but my spirits soared. It was the first time I'd heard Gregory talk about his lover in anything other than sloppy terms. 'She'd get the wrong idea if she knew I was speaking to you. She's highly strung. Hot Italian blood. On her mother's side. From Naples originally. Whereas, on her father's side, the Harringtons, they're old money who…'

'As much as I'd love to spend what's left of the night doing a *Who Do You Think You Are?* on your girlfriend's family,' I said, 'I *was* hoping to get some sleep. What do you want?'

'We can't go on like this, Trish. We should talk.

About us. About the practicalities. About the future.'

Hate to admit it, but Gregory had a point. I couldn't go on blanking him. It was childish. We had important things to sort out. There was another reason. Less noble. I wanted to find out more about the wondrous Madison-Rose Harrington. I had a feeling the longer Gregory talked about her, the more inclined he'd be to dish the dirt. I was looking forward to a dose of that lovely stuff they call *Schadenfreude*.

'I'll give you exactly ten minutes.' I pulled the covers up to my chin.

Ten minutes, naturally, became thirty, then forty-five and Gregory was still going on. Not about how we were going to manage the split but about her, Maddy-Rose. At first, he sung her praises. How fabulous in every possible way she was. How she'd bowled him over since they began their whirlwind romance – yes, he did use them … those tabloidy words. I was about to call time when his mood darkened, and he started properly bitching.

I snuggled further down in the bed. First he slagged off her family. 'Her mother's here all the time. Has a key. Lets herself in and proceeds to take over.' Then he poked fun at their New York lifestyle. 'They eat out every meal, every day. I'm not exaggerating. Breakfast, brunch, lunch, tea, dinner, and supper. Only use their gleaming island kitchens to brew coffee, pop popcorn, and mix up disgusting mac 'n' cheese snacks. And she's incapable of having a civilised discussion without taking every remark to heart and calling her therapist immediately afterwards at God knows how much per hour.'

He moaned about her moods. 'I never know where I am. She'll cold-shoulder me all day and refuse to say why. Then she'll appear from the bedroom, all dressed up, as if nothing has happened, and sweet-talk me into taking her dancing.' He gave a nervous titter. 'Life's certainly not boring, that's for sure!'

I took this, as I am sure I was meant to, as a comment on the dullness of life with me. We never went out dancing on the spur of the moment. I never had a therapist. I let him talk on, until he said, 'Truth is, even with the mood swings and the mother and everything, there's not a single thing about my new life I'd change. I feel more alive now than I have for decades.'

Had he completely forgotten who he was talking to?

Time for me to speak up. 'I thought you wanted to talk about us?' I said, icicles hanging from my words. 'Instead it's been all about you, as usual, and her. I no longer expect you to care about my feelings, but what about the girls? You could at least pretend to be concerned about what this nightmare is doing to them.'

'You're angry. I get it.'

This only infuriated me more. 'Angry is not even close, Gregory. I'm destroyed, wrecked, obliterated. I don't know what I'm doing any more. Or who I am. I'm … I'm …' I sat up, pressing my fingers into the sockets of my eyes.

'Actually, Pats …'

'For the last time, Gregory, stop calling me that!' I screamed into the phone. 'In fact, don't call me at all. Leave me alone. Just fuck the shut up!'

At the other end of the line, I heard a strange sound. It took me a second or two to work out what was going on: Gregory was laughing at my pathetic swearing.

I hung up, laid my head on the pillow and had the best night's sleep I'd had in weeks.

Eighteen

Lesson 6 – Inspiration *En Plein Air*

'It's getting worse, isn't it?' Amanda said, by way of greeting.

'Seems to me,' I said, walking through the house holding my nose, 'the hotter it gets, the stronger the pong. Smells like something's crawled in under your floorboards and died.'

Amanda, in a blue striped cotton sundress that showed off her tanned shoulders, flung out her hands. 'You genius, Trish! The floorboards! Of course. Pavel!' she yelled. 'Get a crowbar or a chisel or something. Got a job for you.'

'He's still here then?'

'Work never ceases with a house of this vintage. It's certainly too much for one woman. The sensible thing would be to sell up and move somewhere more modern but my aunt left Woodview to me and I was very fond of her. It brings back memories of long, hot summer holidays I spent with her, exploring these woods. I couldn't bring myself to part with it. Sentimental of me, I know, but that's me all over.'

***

We sat in the drawing room, French windows wide open, me struggling to concentrate due to the heat, the stink and, before long, the off-stage sounds of splintering wood and Eastern European cursing.

Amanda talked authors, specifically Lee Child, her favourite. She's always on about him, though I'm never sure whether it's the quality of his writing she admires or the size of his bank balance.

'Unapologetically commercial. Doesn't mess about with long sentences. Sparing with verbs. Prolific. Business-like. Multi billionaire.' She sighed with approval. 'What a man!'

Unwisely, I attempted to champion my latest discovery: Barbara Kingsolver. But I don't have Amanda's clever way with bullshit. Only got as far as mentioning how she juggles big themes with rattling good tales, before Amanda stopped me.

'Swaggers too much on the page for my liking. Too self-consciously showy, shoving her talent in your face. The Meryl Streep of literature.'

Was trying to recall how many Oscars Meryl Streep had bagged, when *he* waltzed in, Pavel. Would it be too much to ask for him to knock? He wanted to know how many of 'the flooring woods' he should take up.

They discussed this riveting subject for some minutes, using up more valuable lesson time. Then Pavel did something puzzling – at least I think he did. I wasn't paying proper attention. I was mentally still totting up Meryl's Oscars. But what I think he did is, when he walked behind Amanda's chair, he trailed his fingers across her bare shoulders.

It was over before I could be sure I'd seen what I'd seen.

Whatever did or didn't happen, Amanda had lost all interest in the lesson.

'It's so stuffy in here. Let's go for a walk. We have these gorgeous woods around us. We should take advantage. There's many an inspiration to be found in nature, after all.'

Soon we were in the lane, walking briskly. Amanda took out an e-cigarette.

'Didn't know you indulged?' I said.

'I don't. At least, I didn't. Not for twenty years. Took it up to cover the whiff in the house. Turns out, I quite like it.' She blew out a cloud of condensation. 'Cotton Candy Kisses. Fancy a puff?'

'Not at all,' I coughed.

We made our way up the lane to join what's known as the Old East London Road, her striding, me struggling. Strange name. It isn't a road, more a track. And it doesn't go to London, at least not any more. But it does head east and is old, I'll give them that. Two parallel tracks of pounded earth cut a dead straight line between the hedgerows. They are all that's left, as Gregory used to tell me and the girls in the days when we walked there, of a time when this was indeed the main thoroughfare to the capital.

'And the haunt of many a wicked highwayman,' Gregory would say in an *oooh-arrrh* accent. I think he was confusing highwaymen with pirates.

The girls would walk ahead, as Gregory chuntered on, with an imaginary dog they named Rowdy, shouting to him, throwing sticks and chuckling.

'Better than a real hound,' Gregory would say. 'No poo to pick up.'

Amanda breathed out another fog of condensation, temporarily shrouding her top half.

'Look down,' her headless body commanded, 'at the soil here, the molehills in particular. Ever wondered why they're that peculiar colour?'

She was right. The path and the molehills glowed a bright orangey-red in the sunshine.

'Ochre,' she explained. 'Oxford Ochre, to be precise, at one time the purest and most prized in the world. Seams run under the Country Park. I'd have thought you'd have known that.'

She can never resist!

'News to me.' I kicked at the dry earth. 'And they used this orange dust for what exactly?'

'Orange dust! I'll have you know, the mineral pigment from the pit here was used by artists for many thousands of years, from prehistoric cave painters to Da Vinci and Turner.'

As we walked, she told me more about the history of the ochre pit and how the invention of synthetic ochre had killed the Oxford industry stone dead in the 1920s.

'Since then, the workings have been left in the care of Mother Nature,' she said, 'and she hasn't been making a very good job of it.'

I was enjoying myself. Why hadn't we done this before? It was so good to be in the Country Park and away from Woodview, shaded from the sun and with perfect fluffy clouds – like at the start of *The Simpsons* – in the flat blue sky. A dead tree, smooth and white, lifted its branches to the heavens, like it was giving ghostly thanks. Cattle the colour of clotted cream grazed in a nearby field, lowing and crunching on grass as they ambled forward, pale against the dark thicket of trees some way behind them. They lifted their fine heads and gave us a snooty stare as we passed, as if they knew how valuable they were – but not how that value would be realised.

I took in a breath. And best of all, there was no nasty niff.

'This way!' Amanda bellowed, taking a narrow side path, bordered by trees, their branches meeting overhead.

Bosky. The word came into my head from I don't-know-where. Grace, I imagine. It was a lovely, bosky path. We walked on, Amanda sucking on her fake fag, me loving the way the sunbeams played on the ground, flickering against my eyelids like the frames of an old-fashioned film.

Was about to come over all intelligent on the subject of the origin of the word *flicks*, when Amanda veered off the path. I trotted in her wake, picking my way through knee-high nettles, following the trail of candy-flavoured puffs left hanging in the air, as if she was a miniature steam train.

Rounding a tangle of blackberry brambles, I found Amanda staring at a recently fallen oak, its fat stump rearing up to expose jagged, pumpkin-yellow innards.

'Victim of the winter gales,' she said. 'Snapped like a matchstick. A sad end for such a venerable beast.' She gave its trunk an affectionate pat as if it were indeed a dead animal.

'And now this drought,' I fanned my face. 'Hope they don't lose any more trees. What would Oaker Wood be without its oaks?'

Amanda exhaled another cloud. 'No, no, no. A common misconception. Oaker Wood isn't named for its oaks, despite the spelling. It's for the ochre.'

'Where is this pit then?' I said, shading my eyes. 'All I can see are trees and more trees.' I bent to scratch my ankles. 'And a load of vicious nettles.'

Amanda advanced a few paces. 'Behold,' she

declared, holding out her arms. 'The ochre pit.'

'Oh,' I said.

Let's just say, the Grand Canyon people don't have a thing to worry about. Oaker Wood's ochre pit won't win any prizes as a tourist destination any day soon. Before me was a depression in the ground about ten metres deep and the same across, though it was hard to make out where it began and where it ended, owing to the trees and scrub that crowded in, and the thick carpet of twigs and leaves that covered the whole area.

'It's just a hole in the ground, and not a very big one at that.' I laughed. 'You could say, the pits are the pits.'

Amanda sniffed. 'I've brought you here, Patricia Lightowler, not to make feeble jokes but to fire your imagination, if you've got one. The pit might not look much today but it was once the hub of a thriving industry. Can't you sense the weight of history?'

I didn't think I did.

'Imagine it in, say, the eighteenth century when ochre mining was in its heyday and the pit was much deeper,' she went on. 'Men stripped to the waist, muscles glistening, hewing raw ochre from the sheer cliff wall with hand-picks. Children at their feet shovelling it into carts. Stray dogs begging for scraps. Women handing over cloth parcels of bread and cheese and flagons of ale to their menfolk. The whole scene – men, women, children, dogs, trucks, even the bread and cheese – coated in a thick layer of ochre dust. Right. You take it from there, Trish. Make me see that wall of colour rising high above them. Employ some metaphors. Be as fanciful as you like.'

Here we go again, I thought, heart sinking, 'I see …'

'Don't you dare say a hole in the ground,' Amanda interrupted. 'Close your eyes and set your imagination free.'

I tried, I really did. I squeezed my eyes shut and strained to be in the moment. 'Erm, I see a plethora of reddish-orangey streaks.' I wasn't at all sure about *plethora*, and *reddish-orangey* seemed clumsy and, well, not very imaginative, but it was all I had, so I pressed on. 'Flowing together.' I weaved my hands in the air, searching for an exciting climax to my, so far, quite unexciting description. 'Putting me in mind of …'

'Yes, yes. Go on,' Amanda encouraged. 'Pursue the concept. Dig deep within yourself.'

'… a dreadful old pair of curtains my mother used to have.'

'Honestly!' Amanda puffed out a cloud of candyfloss.

'If you're so clever, what comes to your mind?' I sulked.

Amanda considered. 'I see a waterfall of blood.'

By the time we'd walked back to the car park, an ice-cream man had parked his van and set up shop. It was only that whipped-up stuff that tastes of soap and is more air than ice-cream, but it was cold and welcome in the heat. We sat eating, side by side, on a gnarled old bench, looking over a hazy Oxford. Amanda ended the session with a brief foray – is that the word? – into plot devices. *Tips on how not to bore the pants off the reader,* she called it.

'Lull them into a false sense of security. That's the way to do it. Create a hiatus, a moment of calm, then lob in something totally unexpected to get their hearts pumping,' she said, crunching down on her cornet.

102

Nineteen

Pavel's pubic hair is a surprisingly vivid shade of ginger. Wasn't expecting that. I don't mean the colour. I mean seeing his pubes. It was hard to avoid them. When we got back, there he was, stood at the top of the stairs, naked as the day, towelling his hair and preening. They do that, don't they, men? Preen when they don't have their keks on.

With a yelp, Pavel clutched the towel to his groin and ran, bony buttocks a-quiver, across the landing.

'Well!' I said, exhaling like an outraged nun.

Amanda was bent double, laughing. 'Didn't I mention? Pavel's moved in. I've got plenty of room and he's miserable in that poky B&B in Oxford.'

'As your lodger?'

'No. More like my ... can a man be a housekeeper?'

'Why you not tell me, Mandy,' Pavel shouted down from the bedroom, 'that you bring Trish back with you?'

Mandy? Did you clock that? He called her Mandy!

I tried again with the novel. Had a glass of wine inside me this time. Only the one. Typed for half an hour. Stream of consciousness stuff. Left it to 'cook' while I watched a genius sci-fi movie. I could tell it was genius because I couldn't make head or tail of it. After the film came to its baffling conclusion, I risked a look at what I'd written. Utter bilge. Deleted.

I've been sitting up in bed, laptop on a pillow, looking up Amanda. Nine books she's got listed online. Mostly family sagas – used copies available from two pounds 99p, including postage – and two romslashers.

She was right. She was admired for her plots. Readers described her early stuff as *clever, gripping,* even *enthralling.* Her more recent books, not so much. *Kiss of Death*, the first of her blood-soaked romances got mostly three and four stars. *Multilayered and complex*, said one review. *Confusing,* said another.

The latest, *Love You to Bits,* fared even worse. A dozen reviews, a couple of them stinkers. *A confusing mishmash. Couldn't work out who was doing what to who – or care.* And the final nail in the coffin: *DNF.* Had to look that up. The ultimate ... what's the opposite of accolade? Is it bummer? That, anyway. DNF stands for: *Did not finish.*

Amanda is losing her touch, that's clear. Doing what she's always criticising others for: showing off.

But who am I to judge? My duck remains unbroken.

Twenty

It was another pleasant evening and the two of us were strolling to the film club. Felicity had talked me into joining, to widen my cultural references and improve my writing, she said. I only agreed when she told me how cheap the wine was and how efficient the air con.

As I'd sat through the previous week's Estonian comedy without cracking a single smile, I didn't hold out much hope that this evening's Iranian New Wave offering would be a riot.

As the English subtitles passed before my unfocused eyes, I found my attention wandering and my thoughts returning to research. I should do some. Get in some practice. Show some initiative. Surprise Amanda, in a good way this time. I was still smarting from the *old curtains* incident.

I've settled on Oaker Wood as a topic. Got copies of *Royal Forests of Medieval England* and *Mineral Pigments of the Lower Cretaceous* from the library. Can't say I'm gripped but I'm giving it a go. The next voice you hear will be that of budding his-fic author, Patti Nightowl.

The grass under his feet feels soft, soft as velvet. Walter wriggles his bare toes, enjoying the sensation against his skin. Not that he's ever touched velvet. One day, he promises himself, he will be able to afford a velvet jacket and shoes of softest leather, like the pit managers' sons wear. And a horse. So he can ride through the 117 hectares of hunting forest in style, admiring the spectacular views over three surrounding counties.

As he walks he looks about him at the indigenous trees and bushes of Oaker Wood, as familiar to him as the lines on the palms of his work-hardened hands. How he loves these woods, unchanged since Saxon times!

Even during the English Civil War (1642 to 1651), so Walter has heard tell, work in the forest continued uninterrupted. What a pity, he ponders, that it lost its royal status in 1660. Not that the woods are not used. Oh no! Nobles still pound through the clearings on sweat-foamed steeds, intent on pursuing their quarry of deer and wild boar. The townsfolk still graze their livestock, gather winter fuel, and fell mighty oaks to provide timber for their humble dwellings and grander communal buildings.

What another pity, Walter muses further, as he climbs the path to the pit workings, that European brown bears, the British lynx and wolves no longer roam the region. They would surely have made fine sport, if they had not become extinct in the early Middle Ages due to over-hunting and habitat destruction.

But this is no time for nostalgia. Walter increases his pace. With his father, Abe, hardly cold in the ground of the nearby picturesque village churchyard, and his mother, Maria, gone so long ago, Walter can no longer remember her face, only the sweet perfume of the wild burdock she would tuck into her kirtle, Walter has taken on responsibilities far beyond his tender years.

Though he is but a boy, he has inherited from his father the role of foreman of the renowned Oaker Wood pits, the most productive in the whole of England and worked for generations by members of his family. A lot rests on his narrow young shoulders. He straightens his spine. He has a job to do.

Not that Walter is one to shirk responsibilities. He may be illiterate and no more than sixteen or seventeen seasons old – birthdays are not big at this time – but he is far from ignorant, on one topic especially. He knows all there is to know about the production of ochre at the end of the Elizabethan era and the beginning of the Jacobean and Stuart periods.

He's probably not aware – they were not that great on geology and palaeontology back then either – that deposits are composed of yellow iron oxyhydroxide mineral goethite, laid down during the lower Cretaceous period.

But he does know his ochre is prized above all others by artists for use in their oil paintings as the purest to be found the length and breadth of the land. Furthermore, he knows the ochre lies in thin layers, embedded within sandy and clay-ey layers. These must be removed before the yellow, orange, and scarlet earth pigments can be dug out. After that, the ochre is washed, dried, and milled into a fine powder before being mixed with oil, ready to be squeezed onto the pallets of great artists like Mr. Aloysius Dalrimple.

Mr. Dalrimple! Walter gives a start and squints up at the sun, attempting to gauge the time, for wristwatches are yet to be invented. It is approaching noon, he judges, the time of Mr. Dalrimple's appointment. Prior to placing a substantial order, the famous artist had insisted he must inspect the quality of the ochre at first hand and, no doubt, that of the young and inexperienced pit foreman.

Walter strides out. Time to stop daydreaming and get a wriggle on.

Gawd! To think I thought she was improving.

Twenty-One

Lesson 7: Do It. Check It. Forget It.

'Beware the info dump,' Amanda said, 'There's nothing worse.'

It's uncanny. She's done it again. There I was, minding my own business, working on my research skills, and what does she focus on in today's lesson: research! How does she know what I need to know, exactly when I need to know it? Uncanny!

'Picture it. You're a reader getting stuck into a story,' she continued. 'Plot merrily motoring along, characters making their entrances and exits, when *Bam!*' She thumped the table. I jumped back so hard I bit my tongue. 'The author slams on the brakes to shoehorn in a slab of indigestible detail. Why? They've done the research and they don't want it to go to waste. Spent hours on the internet, or in the library, or talking to so-called experts, or – God help us! – roaming foreign parts on tax-deductible, fact-finding trips.'

'You're saying you don't need to do any research?' I said, thinking of the hours I'd spent trying to make head or tails of those boring books.

'Of course one must research, but one's resulting knowledge must be sprinkled like flat-leaved parsley on a lasagne, not dolloped all over like ketchup on a fry-up.' She lowered her voice. 'But – and I'm giving away a trade secret here – seemingly irrelevant little diversions, that readers are inclined to skim over, do have their place. They provide useful hidey-holes for that insignificant nugget of info that will later prove integral to the plot. And the plot, as always, is king, the twistier the better. It's a trick I often used.' She chuckled. 'Not for nothing was I dubbed the Queen of the Double Bluff.

'Readers don't care, Trish, about the dates of the English Civil War. What they want to know is, why the beautiful Lady Gwendoline, wife of the Royalist hero Sir Oscar High-and-Mighty, may be dancing at the ball with her dull but worthy spouse, but only has eyes for the mysterious George Challenger. And why has she named her children Georgie and Georgiana?'

'1642. When the Civil War kicked off.'

'I think you're missing my point, Rosemary Sutcliff!' Amanda said. 'Add her name to your list of must-reads, by the way.'

'So many books. So many names,' I said. It reminded me of something that had been playing on my mind. 'Do you always write under your real name, Amanda. Have you ever used *nom de whatsit*?'

Should have known better than to expect a straight answer.

'Interesting business, choosing a pseudonym. Something of a dark art.'

All of a sudden, I was struck with a brainwave so totally hilarious, I had to share it. 'You could call yourself…'

'Don't, for pity's sake, say Paige Turner,' Amanda

said, shooting me a look to curdle milk.

'Wouldn't dream of it,' I said, although it was exactly what I *was* about to say.

'No, if I had to pick a new name,' she patted her chin, deep in thought, 'I'd go for something androgynous, like … erm, Leigh. Leigh Baker. How does that sound? Leigh to add a smack of the omnisexual, and honouring the great Lee Child, and Baker to put me at the top of any alphabetical list and close to him on the bookshop shelves. Only, and here's the clever bit, I'd spell Lee, L E I G H and add an extra K to B A K K E R, to make it unique.'

'Lee Child, the American thriller writer?' It wasn't the first time she'd dropped his name.

'Not American,' she corrected. 'Born in Coventry, as a matter of fact. Creator of the Jack Reacher series. What I would give for a hundredth – nay, a thousandth – of his success? Real name, Jim Grant. It's quite an amusing story, how he came to choose his pen name.'

So amusing that, though I left a pause, she didn't bother telling it.

'Should I change *my* name?' I asked, noting down Lee Child and Leigh Bakker, spelled in that peculiar way, to remind me. 'Patricia Lightowler is such a mouthful.'

'Don't even think about it!' Amanda cried, leaping from her seat. 'It's the best thing you've got going for you. Now, coffee I think.'

Did she mean, the *only* thing?

Amanda sent me off to make drinks, like I'm the domestic help, rather than … whatever it is I am. Pupil, mentee, straight woman? While I was in the kitchen, I decided to sharpen up my observational skills. The next voice you hear will be that of apprentice lifestyle writer Patrizia Gufo di Luce.

It's not what you'd call a flash kitchen. Or modern. Not even clean. No hand-painted cupboards in *Weasel's Ears* or *Starling's Flight*. Hers are hand-painted, but in quite a different way. Covered in brush marks, paint runs and stray bristles. I haven't mentioned the colour. For a good reason. It pains me to report, it's orange. *Carroty Carrot Orange*.

Combined with the awful overhead strip lights, the colour burns into your retina. If you stare too long, you get black spots before the eyes, like when you're young and reckless and try to look into the sun.

Ugly silver handles, when you don't even need handles these days, on kitchen cupboards. You press in the right place, and bingo, they open with a sigh, as. if of their own free will. Her worktops are wood effect, not the real thing. You can always tell.

What else? Equipment. Nothing special here either. An enormous range to cook on. Of course, she'd have one of them. In magenta, clashing horribly with the cupboards. Takes up half the room, though I've haven't seen her use it for anything other than boiling a kettle which, I must admit, it does most efficiently, if you don't mind being parboiled yourself at the same time.

She has got one bit of new kit. The coffee machine. An absolute monster. It reigns there, looking incongruous – is that the word? – among the tired surroundings, its black and silver shininess glowering at anyone who dares to come near. She loves it. 'Italian coffee machines are not equipment,' she told me. 'They're 3D works of art.'

I hate it. It's a work of art with a foul temper.

Instead of gently dribbling into the cup like a normal machine, it hisses and splutters, as if it begrudges giving you anything. Then it stops. *Aha,* **you think,** *That's it. Nice cup of fresh coffee.* **Don't be fooled. It's only waiting for you to reach out, so it can erupt back into life and hawk lava-hot liquid onto the back of your hand. Gets me every time. Comes to something when even the coffee machine has it in for you.**

That wretched machine got me again today. I was looking in the kitchen cupboards for some burn cream for my poor hand when I spotted something jammed in the gap between the range and the cupboard. Curious, I fished it out with the kitchen tongs.

A brochure, pages curled and baked crisp by the heat. I was a bit disappointed. A holiday leaflet, flogging the benefits of white sand, turquoise seas, and enormous cocktails. The cover showed a cluster of pastel houses, gardens dotted with the blue rectangles of swimming pools, tumbling down a picturesquely rocky slope towards a beach.

'The Republic of … Kweq … Kweq …Kweq-eye-oh,' I read out loud, struggling to pronounce more vowels than any self-respecting word has a right to. 'An archipelago of jewel-like paradise islands with sugar-sand beaches and exactly the right amount of cotton-wool clouds flitting across perfect azure skies. Not only a haven for the discerning. A real home.'

I flicked through the pages, thinking, if they mean *for the stinking rich* why don't they just come out and say so. On the booklet's back page, was scrawled, in Amanda's handwriting, the word 'Extradition?????' exactly like that, with five question marks. I tutted. Amanda is always telling me off for overdoing the punctuation.

'Actually, it's pronounced Kweck-kway.'

I whirled round. I hadn't heard Amanda come in. Next thing I knew, she marched up and snatched the booklet from my grasp, saying, 'Wondered where that had got to.'

'You planning a trip?'

'Research. Probably won't come to anything,' she said, offhand. 'Don't forget to froth the milk.'

Twenty-Two

I'm quite getting into this writing lark. Practice makes perfect, as they say. Today's Mum's birthday. Here's my tribute to her. The next voice you hear will be that of rookie saga writer, Pat Murphy.

People call her Grace but that's not her real name. Jean she was christened but Jean didn't suit her idea of herself, so she ditched it when she was in her teens and has been Grace ever since. Thin as a whip at seventy-eight, able to do a full lotus at the drop of a hat – even if no hat is available – she is frequently described as an inspiration by people who don't realise what hard work she can be.

She was always different from the other mums. Wore flowing skirts she ran up herself and flat plastic shoes. Never shaved her legs or her pits. Vegetarian long before it was fashionable. She took her only child, a daughter, about on a tricycle with a trailer at the back. These were all things that regularly caused her child to die of embarrassment at the school gates. An old-fashioned hippy, you

115

could call her, but not yet full-on bonkers. The bonkersness only took off after her husband, Paddy, died in his sixties.

No tightly curled cauliflower hair or bi-weekly bingo for Grace in what she would *never* call her 'twilight years'. Instead, she let the dye grow out and wore her hair in a long grey plait and took umpteen courses at the FE college. In time she became a competent aromatherapist, potter, and vegan cook. She took up Spanish and, ten years ago, announced she was going to move to Northern Spain.

'There ain't nothing for me here, me ducks, without dear Paddy,' she said.

Nothing except a daughter, a son-in-law, and two beautiful grandchildren, the daughter thought, but said nothing. In time, her daughter got over it. In time, she understood. Grace had her life to live and needed to start afresh. It was a brave step at her age. It was only later the daughter discovered there was a man involved. Grace had met him online, if you please. On a poker site. A builder turned psychotherapist, originally from Watford, with dreams of renovating a tumbledown *finca* and living a lotus-eating life under the Spanish sun. If, that is, you can eat lotus flowers, which the daughter doubted.

He was a fair bit younger than her and not on the scene long enough to merit a name-check. Quite soon the call of Watford proved too strong, and he scurried back to the UK.

By then Grace had found a new love: Spain. She stayed on in the Galician sunshine, throwing herself into her new life. Not only did she become the star of the ex-pat mind-body-spirit community – oh yes, there is such a thing – she took on the Watford man's half-completed building project and, with the help of the locals, by now friends, transformed his ruin into a charming, if eccentric, *cabana* in the woods.

If that wasn't enough – and for Grace nothing was ever enough – she cleared a section of the garden and grew her own vegetables and fruit, and in any spare minutes fostered and rehabilitated abandoned dogs with behavioural issues, that is, a liking for giving strangers a nasty nip. All this activity gave her the toned, nut-brown body of a forty-year-old, the mind of a twenty-year-old, and the energy of a ten-year-old.

Grace never approved of her daughter's choice of husband. She was a good judge of character.

'I ain't never let meself be defined by other people, not even your father, and he were a sweetie,' she told her daughter. 'Your bloke's too full of hisself. And a prissy eater. You can't trust a man who cuts his breakfast toast into little squares, dotting each one with a blob of butter and a blob of marmalade.' Grace gave a shudder. 'Fair turns my stomach, he does. Give me a man who crunches into a fat doorstep, butter running off his chin.'

To start with, the whole family would visit in the summer holidays. Then, when the daughter's husband said he couldn't spare the time because of his job, just her and the girls. But Grace was always on at her daughter to go out there on her own.

'Park the kids and come in the winter,' she'd say. 'It's still T-shirt warm and we get these amazing Atlantic storms. You ain't lived till you've walked along a beach with the waves crashing so loud you can't hear yourself think and the wind tearing your hair out by the roots. Makes you feel alive.

'I'll introduce you to Skylar. She runs a wellness centre. She'll work wonders for that stooped back and that closed-in chest of yours.'

At last, one October, the daughter took Grace up on her invitation.

'Booked us in with Skylar tomorrow,' Grace said, as she drove them in her ancient Seat from Santiago de Compostela airport. 'She'll sort you out.'

The daughter had been secretly hoping she'd forgotten about the wellness centre.

Though reluctant, she had to admit, they had a great day. She listened to Skylar talk about crystals, hot stones, Egyptian cups, and Hopi candles, and although she didn't believe a word of it, when it came to trying them out, she found their effect magical. Her shoulders dropped, her forehead un-corrugated itself, and her brain dialled down from *stressed* to *aaaaaahhhhh*.

'It's a treat to see you with a proper smile,' Grace said, in a gap between treatments. 'One that starts with your lips and moves right down to your ...'

'All right, mum. No need to go into detail.'

'Honest, love. You look twenty years younger.' Grace reached out for her hand. The daughter covered it with hers. 'So, let's hear it,' Grace said, sitting back. 'Tell your old mum what's troubling you.'

'I don't have any troubles, Mum. Not so's you'd notice.'

'Everyone has troubles, ducks. What about that husband of yours? Still got his head stuck up his own backside? And the girls? Still walking all over you, like that fat cat boss?' Grace knew her daughter only too well.

Hesitant at the beginning, the daughter soon got

up a head of steam and it all came pouring out. How the husband smothered her with his ambition. How the girls looked down on her. How the man she used to work *with* had become the man she worked *for*.

You'd think laying out her insecurities would have added to her anxiety. Maybe it was the hot sun, or maybe there was more power in the crystals and candles than she gave credit for, but the more the daughter talked, the calmer she felt. They finished the day laying side by side on massage tables, coated in Dead Sea mud and swaddled in thick towels, like newborns. From time to time, Grace smiled over, teeth Hollywood-white against the black mud. The daughter smiled back.

'Found your bliss yet, me ducks?' Grace asked.

The shine was somewhat taken off the whole blissed-out thing when I got home to find a bill from Skylar's Spa in my inbox. I'd taken it for granted it was Grace's treat but I paid up and never mentioned it. Money well spent I reckon. Especially after what happened next.

Undetected brain tumour, the medics said. Grace was found in the garden, trowel in hand, an elderly whippet baring its teeth at anyone who came near. I wonder if the bliss we shared that weekend was thanks to the real Grace, or because of the triffid-like thing growing in her brain. I hope it was the real her. I hope she was happy. I know she was loved. I know because of the funeral they held for her in the tiny Spanish square.

Is it OK to say Grace's funeral was fun? Because it was. We drank sticky, red wine. Strangers came up, speaking in Galician. I didn't understand a word but knew what they were saying as, men, women, and children alike cried and kissed me on both cheeks. Then came the singing. And the dancing. And the laughter. I caught a glimpse of what it was that had kept Grace in her little Galician village.

The capacious – love that word! – leather handbag, that's hers. Grace's, my properly bonkers mother. I dip my nose inside it to sniff her face powder when I'm having a bad day. My head's hardly been out of it recently! It's the only thing of hers I brought back. She had it made out there. It's worn, the stitches are coming apart, and I keep losing things in the lining, but I won't be parted from it.

Amanda has a neat little bag, shiny black with a sharp silver clasp that could have your fingers off. There she goes again, Amanda flipping Turner, elbowing herself in, pinching the limelight, when I'm trying to celebrate Grace.

It'll be two years this autumn. Today would have been your eightieth birthday. Miss you, Mum. Bet you'd have had some choice words to say about Gregory. And Amanda.

> *Trish ain't ever gonna tell you this, but I will. For months after Grace died, it weren't me, Ivy, she hears in her head first thing in the morning, last thing at night. It's her, Grace. Trish wakes and, sad and confused without at first knowing why, she calls out, 'Mum? Where are you?'*
>
> *'Sorry, me ducks,' Grace replies. 'Still dead.'*

Twenty-Three

Lesson 8: Take That, Poetry!

Forewarned is … I forget what. Amanda texted me. 'Next week's challenge: choose a favourite poem to discuss.'

Yikes! I have two problems with this. I don't have a favourite poem and, even if I did, I wouldn't be able to talk about it. Anything I understand, like Edward Lear or Spike Milligan, or that one about the woman wearing purple, doesn't have the, you know, *gravitas* to impress Amanda. And I want so much to impress her.

Poetry, I realise, is a language whose basic rules I've never got to grips with. Like German.

For a little while, I considered the one with the church clock and the honey. Or the one with the daffs. Too obvious, I decided. I needed something more arcane – is that the right word? It would make a nice change to see a smidgeon of respect in Amanda's eyes. I hatch a plan but I don't know if I've got what it takes to pull it off.

***

'Right. Let's hear it.' Amanda closed her eyes and listened as I read out loud.

Channelling, as far as I could remember, my performance as Perdita in *The Winter's Tale* – described in the school magazine as 'vigorous' – I attempted to give every word its full *oomph* of passion and poignancy. I ended in what I hoped was a heart-melting whisper.

Silence.

I looked up. Amanda was motionless and quite possibly damp-eyed. Had I achieved the impossible? Had I touched her? It seemed so.

She cleared her throat. 'Thank you, Trish. That was unexpectedly moving. Over-the-top performance but one can forgive you for that. as the words themselves were simple and sincere, and hence all the more affecting. Remind me, who is the poet?'

'Barlow,' I murmured, and waited for the explosion.

It didn't come. 'Marlowe, did you say? Christopher Marlowe? Are you sure? It sounded contemporary.' I kept quiet. 'Perhaps you mean a different, more recent Marlowe?'

'Something like that,' I mumbled, unable to meet her eyes.

'I shall have to look him up. His work is permeated with such an aching regret. Beautiful.'

We spent what was left of the lesson dismembering the words. Time whizzed by. For once, I knew what I was talking about. Feeling cheeky, I was even able to throw in other quotes from the same writer. I kept catching Amanda glancing over, her expression stuck somewhere between puzzled and impressed, but she never sussed what I was up to.

Trish, you absolute legend! She did it! Got one over on Amanda! And why not? Many a PhD thesis has been written on Dylan or Cohen. Why not Gary Barlow? Much more of this and I'll have to start thinking Trish ain't a complete waste of oxygen after all.

Except ... I wonder if she's grasped that the pop song she picked, out of the thousands that clog up her grey matter, is the one about someone longing to get back with their ex? Is her subconscious trying to tell her summat? Does she really want that pompous, two-timing slimeball back? Please tell me she don't!

Twenty-Four

Trish is stressed. Like an overstrung violin, another twist of the tightening-up thingy and she's gonna give. Not that I have the faintest how violins work, but it's gotta be summat like that, ain't it? Anyway, you get my drift. Trish is at twanging point.

I'm a fretter. Always have been. I fret about the big things: the death of the oceans, young people and the housing problem, and don't even get me started on Brexit. WTF, as the girls used to say, when saying it was cool. I also fret more than I should about the little things: the ethics of buying own-brand for the food bank, how much to tip the Big Issue seller; and who to complain to about the potholes.

Potholes? Food banks? What is this? Wish she'd spit out what's really troubling her? Cos it sure as hell ain't the fortunes of a street seller.

But most of all I fret about the girls. Flo phoned.

She's coming home. I was expecting that but there was something in her voice that got my mum antennae twitching, though I tried not to let on.

'That's great. It's much too quiet here without you and your awful music.' I laughed, wishing she'd stuck with the madrigals. 'I expect I can put up with you for a few weeks.'

'More than a few weeks,' Flo said. 'I'll be there for a year, Mum. I'm deferring.'

It took a few seconds for it to sink in. Then, anger rising, 'Dropping out, you mean. That's what young people do before university, Flo, or after they've graduated. Not in their first year, when they're getting started. I can't believe this. Now if it had been your sister …'

I'd hit a trigger. 'Why do you always compare me with her?' Flo snapped. 'Anyway, it's all settled. I don't need your approval. My tutor doesn't want to see me until a year this September.'

'But you told me you loved your course,' I said, on the brink of waterworks.

'Don't get your thong up your crack, Mum. It's no biggie. Just wanted to keep you in the loop.'

'I can't pretend I'm not disappointed,' I said, rallying like the trooper I try to be. 'But this is your home. Of course you can stay here. Stay as long as …'

'We'll talk some more when I'm home,' she said, and was gone.

The strings creak.

Something's wrong, I know it. She's here, Flo, all bulging bags and fluster. She won't look me in the eye. I try not to cross-question her the minute she's through the door, yet there is so much I need to find out. What's behind this sudden change of heart and what will she live on, for a start? I mean, I'm not earning and who knows when or if Gregory's lawyers will stop willy-waving and agree a settlement.

I risked bringing up the subject of money.

'Zara,' Flo said, as if that answered everything. 'There was a poster up in the bus. I'll go first thing on Monday and get a job serving in the shop. Or Topshop or wherever. Does it matter? I won't starve.'

To be honest, that's exactly what it looks like she's been doing. So thin! Never a podgy girl, unlike her sturdier sister, Flo's T-shirt hangs off her like washing on a line, and her denim shorts reveal thighs that are all bone and no meat.

The strings fray.

I was bursting with questions I don't get to ask because then Flo made herself a sandwich, went upstairs with it, and had a long soak in the bath.

'You want dinner?' I shouted upstairs after she's been up there for ages.

'Not for me,' she shouted down. 'Knackered. Going to get an early night.'

That took care of my evening. Spot of dinner, bit of undemanding telly, colossal fretting.

I slept in. Came downstairs to find the house empty. Flo texted. She was off job hunting. On an empty stomach, by the evidence she'd left on the draining board: one used lemon and ginger teabag. Nothing else. It was mid-afternoon before she got back, with news that was worse than I feared: the Zara job had gone. She was starting the following week at Primark.

'And I was lucky to get that,' Flo said, defiantly. 'Don't be such a snob, Mum. What does it matter where I work? It's only to tide me over until ...' Her words faded away.

'Until what?' But she looked away. 'Listen Flo, it's not that I don't want you here. I love having you around. It's just ... I'm struggling to understand. Why have you chucked up everything on a whim?'

Her eyes locked onto mine. 'It's not a whim, Mum. It's a baby.'

The strings stretch, hold for a sec, then — twaaaaaang! — they break.

***

We sat for hours. I stroked her hand. I asked calm, careful questions and she answered in a similar manner. Inside, I was bawling my eyes out.

Eight weeks gone. The father is, and I quote, 'an arrogant, irrelevant idiot.' She hadn't yet told her dad. Or Nell. I was the first, apart from the idiot. I realised she must already have been pregnant the last time she was home. 'Why didn't you tell me then?' I asked.

'What? You serious? I was only a few weeks late. Anyway... how could I throw that in, in the middle of that omni-chaos? No thanks.'

'You've... made up your mind?'

'To keep her?' Instinctively, Flo's hand went to her belly. 'Believe me, Mum, this is not how I saw my life working out but, yes, I am going to keep her. This is something, someone, for once I don't have to share with anyone.'

I understood. She meant Nell. And that made me feel

even sadder.

'So,' I said, struggling for composure, 'a little girl?'

'Don't know till I get the scan. But I think of her as a girl.'

'Well, that's the first thing we must see to. Get you signed up to the hospital to find out if it's a little Miss or Master Lightowler you've got in there. And the next thing is to tell your sister and your dad the news. You going to do that or would you like me to?'

'Would you? Thanks, Mum,' Flo said, eyes glistening. 'I should have known you'd be cool with it.'

Cool with it? Cool, she says. If only she knew. Flo goes to bed, Trish hopes, reassured. Trish sits up alone, thoughts and feelings churning like they're on a heavy duty wash cycle. Late into the night she puts on the funniest episode of the funniest TV sitcom she can think of. Too late she remembers it's the one where the dog dies.

Twenty-Five

Lesson 9: Feeling The Pace

No sign of rain. Hottest summer on record, weather people reckon. The lawn Gregory used to be so proud of crunches like cornflakes when Trish crosses it to get to the compost.

She's been feeling weirdly detached since the news about Flo. So much to get used to. So many things to go wrong. So much to worry about. Flo on the other hand, seems detached in a different kind of way, floating above it all on a cloud of antenatal Zen.

'Relax, Mum,' she says with a grin, if Trish ever tries to talk to her about iron tablets, haemorrhoid cream, or heartburn remedies. 'I'm good. She's good.'

'But ...' Trish says, then stops herself. Dozens of 'buts' run through her head. Flo don't need to hear none of them.

***

I didn't want to go but Flo insisted. 'You need to get out of the house, Mum.'

It was unbearable inside Woodview, what with the heat and the hum. Amanda didn't fancy another walk. Instead we tramped up the garden to the summerhouse in search of air. Like the rest of her place, the summerhouse was in desperate need of TLC, a coat of varnish at the very least. The doors were bleached and warped, their bottoms ragged where the damp and probably mice had had a nibble, the windows were thick with spider webs.

I offered to wipe the cobwebs away but Amanda wouldn't have it. Said a dusty curtain would soften the light. And if anyone needed a flattering light today, it was her. She was heavy-eyed and red-faced. Very un-Amanda-like. The menopause she'd been so snooty about seemed to have caught up with her.

I've no wish to turn this journal into a moan-o-pause memoir but it is an absolute bugger, isn't it? The horror of scarlet blotches creeping up your chest and throat when you're at a dinner party, the humiliation of being stood next to a young man in a lift as your armpits drip, the misery of doing ten rounds with a tangled duvet every night! And as for the brain fog, the mood swings, and the random tear gushings … As I said, an absolute bugger.

And Amanda will make matters worse by wearing the wrong clothes. What's that saying? *There's no bad weather, only bad clothing.* It applies to Amanda in spades. With the thermometer in the high 20s, today she was in a long-sleeved dress and a cardigan, a chiffon scarf wound round her neck. I ask you!

She fanned herself with a sheet of paper, whilst struggling to explain narrative drive. Whatever that is – and I'm still not sure – she's lost hers. Today's class was more like a narrative aimless meander and – a first for

Amanda – dull, dull, dull.

After several minutes of watching her struggle, I'd had enough.

'It's not surprising you're so uncomfortable, Amanda. Bundled up in that cardy. Allow me.' I stood, preparing to help her peel off the woolly.

'Leave it!' she barked. 'I'm perfectly comfortable,' though I could see drops of perspiration on her upper lip.

She did deign to allow me to open the summerhouse doors wide and got that man Pavel to plug in an ancient and noisy electric fan. With that rattling in the background, Amanda stumbled on, pausing every now and then to shake out her hair. Needless to say, Pavel was lingering in the garden, edging towards the summerhouse, making a show of raking the lawn. But I knew what he was up to: earwigging.

I'd been trying – fighting against the fan – to tell Amanda about a novel I'd just finished. It was written by a South American writer and a classic of the genre, Felicity had informed me. I'd only 'got' about a quarter of it, though I wasn't about to let on to Amanda. Consequently, my in-depth analysis consisted mainly of slipping the words 'magical realism' into the conversation at every opportunity.

I was in full flow when Pavel interrupted. 'Why you talk about this bullshit book? Why you not talk about a good book? Why you not talk about Harry Potter?' He dropped his rake and strolled over. 'I read Harry Potter in my country. Harry Potter is bloody excellent book. The films also I like.'

'Harry Potter, I think you will find,' I said coldly, 'is for kids. We're discussing grown-up literature.'

Amanda held up a hand to silence me. 'I'm surprised at you, Trish,' she shouted over the clattering fan. 'Pavel's reading choices are as valid as yours. In any case, Harry Potter ...' She broke off. 'Will someone *please* switch off that fucking fan?'

There she was again. Standing up for her live-in lackey rather than siding with me, my paying pupil. My nose was properly out of joint.

***

Something good did come out of today. I made a new friend. A little black cat, not much more than a kitten. I found him at Amanda's back door on my way to the house for one of many comfort breaks. I swear that man Pavel irritates my bladder.

Anyway, I called to him – the cat, that is – and he came over, winding himself round my ankles, purring like a tiny sewing machine, much too loudly for someone so small. He's a friendly thing. Almost too friendly. If I hadn't been quick, I reckon he'd have slipped into the house. Then I had one of them ... those lightbulb moments.

'Is it you?' I said, picking him up to stare into his golden eyes. 'Have you been sneaking into Amanda's and widdling all over the place? Are you the cause of the big stink?' He purred even louder, seeming to confirm my suspicions. 'Naughty, naughty.'

I know I should have told Amanda. I'll tell her next time. Probably. With my life in ruins, and her lessons more useless by the week, it feels good to have something over her at last. Don't have much to give thanks for these days, but at least my house doesn't reek of cat piss.

Twenty-Six

Lesson … Oh, there isn't one

Trish don't get a chance to tell Amanda about LBK, Little Black Kitty – that's what Trish has named him – on account of Amanda wrongfoots her by serving an underhand stroke.

I arrive on time, to find Amanda in a flowery dressing gown and gold slippers, flitting about the kitchen, slurping Fruit 'n' Fibre, singing to herself, giving no indication whatsoever of getting ready for a class.

'Running late?' I asked pointedly, making a show of wrinkling my nose. 'Still hums like a gents' urinal in here.'

'The mystery continues,' Amanda said, dumping her dirty breakfast things in the sink. 'Do you know, one hardly notices the smell after a while. In any case, you wait, Pavel will soon have it sorted.'

I allowed myself a little smirk. I mean, if she couldn't be bothered to get dressed, why should I be bothered to let her into my secret?

133

Amanda left to get ready and yet again, I was left watching the clock, picturing my bank balance ticking down towards 'insufficient funds'. When she returned, to my surprise, she was in tennis gear, long hair tied back and short white skirt fluttering against her slim, brown thighs. I was thankful I'd put leggings on under the faded Laura Ashley dress I was wearing. She was carrying a racket.

'What's with the outfit?' I asked.

'I'd have thought that was obvious.' Amanda looked past me and her face lit up. 'Why, here he is! Eat your heart out, Rafa.'

It was that man of course, Pavel, also dressed for Centre Court. 'Look at him,' she crowed, 'never picked up a racket in his life but, with those shoulders, a natural if ever I saw one. Caroline and Sandra will go positively avocado when I walk in with *this* on my arm.'

I was outraged. 'You're going to play tennis with your handyman, instead of giving me my lesson?'

'I expect I should have let you know, Trish, but it was a last-minute thing and … Christ, look at the time! Have to dash or we'll miss our slot.'

'I assume,' I said, through tight lips, as she gathered up her things, 'that as I've already paid, you'll be adding on …'

'Do me a huuuuge favour, Trish,' she butted in, 'and pull the front door shut behind you when you go. Byeee!'

And in a flurry of sports bags and laughter, they were gone.

I strode about the kitchen, talking to myself and seething. *The cheek of the woman! Who does she think she is? Taking liberties!* Then I decided, if she can take liberties, so can I. I might never get another opportunity like this. I headed for the stairs to find out, once and for all, if Pavel had, as

I suspected, been promoted from handy man to *handsy* man.

I imagined snooping would be one of those things, like squeezing a blackhead, that you really shouldn't do but are so satisfying if you break the rules and do them. It wasn't. I felt grubby and guilty, opening her cupboards and drawers, poking about, touching her things. I'd make a rubbish burglar.

But, determined to uncover the truth, I gritted my teeth. It didn't take long to come up with the answer. They weren't exactly discreet. Amanda's big bed was a mess, covers thrown back, pillows all over the place, and sheets ... actually, I couldn't face inspecting the sheets. I didn't need to. A pair of men's boxers hung over the side of the linen basket. And when I went to the spare room to check, I found the bed there hadn't even been made up, let alone slept in.

It couldn't have been more obvious. Unlikely as it may be, Pavel and Amanda were lovers.

Well, that was an eye-opener and no mistake! With it, came the realisation that, after all these hours together, I still had little idea of what went on behind Amanda's arrogant mask. Who was this woman I paid to humiliate me, week after week? Who, one minute seemed to 'get' me like no-one I'd ever met before, and the next, left me twiddling my thumbs while she bunked off to cavort with her toy boy? Now was my chance to find out.

I moved on, with a shudder, from the post-shag bed to the cluttered dressing table. In pride of place was the biggest bottle of perfume I'd ever seen, with an extravagant glass stopper made to look like folds of floating fabric. I put on my glasses to read the label. It was called *Ce Que Tu Sais* and was, the gold label proudly declared, *Parfum personnalisé et exclusif de Paris*. Must have cost a bomb, though the liquid that half-filled the bottle was, I must say, an unattractive dark stewed-tea colour that didn't invite the sniff test.

Red Hot Nights, her lipstick was called. Surely too red and too hot for a woman of Amanda's age! There were jars of stuff called base layer. I didn't even know what that was. Another, smaller, promised 'weightless shine correction.'

Gravity defying makeup, I thought. *Whatever will they think of next?*

I unzipped a white cosmetics bag. Mascara. Eye pencils. More lipsticks. Foundation. Blusher. Shadow. Powder. The usual stuff and all brands I'd never heard of. Not a Rimmel or a Number 7 among them.

Losing my inhibitions, next I burrowed into her underwear drawer. This was puzzling. Where I was expecting bright froths of Agent Provocateur or La Perla – oh yes, I know the best knicker brands, though stick to M&S myself – I found only cheap chain store, grey with age and saggy with washing.

Tucked away at the back of the drawer, under a well-worn pair of what Grace would have termed 'apple catchers', I found another jar, bigger and cheaper looking than the rest with a scratched silver lid. I dug out a blob of cream and rubbed it between my thumb and finger. It was very pink and very gooey. Squinting at the writing, I read: *Total coverage concealer. Guaranteed to mask acne, post-surgical bruising, tattoos, scars, birthmarks, and other blemishes.* What was Amanda doing with that? Her skin was flawless.

I needed to reflect on what I'd discovered and one of Amanda's e-ciggies lay on the bedside cabinet. I don't normally approve of smoking but these weren't normal times. I picked it up and went downstairs and out into the garden to clear my head, and see what all the vaping fuss was about. I didn't like it. It was like smoking a Haribo. Hearing me cough and splutter, LBK appeared from under the hedge. After massaging my ankles, he threw himself down on the ground in a sunny spot, purring.

'Don't think you can get round me like that,' I warned, reaching down to caress his leathery little ears. 'And if Amanda Turner ever catches you, I dread to think.'

Trish sits stroking the cat, having the occasional suck on Amanda's fake fag, sticking her tongue out in disgust each time. What is she thinking about? Mostly about the differences between her and Amanda. Wondering what her life would've been like if she'd been as un-embarrassable as her, if she didn't give a flying fig for what people thought. Would they have stopped pushing her around? Would her marriage have survived? She asks LBK, but he don't have no answers. He's a cat, for Gawd's sake.

She puts Amanda's e-ciggie back where she found it, wiping the end with a tissue. Then she bolts the back door and, as instructed, pulls the front door shut behind her.

Twenty-Seven

Love at first sight, that's what it was. And don't you dare say it wasn't; that it doesn't happen like that outside of romcoms. I know what I felt. I can feel it now. The tightness in the chest, the pounding of the blood in the ears, the pricking behind the eyes. No, not a heart attack! Love, true love. The second I saw that fuzzy black and white image, I was a goner.

'Here, this might cheer you up,' Flo had said, holding out her phone, like a four-year old shyly presenting her first potato print. 'We got scanned today.'

I bent over and − kapow! − totally smitten. How could anyone resist such irresistibility? The curve of the head I long to cup, the snub little nose I long to stroke, the white blurs that are the wriggling fingers and toes I long to smother in kisses. My grandchild.

My. Grandchild.

As I lay in bed writing this, I pause every so often to rub my thumb over the image on my phone and feel … what? *Euphoric* isn't the word. Too impersonal. Too Amanda. What I feel is, nothing else matters. The troubles weighing me down have floated off on the breeze. I have more important things to think about. I feel, at least I begin to feel, blissed out. Just like Grace said.

Blissed out and nostalgic for a time some twenty years ago, when I was a new mother and I'd never been so happy. I stood in front of the big mirror in the bedroom, a gently snoring newborn tucked under each arm, saying to myself: This is me now and for the rest of my life. What an amazing thing I have done!

Didn't last of course. My bowels seized up. My nipples cracked, feeding more blood than milk to the infants. They, the little tyrants, decided sleeping at night-time was for wimps. Before long I was stood in front of the big mirror, struggling to hold onto two squawking, squirming babies, saying to myself: This is me now and for the rest of my life. What the bloody hell have I done?

Trish don't share none of this with Flo of course. No-one ever does, do they? It's the worldwide conspiracy that keeps the human race going. Instead, she throws herself into housework. She cleans and tidies, dusts and disinfects, straightens and stacks, irons and folds, and rearranges her books by jacket colour, like Ms. Rowling suggests. She buys fresh flowers. The house looks fabulous. Trish don't.

Then, exactly when she's at her lowest, Nell phones. In tears.

'What do you mean you've lost your bank card?' I said.

'What else could I mean, Mum?' Nell somehow managed to be weepy and in a snit with me at the same time. 'It must have fallen out of my wallet in the taxi. Or something.'

'Have you tried …?'

'Yep,' she cut in. 'I have tried contacting the taxi firm. I'm not an idiot.'

'Idiot enough to leave your card in a taxi,' I thought and, for once, *did* say.

'Sorry, Mum. Jack was saying something. What was that?'

'Jack? I thought he was called Johnny. Listen, you need to call your bank.'

'We're supposed to be meeting up with a whole bunch of people and going down south for this thing on the beach. We can't miss it. It'll be awesome. If we don't get there, I'll just die. Can't you do it for me?' she wheedled, in a voice that always used to work. 'I would, but we're in the middle of nowhere.'

'Amsterdam is hardly the dark side of the moon, Nell.'

'We're not in Amsterdam. I told you. We're on the move,' she said, pendulum swinging back to snitty. 'We're in … Jack, where is it we are now?' I didn't hear Jack's answer. 'Can't you talk to them, Mum? Pleeeeease!' she said, dialling up the wheedle factor. 'You're good at that sort of boring stuff.'

'Nell.'

'Tell them to cancel my card and send me another. I'll message you an address when I know where we'll be.'

'Nell.'

'Have to go, Mum. Battery's about to expire and Jack's giving me evils. We're trying out this new karaoke bar tonight. He's got *such* a great voice. After two or three mojitos, you'd swear Harry Styles was right there in the room. Oh, and get them to courier it. The post will take ages. I can mooch off Jack for a couple of days but after that it'll get *really* awkward.'

'Nell. No.'

'Sorry. Say again?'

'I said, no. I won't be talking to the bank and I won't be asking them to courier you another card. You're old enough and clever enough to get yourself all the way out there to … wherever it is you are. You do it.'

Nell's not a girl to give up easily. 'But Mu-um! You can't expect me to …'

'What? Interrupt your fun and games to sort out your own mess? Oh yes, I can. In case you haven't noticed, I've got quite a few problems of my own right now.' *Not to mention the small matter of becoming a grannie before long and you, by the way, an auntie*, I thought about saying, but restrained myself. 'Frankly, Nell, your little hiccup doesn't even register on my anxiety chart right now. Have a great time at the beach party. If you make it. Good luck with the bank. Love you, darling. Bye.'

I was buzzing when I put the phone down, wallowing in a new sensation: saying no to my lovely but demanding daughter.

Bravo Trish! As long as she don't weaken. Step away from that phone, right now!

Twenty-Eight

Lesson 10: Unreliable, *Moi?*

To my surprise, she don't. Weaken that is. Thank Gawd! What she does is, she climbs up on a chair and sticks her phone at the back of the most out-of-reach cupboard in the kitchen, the one above the fridge freezer. Then distracts herself by sitting at her laptop. And stares. Was gonna say 'And writes'. I scrubbed that. Not a sodding word appears on the screen. Not one worth keeping at least.

A thousand quid! A cool thousand quid Amanda has creamed off her. Money Trish can't afford. Money she should be putting away to lavish on her grandkid. And still there's no progress. Trish ain't written a single word of her novel. She's an inspiration-free zone.

Now's not the time to quit, she tells herself. Not after she's put in all that time and all that dosh. And Amanda, of course, insists if she sticks at it a little bit longer, a few more weeks, she'll start to see real results. She would though, wouldn't she?

Meanwhile, things at Woodview have become tricky,

142

since Amanda and that man have been, as they say, seeing each other. Seeing to each other, more like!

Unreliable Narrators, it was today. Again, we were ensconced – is that the word? – in the summerhouse. The session began promisingly.

'It's a popular technique,' Amanda said, 'especially among thriller writers, as a way of keeping the reader in the dark, so one can spring the big surprise later. Let us compare two classic examples: *Rebecca* and *The Talented Mr. Ripley*.'

We got no further, because *he* walked past, Pavel, a spade and fork over his shoulder. On his way up the garden, to do whatever it is he does there. Not planting veg, that's for sure. The patch is as bare now as it was when he started. Without a word, Amanda got up and marched over, a determined look on her face. I couldn't hear what they were saying but the body language – his neck tense, her back rigid – suggested it wasn't sweet nothings they were murmuring.

The difference of opinion went on for some time. Luckily, I'd bought a book. The first volume of the complete works of Dashiell Hammett. Weighed a ton. Another Felicity recommendation and this time, she'd hit a bullseye. 'Hard-boiled' they call his style. Makes me wonder what my style would be, if I had one. 'Soft-poached', maybe?

Amanda was properly out of sorts when she got back to me.

'So he's your boyfriend now, is he? Pavel,' I asked, not in the mood for being subtle.

'Not that it's any of your business,' she said. 'But, yes. We're in a relationship. Shall we resume?'

She began explaining all over again about Mrs. de Winter

and Tom Ripley. When I pointed out she'd already done that bit, she got right tetchy with me.

'Lovers' tiff?' I said, trying to jolly her along. 'Is it because Pavel trounced you in front of your tennis club groupies? Never had you down as a poor loser.'

Amanda, who until then had been leaning at the open door, scowling and vaping out clouds of overripe peach, or possibly mango, sagged into the canvas chair beside me.

'Contrary to expectations, he was hopeless, if you must know,' she sighed. 'Toe-curlingly bad. Played as if he had a hole in his racket. Whiffed even my gentlest serves.'

Didn't dare ask what *whiffing* was.

'What then? Weren't those girlfriends of yours impressed with your new squeeze?'

'Rather *too* impressed, as a matter of fact. It started when they joined us in the bar after the match. One could hardly blame Pavel,' she said. 'His pride had taken a knock. Then along came Caroline and Sandra, middle-aged Stepford wives with their filler-lips and egg-smooth foreheads, who proceeded to flirt shamelessly. What was a red-blooded young male expected to do?'

'Lapped it up, did he?' I said, knowingly. 'And that's what's got your goat.'

I was close enough to see Amanda's jaw tighten. 'You should have seen them, Trish. It was horrific, watching them circle, waiting to go in for the cougar kill. One couldn't stand by and watch them devour the poor boy in front of one's eyes. So I told him to pick up the rackets and we left.'

'And Pavel was OK with that?'

'Of course not! Kicked up the most terrible fuss. But I insisted.' She stared thoughtfully down the garden to where Pavel had gone back to prodding feebly about in the soil. As I watched, he picked up a stone and threw it at the fence. Hard. So hard, even though it ricocheted nowhere near us, I ducked.

'See? He's still sulking. One could have handled it better, I suppose. Too late now. I only wish … after we got back home …' She hesitated. 'Can I trust you, Trish? If I tell you something, it mustn't go any further.'

'Of course,' I said, trying not to sound too keen.

'It was as if he were a different person.' There was a catch in her voice. 'Not the man I know.' Amanda looked out at the cloudless sky. 'Pavel's a passionate man. That's part of the attraction, if I'm honest. His unpredictability. His flashes of temper. Not knowing what he'll say, or do, next. You know what I mean. No matter how liberated we women like to think we are, an alpha male is irresistible, don't you think?'

'Never seen the appeal of the caveman type myself,' I said, curling my lip.

Come off it, Trish. What is Gregory but a pass-agg caveman in a designer suit? The only difference is, he's more subtle with it. He does his damage, not with slaps and punches, but with cheap shots and snide digs. He never let Trish forget she's state school trash, whereas he went to a 'good school'. He nagged her into southern-ising her East Midland accent, though it lurks not far beneath the surface. But that weren't enough for him. She still got it in the neck for listening to cheap pop music and watching awful TV reality shows, serving dinner guests 'peasant fare' and not laughing at his friends' so-called witticisms, cos she didn't have 'the background.'

Amanda had gone silent on me.

'What happened, Amanda?' I encouraged. 'What happened after you got home?'

145

She put a hand to her throat and, with much gulping and sighing, spoke at last. 'You mustn't blame him, Trish. He was angry. I'd shamed him, by beating him in the match, and then dragging him away when he was having a good time. He said I'd treated him no better than a dog. His eyes – those beautiful blue eyes – they were so cold. Oh Trish, they were almost black with anger!' She squeezed her own eyes shut.

'Did he hurt you, Amanda?' I insisted. 'If he did …'

'Take no notice of me. I'm being silly. I'm falling for him, you see, Trish. Really falling. And it was only …' She swallowed hard, muffling her next words.

I leant in. 'I didn't catch that. Only what, Amanda?'

But the moment had passed. She pressed her lips together and wouldn't repeat it. Rousing herself, she said, 'Never mind. It was nothing. Let's get back to narrators, reliable and unreliable. Which one is Nick Carraway, would you say?'

For the rest of the lesson I was a mess. Couldn't concentrate. Couldn't think of anything except what I thought I'd heard Amanda say.

Twenty-Nine

OK, so after a couple of hours I did give in, clamber up and scrabble among the sandwich boxes and food bags to retrieve my phone. But I didn't contact Nell till the following day, and then only by text, and I didn't even mention the lost plastic.

How's Harry S? How was beach party? Hope you remembered sunscreen.

I added a heart to show 'no hard feelings.'

There was no reply until late evening, when half a dozen messages pinged in, one after the other. A load of blurry beach photos taken at night, the sky black, a huge bonfire blazing in the background. I think Nell featured, though one drunk young person dancing out-of-focus in front of flames looks very much like another.

Then an incoming message, displaying Nell's customary offhand way with language: *Fab ta. All gr8. Sknny dippg till 6.*

I assumed she meant a.m.

Then a pause before: *HS histry btw. Miguel helpg me brsh up my Spnish.*

Together with a lip-smacking emoji that left little to

my imagination. I heaved a sigh of relief. Nell was fine.

***

I was mooning over the baby scan, when I heard the front door open.

'Flo? Is that you?' I called out, coming through from the kitchen. 'What are you doing back so early?' I skidded to a disappointed halt. 'Oh! You!'

'Nice to see you too,' Gregory said, parking a suitcase and a carrier bag at his feet, and slipping a computer bag from his shoulder. 'Hi, Pats.' He threw his arms wide, inviting a hug.

Ignoring his invitation, I folded mine across my chest, like a bad Les Dawson impression.

'What are you doing here?'

'Did try to warn you but you've been ghosting me. I'm giving the keynote talk at Bicester Business School.'

'You know what I mean. What are you doing *here*, in this house?'

'Do we have to stand in the hallway like strangers? How about we move to the kitchen and you make me a coffee?'

'How about you bugger off, Gregory?'

Gregory's fuse is short at the best of times. And this was the worst of times, as someone famous once wrote.

'I know it's hard for you but do try to act like an adult,' he said. 'I own half this house in case you've forgotten. I have every right to be here.'

I planted my feet more firmly. 'That's strange,' I said. 'My lawyer tells me exactly the opposite.'

Who would that be, then, Trish? Your imaginary lawyer?

148

Gregory pushed past me into the kitchen, plonking himself down at the breakfast bar. 'Look I've been flying half the night,' he said. 'And you know what airline food does to my digestion. Let's not fight. Put the coffee on, please, Pats. Don't make a scene.'

I shook my head. 'I've wasted far too many years of my life not making scenes. Not any longer. I want you to get out, Gregory. Now.'

'I promise you, I don't want to stay in this Wendy house a moment longer than I need to. I came to talk. We have important matters to discuss.'

He had a point. 'A talk,' I said. 'That's all. And a coffee.'

He gave a sly smile and, too late, I saw I'd blundered.

'And to go with it, this.' He lifted the carrier bag. 'Champagne, quite a good vintage for Heathrow. And OJ, of course. Sorrento? Remember?' Gregory waggled his eyebrows. 'It is brunch-time after all. Buck's Fizz o'clock.'

'I don't know how you've got the nerve,' I said, on high alert.

'What's the harm in a friendly little drink?' He got up and started to poke about in the kitchen cupboards. 'OK, I give up. Where've you hidden that big glass jug?'

I slid off the kitchen stool and dug out the jug. The one I use for flowers. It's a pretty jug and the only thing Dad left me when he died. He won it in a fishing competition before he was married. Before I was born. Before he'd even met Grace. Before she even *was* Grace. Had I given the jug a rinse last time I used it? That was the question. Not, judging by the scummy green ring round the inside. I handed it to Gregory. 'There you go,' I said brightly. Served him right.

The barefaced cheek of the man, dredging up Sorrento! I expect you wanna hear the gory details? She's never gonna tell you, so it's down to me. Hope you've got a strong stomach.

It's 2002 and Gregory and Trish are on holiday in Sorrento, newly married and childless. The hotel is cheap but its big thing is, they serve prosecco at the breakfast buffet. Every morning the young couple queue for their warm bread rolls, salty Parma ham, sweet tomatoes, and neat little pastries, all washed down with prosecco and orange juice they squeeze themselves in a scary silver juicer.

It's inevitable really. Soon as they've eaten, they scamper back upstairs to their still warm bed for what Gregory calls, 'seconds'.

Last morning of the holiday, after they've knocked back even more booze than usual, there's no time for any funny business before they have to catch the airport bus. They just about make it before the last call. Trish is dozing drunkenly in her seat on the plane when Gregory shakes her arm. 'Follow me,' he hisses, taking her hand, a twinkle in his eye. Half asleep, she weaves her way down the aisle to the tiny toilet. 'Fancy joining The Mile High Club?' he says. 'It'll be a laugh.'

Laughter is their downfall, as it happens. Jammed together, Gregory accidentally sits on the tap and gets a wet bum. Trish gets the giggles. They don't get the chance to complete the Club's basic requirement, cos their merriment alerts the cabin crew. Someone bangs on the toilet door and Gregory and Trish emerge to take a Walk of Shame back to their seats, Trish still giggling.

Oh Trish! Whatever happened to that up-for-anything man and that oh-go-on-then-if-you-insist woman?

Thirty

Unlike many nightclub crooners, I've had far too many regrets to mention. Letting Gregory over the threshold that day was certainly one of them. Striding about the place, inspecting, sniffing, running his finger along the shelves, as if he was still master there. And talking. Always talking.

'What about Florence? Going and getting herself …?'

'If you say, "knocked up!" I said, 'I won't be responsible. Actually, I'm fine with her getting pregnant, if that's what she wants. Very much looking forward to being a grandmother, as a matter of fact.'

'Maddy-Rose thinks it's a waste of her potential.' He busied himself mixing up the drink in the old glass jug. You'd have thought, he'd have remembered it only got used these days for flowers.

'Does she?' I asked, grinding my teeth, 'So kind of her to be concerned.'

'Maddy-Rose doesn't approve of alcohol.' Gregory poured us both generous measures. 'Plays merry hell with your *chakras*, apparently.' He held up his glass. 'Here's to playing merry hell. Chin chin.'

Not wanting galloping food poisoning, I didn't touch my drink. Funny, I'd never noticed before how Gregory's Adam's apple bobs up and down when he drinks. I sat opposite, watching as over the next hour his Adam's apple went crazy while he drained almost the whole jug.

He beamed drunkenly at me, as if anticipating the punchline to his own jokes, and talked and talked. Mostly about Madison-Flaming-Rose. After the first couple of glasses, he said she was 'intense and highly principled'. A few glasses later and she was 'exciting and full of life'. Finally we got to the nub: she was 'needy and high maintenance.'

It was tactless and insensitive of him to go on about her to me of all people but oh, how I was enjoying it! Hearing my replacement being bad-mouthed once more cheered me up no end. It wasn't, however, why I'd let Gregory in.

'Weren't we supposed to be talking about us, not her?' I asked, when Gregory was well and truly plastered. 'Working out finances, the mortgage, and stuff?'

To my surprise, Gregory reached forward from his stool and took both my hands in his. With the seriousness of the dead-drunk, and speaking very deliberately, he said, 'I have no illusions. Running two households will take its toll.' He swayed. 'But I will make it work,' he said, steadying himself. 'You won't suffer. I promise you that. Nor Florence and Eleanor.' He burped a mist of orange and champagne into my face, and whispered, 'I'll see you all right, Pats. You can trust me.' Then, before I could stop him, he wrapped his arms around my shoulders. I felt his grip tighten and pulled away.

'What *do* you think you're doing?' I said, giving him a gentle shove, all that was needed to unbalance him. He landed on all fours on the little rug I'd haggled for in

Marrakesh.

'Did you think,' he slurred, 'I was making a pass? You did, didn't you? I can see it in your face. Jesus, Pats! You're twice her age.'

Then he hunched over and puked his guts up over the rug.

I was fond of that rug. 'Get out. Get out now,' I yelled. 'And don't come crawling back.'

'Don't you worry, I'm going,' Gregory said, wiping his mouth and lurching to his feet. 'Only came round to say, as you continue to refuse to accept divorce papers in the mail, I've got no alternative but to get them served on you in person. Expect an official knock on the door any day soon.'

I'm watching him now from an upstairs window. He's sitting on his case outside, on his phone, head drooping. I expect the hangover is beginning to kick in.

I'm seeing him with new eyes. You get used to someone after twenty-one years. Like a pair of worn-down slippers you take for granted: they kind of do the job, but aren't anything special any more. Am I ready to chuck in my old slip-ons for a pair of – what? – high-heeled mules with an ostrich feather trim? Is that my style?

Ah, a taxi's drawn up. He's getting in. He's gone. I dust my hands together. He's no longer my problem. Except, of course, I know he very much is. While I'm thinking what to do, might as well get a bucket and sponge and do my best with that rug.

***

Hate to admit it but Gregory had me spooked. That night

I ended up with a corker of a three a.m. anxiety dream. I was on the street, rain splottering onto black binbags at my feet. Nell and Flo, little girls once more, were clinging to my legs, crying. For some reason, I had to get to Primark urgently, but the girls wouldn't let go of me. I pulled desperately against their little bodies. They, rain dripping from their pigtails, howled, 'Mummy, Mummy, don't leave us.'

I was howling too when I woke up.

I get it. It's a sign. Have to face facts. The divorce is going to happen. If I don't want to be shafted by Gregory, I have to deal with those flipping brown envelopes on Gregory's desk. Open them, or – a sudden brainwave! – get someone else to open them for me. I need a solicitor. I've made an appointment. Picked him off the internet. He looks perfect, even down to his name.

Thirty-One

She met him today, the solicitor. Mid-twenties. Floppy, upper-class hair. The beginnings of a belly. Lots of nervous energy that shows itself in a twitch. Name of — get this! — Peter Bungle. Priceless!

Peter Bungle's office was one room above a Turkish barber's. He answered the phone himself — stumbling over his own name — designed the firm's unreadable, multi-font, white-on-black website himself and, judging by the crumbs on his desk, made his own lunchtime sarnies. He certainly ironed his own shirts. There were scorch marks.

He was inexperienced, disorganised, and way too eager. Absolutely what I was looking for. Because what I needed was a solicitor who'd cock things up so royally, the divorce would drag on for years, costing Gregory a small fortune and aggravating the holy crap out of him.

All well and good, but what I wasn't counting on was Peter Bungle's puppylike charm. I liked him, you see. I liked him from the moment he tripped over his folding bike, to when he almost fell into my arms as he went for a handshake. I liked hm even more when he told me, with an embarrassed grin, that I was his first client.

'First *divorce* client?' I queried, dumping a pile of unopened envelopes onto the clutter of his desk.

'Though I have a law degree from Exeter and am positively bristling with qualifications,' he said, with a twitch of his glasses, 'I rented these delightful premises…' He spread his hands to indicate his lowly place of work. '…only ten days ago. And you, Mrs. Lightowler, are the first person, other than a *Watchtower* seller, to visit. You are my first *ever* client.'

'Bristling with qualifications, you say?' I looked around for framed proof.

'I know,' Peter winced. 'My *bone fides* are another thing I need to get round to. To be honest, I'm not much good with hammers and nails and so on. But I can assure you, I am a highly qualified legal eagle. And keen as Coleman's to prove myself. Daddy's only stumped up the rent for this place for six months. After that I'm sailing single-handed. Thought you should know, in case, you felt you wanted a more mature hand on the tiller, so to speak.'

Peter is into boats, as I quickly found out. And oversharing.

'Thank you for your honesty.' I was at my most cool and professional. 'But you are *exactly* what I'm looking for. Only, word to the wise, get someone to do you a proper website, one that people can actually read. And maybe think about changing your name?'

'Oh, I couldn't do that. There have been Bungles in the legal game for four generations. Daddy would go spare! He's a circuit judge, by the by. Mummy's the longest serving magistrate in the West Country and my oldest brother hopes to go for KC next year. He's called Paul. Only thirty-one but already losing his hair.'

See what I mean about oversharing?

I explained what had brought me to visit him and Peter took notes. Not all that efficiently, I was happy to see. The scribbled-on post-its immediately curled off his computer monitor, some landing behind a radiator, never to be seen again, I'll be bound.

Over tea in brown-ringed mugs, Peter ran through a version of *Divorces for Dummies*. 'Things are much more straightforward since the new no-fault law came into force in 2022,' he explained patiently. 'Much less stressful for all concerned, particularly any children.'

It spelt the end, he said, of the blame game. No more mudslinging. No more accusations of adultery or unreasonable behaviour.

'All the court needs is a statement that the marriage is irretrievably over and, after a suitable period of twenty-six weeks for the legal niceties, that is that. The divorce is granted.'

'Simple, eh? And who decides who gets what?'

'You do. You and Mr. Lightowler. As there are no children– your daughters being over eighteen – it's up to you, between the two of you, to come to a reasonable and amicable settlement. Will you be able to do that?' Peter asked. 'Act reasonably and amicably?'

I hesitated. 'Once, I would have said so. Now, I'm not so sure.'

I left Peter Bungle Associates in a buoyant mood. Likeable though he is, I feel confident the scruffy young lawyer will make a pig's ear of the divorce. I mean, how can he handle a prickly transatlantic break-up, when he can't even tuck his own shirt in?

Are things beginning to go Trish's way? Probably not, but she is feeling cheerier. Surfing on this small wave of

*optimism, she has another go at The Novel. Spends all
evening on her laptop, risking no end of back trouble, and
this time does end up with summat. Only one line but it's
a start. You ready?*

It goes: 'Chapter One.'

Have to take it all back. I underestimated you, Peter
Bungle. You may be young, untidy, and inexperienced,
and still call your parents Mummy and Daddy, but you
were onto Gregory quick as.

Peter phoned me, a few days later. 'I've only had a
cursory look but I'm pretty sure Mr. Lightowler is hiding
substantial assets,' he told me. 'I can't stand cheats. He
thinks he's clever but he's met his match with us
Devonshire Bungles. Being sailors, we're good with
knots, Mrs. Lightowler. And if I can tie and untie a
rolling hitch in thirty seconds – and I assure you I can –
I'm confident Mr. Lightowler's business entanglements
should present no problem.'

This was a blow. Problems were what I was hoping
for.

'So you don't anticipate the divorce being a long and
drawn-out affair?' I said, trying not to make my
disappointment obvious.

'I wouldn't say that. With the size of his potential
assets and this level of skulduggery, well, who can tell?'

This was better news, though one thing was
bothering me still. One thing I needed to make clear.

'So you understand,' I said, 'I'm not in it for the
money. As long as I have the house and a bit for the girls.
Gregory and his lady friend are welcome to anything
else.'

Down the line I heard a sharp intake of breath.
'Correct me if I've got any of these facts wrong, Mrs.
Lightowler. You are currently unemployed, with few

qualifications and no immediate prospect of work. Right so far?' He didn't wait for an answer. 'You have no independent means, no rich relative from whom you could request a loan, and little or no savings?'

'I have my redundancy money,' I said. *Rapidly being transferred to the bank account of one Amanda Turner*, I thought.

'Long term, you intend to live on what precisely?'

'I have a plan,' I squeaked.

'Forgive me for being blunt, Mrs. Lightowler, but you can't eat a plan. You can't fill your petrol tank with it.' He was sounding more lawyer-ish and less Bungle-ish by the second. 'And you certainly can't pay your mortgage with it.' He paused for effect. 'What is this plan of yours anyhow? Run it past me.'

Oh dear! I was going to have to say it out loud again, risking another hot flush incident.

'I'm going to write a novel.' And there it was, the blood rising, the sweat pouring. I grabbed a handy pizza leaflet and flapped it in front of my face.

'I happen to have a good memory for figures, Mrs. Lightowler. Useful in my line of business. Do you know what percentage of writers earn a living solely from their writing? Nineteen per cent, according to the latest figures. Less than one in five. Many don't even earn the minimum wage. In fact, the median annual income for a professional author these days is £7,000. You'd be better off stacking shelves at the supermarket.'

'Who's to say I won't be one of the – what was it? – nineteen per cent?' I said, going in for some heavy fan activity. 'Only the other day, a quite well-known author told me I have the makings of an excellent writer.' Well, she had. If you take *not entirely hopeless* to mean *excellent*. I wasn't embroidering the truth, I told myself, I was following Amanda's advice, and showing total and

159

shameless self-belief.

Peter wouldn't let it go. 'She's got you signed to a literary agent and a publisher, has she, this quite well-known author? You have a contract? A multiple book deal? An advance?'

'No, but she says I show promise.' *Improving* is what Amanda had actually said. 'She's giving me private lessons. She wouldn't be wasting her time if she didn't think I had what it takes.'

'I don't mean to pry,' he said, though of course he did. 'But are you paying this woman?'

'Yes, well...'

'If I may summarise.' I imagined Peter on the other end of the line, pacing his tiny office, brows wrinkled earnestly. 'An author, to whom you are paying a fee, has said you show promise. And *that's* your plan?'

'When you put it like that.'

'Let me go into battle for you,' Peter said, voice rising. 'Let me get you more than the house and a little bit for your girls. From what I've seen, your husband can well afford it. And wouldn't it be sweet, Mrs. Lightowler, to teach him a lesson he won't forget?'

'Please call me Trish,' I said, feeling my face at last begin to cool.

Thirty-Two

Lesson 11: Putting The Fizz Into First Lines

What would Trish do for a killer opening? Kill for one, probably. State she's in, she'd probably commit murder for one that was ever so slightly narked off. Then, what do you know? As if in answer to her prayers, out of the blue, Amanda announces today's topic: killer openings. Couldn't have been more timely. At last a lesson that might actually be useful!

We were in the summerhouse again, Amanda wearing tailored black pants and a long-sleeved cream shirt printed with birds of paradise flowers. And me – do I even have to say? The usual T-shirt and tourniquet leggings combo.

She had brightened since I last saw her, enough to request another wodge of money at any rate. One good thing. Got her to agree to payment week by week from now on. Don't dare look at my bank account.

We'd only just got off the starting blocks with 'Marley

was dead, to begin with' – by that writer I can't be doing with, Dickens – when Amanda abandoned me to go and fetch a book she needed. It was another hot day – *Sapphire Sensation* sky with a *Melon Sorbet* sun. I decided to take a stroll. Round the side of the house, I could hear that man Pavel messing about in the rose bed. I'll have a word, I thought. Let him know I've got my eye on him.

Found him, in shorts and vest, secateurs in hand, not so much dead-heading Amanda's leggy blooms, as performing a mass execution.

'Don't think I don't know what you're up to. I do,' I said, catching him unawares. 'And it's got to stop. Right now.'

The stupid man did exactly that. Froze, sunlight gleaming from the blades of his secateurs. 'What I do wrong, Treesh? he said, face expressionless. 'I cut off heads, like Mandy say.'

'Not talking about the roses. That is, not *only* about the roses. I'm talking about … you know, relationships. About not taking advantage. About being honest with each other. About being kind. Get my drift?'

He was staring at his feet. Was he even listening? Deciding a practical demonstration might get the point over, I reached over and took the secateurs from him.

'People, like plants, need nurturing. It's wrong to hurt them, just as it's wrong to hack at these roses.' I began methodically snipping the faded flowerheads, trimming off each one above a bud, as Grace had taught me. 'As far as I can see, you're no better at deadheading floribundas as you are at playing tennis.'

'Tennis?' Pavel's chin jerked up. I had his attention.

'Yes. Amanda told me all about it. She said you played like you had a hole in your racket.'

'What stupid talk is this? If I have hole, how I win match?'

162

'Come off it. Amanda thrashed you.'

'What is thrash, please?'

'Trounced. Crushed. Hammered.' I said, snapping at him as I snipped. He was really getting on my nerves and I was showing it. 'She wiped the floor with you. Made mincemeat of you. Beat you to a pulp. Won, hands down.'

Pavel's lips twisted into a smirk, coming as close to a smile as I'd ever seen. 'Mandy, she tell you this? Naughty Mandy. I play tennis in my country. I am champion of my village. What she say is not true. I win match. She does not thrash me. I thrash her. It was – Mandy she teach me these words – it was straight sets.'

How pathetic! Like most bullies, the man was so insecure he couldn't even admit to losing a measly tennis match. My contempt grew.

'And afterwards, you met Amanda's friends? You had a drink with them?'

'Yes. Funny ladies. We make jokes.' He frowned. 'Mandy, she not like jokes. She is little bit jealous I think. After we go home, forgive me to say, Mandy she is like mad woman. Trish it is ...' He broke off. 'It is bleeding bad.'

'What?' I said, taken aback by his sudden ripe language.

He pointed. 'Your hand. Is bleeding bad.'

I looked down. Blood was dripping from my fingers. Those secateurs were sharper than I thought.

'There you are!' Amanda strode towards us, brandishing a paperback. 'I found it! If there's a more arresting first line than this one in *Earthly Powers,* I've yet to read it.' She halted. 'What in heaven's name are you two up to? It's a bloodbath.'

The morning wore on and the heat became unbearable.

The summerhouse walls creaked, my fringe plastered itself to my forehead, sweat dried in an itchy patch between my shoulder blades and my cut finger throbbed.

'Do you have to do that?' Amanda broke off from Jane Austen to frown at me, writhing in my chair, like a grizzly scratching itself against a tree. 'It's most off-putting.'

'I'm sweltering, Amanda. My back's itching and my finger's agony,' I wailed, cradling the clumsily bandaged digit.

All I need now is a hot flush, and my morning will be complete, I thought. Just then, I felt the familiar boiling of the blood.

'Could I get a glass of water?' I begged, all of a sudden, like the witch in *The Wizard Of Oz*, melting, melting.

'Really, Trish!' Amanda sighed. 'You have the attention span of a five-year-old. All right, we'll take a break. I'll get Pavel to make us a cold drink.' The man's ears must've been flapping because his head immediately appeared from behind the summerhouse. 'Darling,' she said. 'Trish is dying of heat and hormones. Two tall glasses of lemonade, if you please? The real stuff. Lots of ice.'

Pavel glared.

'Please?' she pleaded.

I'd have preferred plain water, not being a fan of citrussy drinks, unless they're accompanied by a shot or two of gin. But, ignoring my protests, Amanda gave Pavel instructions on how to make lemonade. He listened gravely and went back to the house.

Me and Amanda, but mostly Amanda – I was still too hot – were debating the advantages of a provocative first sentence over gentle scene setting, when Pavel reappeared, bearing a clinking tray. He put the tray down on the rattan table in front of the summerhouse.

Shading her eyes, Amanda stepped outside. 'What do you call this?' she said, giving the brownish liquid a stir, sending white pith and dark pips whirling in a mini tornedo. 'Looks like pond water.'

'Is lemon-ade,' Pavel said, without irony. 'Lemon, sugar, water and plenty ice. All mix up in mixing up machine. The receipt like you say to me.'

'You have to sieve out the crap, you idiot. How can you not know that?'

'You not say nothing about no *siff*. I am not cook, Mandy.'

'I'm not drinking this muck.'

Forgotten inside the summerhouse, I sank low in my seat, embarrassed.

'You not want? What I do with it?' He picked up the jug.

'Whatever the hell you like.'

'You ask for drink. Have drink.'

With that, he swung the jug and emptied the contents over her. Amanda screamed. Ice cubes cascaded around her and bounced onto the decking. Lemon peel caught in her hair. Juice dripped from her chin.

'That is not funny,' she said, rubbing her eyes. 'It stings like buggery.'

I tensed, wondering what would happen. What did was the last thing I expected. Amanda grabbed a handful of smashed fruit and pelted Pavel with it. How would Pavel react? I closed my eyes, expecting a roar of rage from him. Instead it was her shrieks I heard. I opened one eye to see Pavel, shoving melting ice cubes down her front. She wriggled out of his grasp and, laughing, raced up the garden. Pavel, blank-faced as ever, sprinted after.

Giddy squeals came from behind the trees. I tried to ignore them and get on with my book, hoping Amanda might remember at some point she was supposed to be teaching a lesson. Then the pair emerged and ran past me, Amanda flicking the backs of Pavel's bare legs with a wet tea-towel, before disappearing into the overgrown shrubbery. The squeals died away and at last there was peace.

The silence was every bit as distracting as the shouting. More so, as I couldn't help imagining what was going on out of my sight. After a while I gave up, walked halfway up the parched lawn and called out a goodbye. They didn't answer. I let myself out via the garden gate.

I don't get their relationship. One minute she's hinting he's been physically abusive towards her, the next she's chasing him round the garden with a wet towel. Is it just a relationship that blows more hot and cold than your average? Or something more sinister. I was out of my depth.

Such an innocent! All relationships are a mystery to outsiders, Trish. All in different ways. Someone famous once said summat along them lines. Take her and Gregory. Together more than twenty-one years, now the only things they have in common are the girls and the divorce.

As for Amanda and Pavel, that's easy. They're using each other. He's in it for the free board and lodging. She likes having the attention and someone to boss about. And both of them are loving the bedroom action. Of course, there's no future in a relationship like that, but what does that matter? As long as they're having fun. If they are. But if he's knocking her about, well, in that case all bets are off.

Thirty-Three

Lesson 12: Give The Reader A Break

Nothing to report, so she don't write anything new in the journal. When she goes to Chateau Woodview this week, Trish finds all is sweetness and light. No rows. No bruises, far as she can see. Pavel and Amanda coo at each other like sick-making turtledoves.

In fact, though he's as pokerfaced as ever, Pavel gives every sign he's as smitten with Amanda as she is with him. So much so that, to Trish's horror, Amanda lets him sit in on their lesson. Bridging scenes, it is today. Pavel holds her hand and, every now and then, gives them the benefit of his priceless literary thoughts.

This sort of stuff: 'Is boring, this bloody book. No fightings. No killings. No car chasings.'

Though he sets Trish's teeth on edge summat rotten and she gets a proper bag on, that's hardly proof of abuse. Unless of the English language. She is so pissed off, Trish fails once more to grass up LBK. Piddle on in peace, little kitty. Trish ain't gonna rat on you. Not yet.

Thirty-Four

Lesson 13: Holding Back

*Trish's excuse is there was no traffic on the ring road,
and ... yada yada yada. We know better though, don't
we? She gets there early on purpose and creeps in through
the back, cos she's hoping to catch him out. And she does.
Kind of. Soon as she pushes open the back door, she
knows there's a situation in progress.*

'What I do? What I do wrong this time?' Pavel was
shouting. Never heard him at full volume before. Quite
intimidating. Amanda's reply was a low mumble.

I was in a dilemma. Conscience told me to make a
quick and silent exit, leaving them to argue in private.
Concern for Amanda's wellbeing and curiosity, on the
other hand, told me to stay put and listen. The latter
naturally won. I crept forward into what Amanda grandly
calls 'the scullery', to me just a dark, narrow room leading
into the kitchen, where she stores her pots and pans.

'Why are you like this to me, Mandy, when I do

everything for you?' Pavel was bleating. 'Tell me, because I do not know. I am clueless.'

I heard Amanda give a snort of ridicule.

'Clueless is right word, no?' he said. 'Why is this so funny to you?'

Careful, Amanda, I thought, detecting anger in his words. *You're playing with fire.*

At this point, annoyingly, they must have moved because their next exchange was muffled. I sneaked closer, straining to hear. Then jerked back as Amanda gave a sudden cry.

'You bastard!' she shouted. Then I heard the unmistakable sound of a hand striking bare flesh. 'That hurt,' she shouted.

Next moment, Pavel dashed past me, head down, almost knocking me over. As he flew past, his elbow caught the handle of a large jam pan, sending it crashing to the quarry tiled floor. The deafening reverberation went on for several seconds. As the sound died, the shadow of Amanda appeared in the doorway.

'God, you made me jump,' she said. 'What are you doing, skulking there?'

'I was early. What's going on, Amanda?'

She didn't answer straightaway. Picking up the jam pan, she replaced it on the shelf, carefully moving it until it was in line with the other pans.

'It's just his way,' she said, her back to me. She moved the pan a half a centimetre to the right. Then to the left. 'It'll all blow over in five minutes.'

'You OK, Amanda?'

'I'm fine,' she said, though there was a tremble in her voice.

'Are you sure? Because …?'

'Drop it, Trish.'

But I know what I heard. Pavel had hit her.

We got on with the lesson, though neither of us with much enthusiasm. Amanda seemed distracted and kept touching her cheek. I couldn't stop thinking about what had happened. It wasn't until I was about to leave, and that man was upstairs, safely out of earshot, that I dared raise the subject.

'You know, Amanda, you can talk to me, anytime,' I whispered. 'Or, if you're ever worried and need to get away, give me a call. You'd be welcome to stay at ours … that is, mine. Flo's home but there's a sofa bed in the spare room. It's a bit lumpy but I could get a whatsisname, a memory foam topper. I've been meaning to. From John Lewis, so it'll be nice and comfy. And at least you'd be safe.'

For several seconds, Amanda seemed unable to speak. Then she whispered, 'That is so kind of you, Trish, but not necessary.'

'You don't have to pretend. I heard everything. If you ever need a witness …'

She summoned up a brave smile. Wan would be a good adjective to describe it. 'I appreciate the offer but, as I say, there's no need. I'm perfectly fine.'

'You scared of him, Amanda?'

There was a long pause before she replied. 'He doesn't mean anything by it, Trish.'

What with the worrying goings on and the tense atmosphere, there ain't much hope of Trish learning anything today. All she notes down from the session is the title: Building Suspense by Withholding Information.

170

Thirty-Five

Trish has been summoned. 'One or two things have come up,' Peter Bungle says, not willing to say any more over the phone. Ominous.

Peter was on a call when I arrived. I sat on a hard chair in the corridor like a schoolgirl caught smoking in the bogs, and waited for him to finish. After a while he appeared, apologising profusely. He couldn't yet afford a proper reception, he said. Or indeed, a receptionist to sit in it.

He'd been talking to Jay, he explained, a chum from school, now based in San Francisco. Normally I wouldn't approve of such chum-ism but when it comes to taking on Gregory, I'm prepared to use whatever comes to hand.

Chum Jay, Peter explained, is a forensic accountant. That sounded impressive, though I wasn't clear what one was, until Peter – to use an Amanda word – elucidated.

'Specialises in divorce investigations, looking into fraud and financial irregularities and advising clients in dispute. And he's based in America, which might come in handy.'

'Hold on. Did you say 'financial irregularities'? So Gregory *is* on the fiddle?'

'It's early days but, yes, Jay confirms my impression. There are definite suspicions pertaining to your case.'

'Oh, I'm a *case* now, am I?' There I was again, resorting to quippery when things looked like turning serious.

'That's what happens when you get yourself mixed up with the law, Trish. You're no longer a person. But that wasn't why I asked you to come over. To cut to the chase, Mr. Lightowler has made you an offer. A settlement. Not an acceptable one in my professional opinion.'

'We turn it down then,' I said. 'Tell him to take a running jump.'

'That would be my advice, yes.' Peter folded his arms, resting them on his nascent – another Amanda word – paunch. He lifted a cautious eyebrow. 'I don't want to raise false hopes but, from what I've seen, Jay is set fair to well and truly take the wind out of his sails.'

'With any luck, leaving him dead in the water,' I said, catching the nautical bug.

Thirty-Six

Lesson 14: The No Lesson Lesson

Amanda does it again! No class this week, she informs Trish in an email. It's Pavel's birthday, if you please. She has summat special planned for him in the morning, summat, Trish has a horrible feeling, that involves a long lie-in and baby oil. In the afternoon, she's having a few people over for celebration drinks. No mention of a refund. Not a word of an apology.

'Of course, you're invited,' she adds, to Trish's surprise. 'Bring a plus one if you like.'

Trish, Gawd knows why, takes Felicity.

I felt bad. Felicity was so excited when I told her, and I was almost certain the party would be a let-down. Most things Amanda has a hand in are, I find.

I found Felicity waiting on the pavement outside her flat, wearing a cobalt blue dress, and carrying a box of Thornton's dark chocs and a bunch of multi-coloured dahlias.

'I didn't know which to bring,' she said, sliding into the passenger seat. 'So I got both.'

'Nice frock.'

'Do you like it? My sister chose it for me. For her wedding last year.' She smoothed the skirt over her knees. 'Most I've ever spent. This was a good opportunity to give it another outing. Get my money's worth.'

I'd made an effort too. Bought a sleeveless shift number in a blush pink abstract pattern. Bit tight round the bum, making it ride up round my thighs when I sat down. But the way I looked at it, in this heat, the less covered up you are, the better.

Felicity grew more antsy the closer we got to Woodview. By the time I pulled up at the gates, she was like a schoolkid on their way to Disneyland Paris. I, on the other hand, was increasingly on edge.

'Look,' Felicity pointed. 'Balloons.'

Two flaccid – is that the word? – balloons hung either side of the gates.

'Jeepers,' I grumbled, tapping the steering wheel as we waited for the gates to swing open. 'I know he's younger than her but he's hardly balloon age. What will we have for tea? Jelly and ice cream?'

'Anywhoo, Trish,' Felicity said, rolling her eyes. 'Can we take it as read you don't like the man and enjoy the party. Please.'

I got a shock when I saw Amanda. She looked terrible. Dark shadows under her eyes and cheekbones as sunken as a supermodel's. As usual her outfit was lovely. An aquamarine, long-sleeved, flowing dress. Classy, except the blue-ish tint made her look even more washed out than usual. Pavel stood close by, his tanned, hard body contrasting with hers.

When Amanda said *a few people* for drinks, it wasn't a figure of speech. Me and Felicity were the only two guests.

'I sent out a load of invitations,' Amanda explained. 'No-one else was free at short notice.'

Had she? Had she really? I seriously doubted it. Apart from the women at the tennis club, and she'd fallen out with them, I've never heard her mention any friends.

I had completely forgotten to remind Felicity about the pong. I'd mentioned it in the past, of course – gone on about it a bit too much, perhaps – but I hadn't prepared her for its stinkiness on the day. It hit her, poor lamb, as soon as she entered the house.

'Urgh!' she gagged, hand over mouth. 'God, that's horrible!'

Give him his due, Pavel had done his best. He'd been unstinting with the room spray. The custard drawing room reeked of lavender, though it totally failed to disguise the powerful underlying notes of Parisian *pissoir*.

Amanda was unfazed. 'I'll open the French windows. That should flush out the worst of it.' She tugged half-heartedly at the double doors. They rattled but didn't open.

'Pavel darling, would you mind?' He stepped forward, throwing the doors open so hard, they banged against the outside brickwork. 'Take some deep breaths, my dear,' Amanda said. 'Is that better?'

'A little. Thank you.' Felicity gulped in fresh air like she'd been rescued from drowning. 'Sorry to make such a fuss.'

'Nonsense! I should be the one to apologise. That unpleasant odour has been hanging round for weeks now. We can't find what's causing it and the council have washed their hands of us. Quite frankly, I don't know which way to turn.'

From across the other side of the room, I decided it was time to 'fess up. 'Actually,' I said, 'I think I might ...'

'Champagne. We must have champagne!' Amanda shouted, clapping her hands and cutting me off before I could make the big reveal. 'Could you do the honours, Pavel darling?'

There was no satisfying 'pop' as Pavel uncorked the bottle. The fizz, like the party, was lukewarm and flat. Amanda hadn't gone overboard on the catering. An assortment of crisps and dips were spread out on what I'd call a sideboard. Amanda no doubt has a fancier name for it. In the centre, looking lost, was a small, supermarket birthday cake. Not even M&S I'd wager. I'm sure an eight-year-old would have been delighted by its football theme and bright green icing. But for a grown man!

Pavel never left Amanda's side, faking an interest in the conversation. Not that conversation exactly flowed. Thank goodness for Felicity. Once she'd recovered from the assault on her nostrils, she kept up a breathless chatter, handing over her gifts to Pavel, who grunted a thanks, and shyly reminding Amanda, a red rash spreading up her neck, where they'd met.

'You introduced me to Trish, didn't you? A serendipitous happenstance for both of us,' Amanda gushed. I made a mental note to look up 'serendipitous' when I got home. 'As a matter of interest, how many of my novels do you carry in your little library?'

The rash reached Felicity's cheeks. 'I'm not sure, Miss Turner. The county buyer is in charge of what goes on the shelves. I have very little say.'

Amanda gave a tinkling laugh, quite unlike her usual hearty chuckle. 'Come now. I'm sure a librarian of your experience has impeccable taste and my books are extremely popular, as you know.' Amanda was shameless. 'I have some copies in my study. You're welcome to take some. Trade price. I'll get them. Trish will give you my bank details.'

'Erm ...' I said.

'Erm ...' Felicity echoed, looking stricken.

But it was too late. Amanda had already left the room.

***

Tink, tink, tink. Tapping a spoon on her glass, Amanda appealed for quiet, though with only four of us in the room, it was hardly needed.

'I'd like to say a few words. This is a big day for Pavel.' Her limpet boyfriend nodded his head, even then not smiling. 'Thank you so much for helping us celebrate with him. Happy birthday, darling.' She raised a glass of warm fizz and Felicity and I did likewise.

'Today he's reached the grand old age of thirty. Congratulations, my darling! But there's more. Not that I understand any of it but, it seems, now he's entitled to a share in the family business back in his home country. How fabulous is that?'

'I don't know. How fabulous is it?' I said, on my third glass and feeling reckless, imagining half shares in a garage in a village where only the mayor owns a car, or in a ramshackle shop that stocks twelve different kinds of turnip. Amanda glared.

'Here, here,' Felicity called out. I turned to see if she was being sarky but I don't think she was. Felicity doesn't do sarcasm.

Amanda pulled Pavel even closer. 'As if that weren't enough for one day, we have even bigger news. Pavel and I are ...' She waggled her left hand.

177

'Are what?' I asked, confused. Then I saw. 'Shit!' A ring glinted on Amanda's third finger. 'You're engaged? To him?' I pointed, so there could be no doubt.

Amanda glared some more. I suspect this was not the reaction she was looking for.

'Don't be churlish, Trish.'

'I'm surprised, that's all, after last week.' It just slipped out.

Felicity wasn't to know. 'Why?' she asked. 'What happened last week?'

Amanda's eyes widened. Was I about to blurt out what I'd witnessed? Of course not. I wasn't feeling *that* reckless. Behind Pavel's back, I discreetly mimed zipping up my mouth and saw Amanda's shoulders relax.

'We were chatting,' she said, 'about marriage and I said what an antiquated institution it was. But I was simply playing devil's advocate. I'm really an old romantic at heart. Trish, of course, holds more cynical views. Not surprising, given her current circumstances. Would you like to …?' She extended a limp hand in a regal gesture.

It was a moment before I understood she was inviting us to give the bling closer inspection. We gathered round.

'Congratulations.' I mwhah-ed in the vicinity of her cheek. 'An impressive sparkler.'

'Family heirloom,' Amanda explained. 'Belonged to my grandmother. More meaningful than some over-the-counter purchase, don't you think?' *And cheaper*, I thought. 'Granny wore it to be presented at court when she was twenty. If only … oh dear!' Amanda appeared suddenly overcome.

'What is it, Mandy? I help you,' Pavel said, guiding her to a chair.

'Sorry.' Amanda said. 'It's been an emotional day. I was thinking of my family. If only some of them could have been here today to share my happiness. Sadly they are all gone. I'm alone in the world.'

'I thought you said you had a …'

'Take no notice,' Amanda interrupted. 'I'm just a silly, old woman.'

Pavel perched on the arm of her chair, stroking her hair, making shushing noises. 'We not talk of sad things today. We talk only of happy things. Tell them, Mandy, about the asking for the finger in marriage. Was so beautiful.'

'The proposal?' Amanda said, rallying. 'Well, it was this morning. It was such a beautiful day, we went for a walk in the woods, up to the old ochre pit. Remember, Trish? You were rather unimpressed. But I find it very atmospheric, and it's nice and private.' She nuzzled Pavel and he kissed the crown of her head. 'I assumed the traditional position among the twigs and leaves, and that was it.'

'*You* asked *him*?'

'Why ever not?'

'At the pit?'

'Yes. What's wrong with that?'

'Nothing,' I said, thinking, *nothing except you said it reminded you of a waterfall of blood.*

***

I spilled the beans – almost wrote 'let the cat out of the bag' – on the doorstep. I don't know why I picked that precise moment. A sudden urge to prick the bubble of smugness surrounding the happy couple, I suppose.

'A cat?' Amanda said, untangling herself from Pavel's arms, suddenly stern. 'You're telling me, all this time a moggy's been stinking us out?'

'To be fair, I've never caught him in the act but he's

often hanging about in the back garden under the bushes, snoozing in the shade. He must have been sneaking in when no-one was looking. I literally only made the connection today.' I wasn't about to confess how long I'd been holding onto my smelly secret.

'I wish you'd made the connection sooner,' Amanda said sourly. 'It would have saved us a whole lot of messing about. So, how does one get rid of cat stench?'

Pavel, who'd been fiddling with his phone, started to read out loud, 'Wash aff ... aff ...'

'Fuck's sake, give it here,' Amanda commanded. '*Wash affected surfaces with bicarbonate of soda,*' she read. 'Right. The minute we get back from Dorset, you'll have to get scrubbing, my darling.'

'Dorset?' I said.

'Yes, my fiancé and I,' Amanda said self-consciously, 'are grabbing ourselves some five-star luxury. Our bags are packed and we're off this very afternoon for a week in a spa hotel deep in the New Forest.'

'A week? So no class today and none next week either?'

'We've just got engaged, Trish. You surely don't begrudge us a little holiday? The hotel's got a hydrotherapy pool, and a Finnish sauna.' She tittered. 'I bought a new bikini specially. Leopard print. I love it! I'll show you before you go. There's every kind of massage and mud treatment and – best of all – absolutely zero phone coverage. It actually boasts about it on the website. Not that we care. We probably won't make it out of bed the whole week.'

I gasped. Without warning, my mind had hurtled back to Sorrento.

'And when we come back,' Pavel said in his monotone. 'We deal with pissing cat.'

Me and Felicity tried to escape without being shown

the blessed bikini but Amanda would insist on running upstairs to get it.

'What do you think?' she said, holding it against herself.

'It's very small. And lime green.'

'Knew you'd approve.'

'Well, that wasn't what I expected,' Felicity said as we drove home, a box of Amanda's books bouncing on the back seat. 'And I don't only mean the pong.'

Thirty-Seven

With Amanda and Pavel out of the way, Trish can at last focus on what's important. Her novel.

Here's a weird thing. While they're off on their Dorset bonk-fest, I've been – I hardly dare say it – writing. The Novel. Yes, I know! Miracle of miracles. Started it, at least. Almost three chapters in. Nearly three thousand words. Three thousand! All out of my own little noddle. Can't tell you how good that makes me feel. Only a first draft, but still.

Could it have been Amanda who was holding me back all along? That would be ironic. Certainly, with her gone, I've been unblocked, like a drain after a hefty dose of Mr. Muscle. I informed Felicity and she was absolutely agog – is that the word? – to see what I'd written. 'All in good time,' I told her. 'I've gathered the ingredients of my cake, but I haven't yet put it in the oven, let alone done the fancy icing and stuck in the indoor firework.'

It was something Amanda had said, about writing a book being like baking a Victoria sponge. I didn't dare point out at the time that Victoria sponges don't generally

182

have icing. To be honest, I was more at the stage of peering into the cupboards, wondering if I have enough eggs and self-raising flour.

The ending worries me. Shouldn't I know how the book ends? Have an idea, at least. At the moment, I'm not even sure what happens at the beginning of chapter four. I mean, don't ask me. I'm only the writer! The main thing is, I've made a start. See, Amanda, you were wrong. I am an improviser, a Jamie Cullen, after all.

I was miles away, thinking about that pesky ending, when I heard a gentle knocking at the front window. Who knocks on a window when there's a perfectly good bell, not to mention a knocker, not six feet away in the traditional position on the front door? Tutting loudly, I went to investigate. A big, burly bloke with no hair and no discernible neck loomed into view as I approached the window.

'Mrs. Lightwoller?' he enquired politely through the glass. I get that a lot, even though the middle part of my name is 'owl', a word you'd think most people would recognise. I opened the window a tiny sliver.

'Good afternoon, Madam,' he said. 'I am under instruction from the firm of Didcock & Weake to serve you these papers to sign.' He held up a familiar-looking brown envelope.

'Are you the bailiff?'

'Strictly speaking,' he said in a gravelly voice that reminded me a bit of Daniel Craig – though in appearance he was more of a Ross Kemp – 'I'm the process server.' He leant forward, attempting to stuff the envelope through the narrow crack in the window.

'Well, strictly speaking, I am not Mrs. Lightwoller,' I said, slamming the window shut. 'So you can sling your hook.' Then I ran upstairs and hid in bed, switching on

Radio 2.

There I stayed, under the duvet, fretting about my bedding plants, worried he'd flattened them with his big combat boots. He looked like the sort of man who'd wear boots with laces up his shins. Size thirteen, doubtless. My poor petunias!

He was persistent, I'll say that for him. Hung about outside for quite a while. I could hear him. First he rattled the back gate. Ha ha! Won't catch me out there. Always keep it bolted from the inside. Then he went round to the front again and began what I can only describe as circuits: tapping on the window, ringing the bell, knocking the knocker. Nothing excessive. Nothing to alarm the neighbours. I expect they are trained that way at Process Server School. Tap. Ring. Knock. Repeat. Tap. Ring. Knock. Repeat. I turned up the radio and slid deeper down, sweating under 4.5 tog's worth of duvet. Eventually I fell asleep.

I awoke with a start. All was quiet. He'd gone. I tiptoed down to check on the state of the front garden. What do you know? Not a petal bruised or a leaf crushed. The bailiff who isn't a bailiff who looks like Ross Kemp and sounds like Daniel Craig must have pirouetted round my plants like Darcy Bussell.

Thirty-Eight

Shit, shit, and more shit! Radio 4 is on. She's only half listening, so it's a complete fluke she even catches it. Usually she finds consumer programmes boring. Not this time. She listens with growing horror.

Gordon Bennet! Have to get hold of Amanda. Urgently. Tried phoning but it went straight to voicemail. I could have left a message. But who's to say she'd listen to it? She's not a must-check-my-messages sort of gal. When was it they said they would be back? I can't remember. *Slow down, Trish, you're probably panicking over nothing.* But what if I'm not?

Going to pin a note on her front door, where she can't miss it. Drive over now and leave a note. What else can I do? Yes, that's it. Drive over. Soon as I find my flaming car keys.

Thirty-Nine

Too late! They're already home when she gets there, She hears them in the back garden as she parks up. Amanda's light chatter. Pavel's low rumble. They're in the corner where Pavel had started and abandoned his veg patch. He's digging. She's leaning against the fence, vaping and ogling.

'Trish!' Amanda said, surprised. 'There's no lesson this week. Did you forget?'

'I know. I …' I stopped in my tracks and gaped. 'That's a big hole you're digging, Pavel. What are you planting? A tree?'

'Is not hole,' Pavel said, continuing to chop into the baked earth. 'Is grave.'

'For that stinking cat.' Amanda blew out a cloud of minty condensation.

'Is sad but the cat it piss in house,' Pavel said, taking a breather. 'Make bad smell.'

'That's why I came over,' I said. 'To tell you. The smell, it wasn't the cat.'

'It most certainly was,' Amanda said. 'Squirting its

186

disgusting pheromones all over my home.'

'But he didn't. I heard it on the radio. Radio 4's Winifred Robinson. So it must be true.'

Amanda smiled. 'I've missed you, you know. You and the piffle you spout.'

'No, listen. You don't understand.' I took a deep breath and spoke slowly. 'The smell, lots of people are suffering from it. Hundreds have complained. There was an in-depth investigation on Radio 4 and they found, it's not cats or drains or dead rodents. It's paint.'

'Paint?' she said, smile rapidly dying.

I gabbled out a version of what I'd heard on *You and Yours*. Something had gone wrong at the factory with the mixing of a batch of emulsion. That, along with the unusual heat, had caused a chemical reaction. All round the country, people were holding their noses and demanding an explanation.

'You're telling me,' Amanda said coldly, 'that all this time, it was the sodding paint?'

'I made a mistake.' I was on the verge of tears. 'A terrible mistake. He's not responsible, LBK. The cat. He's innocent.' I looked from Amanda to Pavel, desperately hoping. 'Please tell me you haven't done anything rash.'

Amanda took a long, slow puff, then said, 'If only you'd been here fifteen minutes earlier.'

My heart sank. No.

'Regrettably, it has already been dealt with.' She lowered her voice. 'That is, *he* dealt with it.' She gestured towards Pavel who, not caring or not understanding, had gone back to digging. 'The stench when we got back was unbelievable. Then the moggy appeared by the back door. After what you'd told us, one had little choice but to act.'

'But he's only a little kitten,' I gulped. 'His family will

be out there searching for him, scouring the woods, worrying, calling his name.'

'Don't look at me like that,' she said, taking another puff. 'Pavel did the deed. I had nothing to do with it.' Touching my elbow, she drew me out of earshot. 'I told him to sort it and that's exactly what he did. You can stop digging now, darling,' she shouted over. 'That'll do. It's a cat not a Shetland pony.'

I hadn't noticed the little bundle laying in the long grass, wrapped in a grey towel. Pavel picked it up and, I have to say, with some reverence, placed it in the hole.

'Shouldn't we, like, say a few words?' I said, swallowing down bile.

'If we, like, must,' Amanda mocked.

We lined up beside the makeshift grave. Me and Pavel bowed our heads.

For a moment Amanda sought inspiration in the cloudless sky before chanting to a sort-of hip-hop rhythm:

'Sorry little cat. You went splat.
It's a crying shame. When the paint–'
She turned to me and, cupping a hand to her mouth, stage-whispered, 'And Patricia Meddlesome Lightowler – Was to blame.'

'There,' she said, 'will that do? Not bad for an off-the-cuff effort, I thought.'

It was inappropriate and offensive, and I'm darned sure it didn't scan, but Amanda seemed pleased.

Pavel began shovelling back the earth, covering the pitiful little body. This done, he bashed the soil down with the back of the spade, crossed himself and headed for the house.

'Did you say, Mandy, you bought biscuits?' I heard

188

him ask.

Amanda's pretty unfeeling, I grant you, but he is beyond words.

Forty

'You did what? Oh, Trish, you didn't!'

I'd been brooding over poor LBK, feeling guilty one minute, outraged the next. Peter Bungle always had the knack of cheering me up, so I gave him a call to check on progress. Also to tell him the tale of the bailiff. To crow about it, if I'm honest, imagining he would find my pig-headedness amusing. Embroidered a bit for effect and waited for his loud guffaws.

'Have I got this right?' Peter said, about as far from guffawing as you can imagine. 'You hid under the bedclothes and refused to take delivery? What, pray, did you hope to achieve by that?'

'Dunno,' I said, like a sulky child on the naughty step. 'Wind Gregory up, I suppose. Make him waste more money on lawyers.'

'You're only delaying the inevitable, Trish. If you don't co-operate, the divorce will still go ahead. Mr. Lightowler can proceed without your signature and the end result will be the same. It's just, Mr. Lightowler will have to jump through various legal hoops to get there.'

'Good,' I said. 'That's no less than he deserves. Or do

I mean 'more'?'

'Is that what you want, Trish? Really? To needlessly delay a divorce from a man who's made it abundantly clear – apologies, but it has to be said – doesn't want to stay married to you, or even in this country? I thought the whole point was to be free of him. Why in the name of ... words fail me.'

I was shocked by Peter's vehemence. Never heard him sound so angry before. In that moment, any thoughts I had of spiting Gregory by refusing to co-operate, disappeared. That would only taint the memory of what our marriage had once been. I was better than that.

'You're right, Peter. I don't want to stay shackled to him for one second longer than I need to. I have, after all, a whole new life to start living.'

'That's the spirit, Trish. Sail on into unchartered waters. See what they have to offer. So, when the process server next comes to call – and they will – you'll do what?'

'I'll take the brown envelope and sign the blasted papers.'

'Good. Glad we've got that clear. Now, do you want to hear how Jay's enquiries are getting on?'

Forty-One

Lesson 15: In Conclusion ... Or Is It?

*Frigging hell. She's not going back there, surely? She is,
the stupid cow! How can she bear to be anywhere near
that man, knowing he's a cat killer? As for Amanda,
bollocks to loyalty. Bollocks to the sisterhood. She don't
owe her nothing, not after the way she's fleeced her,
belittled her, outright insulted her. Amanda's made her
bed. Or unmade it. Let her lay in it. Stay away, Trish.*

Had to go back. Couldn't abandon Amanda.

Jolly good job I did. She was properly low. Not at all
what you'd expect of a newly engaged woman. She could
hardly muster the energy to teach at all. She's lost her ...
what's that word? ... va-va-voom? Only a few weeks ago,
every lesson was an excuse to show off or have a go.
Today, I'm sorry to say, she was boring.

That man was nowhere to be seen, thank the Lord.
Putting two new coats of paint on the study walls,
Amanda told me, sealing in the pong, as instructed by

Radio 4's Martha Kearney.

We did endings today. As far as I could make out, Amanda favoured what she called *The Fatal Attraction Ending*. When you think it's all over but it's not. At least, I think that was it. She didn't explain it very well. And she looked awful. Unkempt. Funny word, that. Is anyone ever 'kempt' I wonder?

When was the last time her hair saw shampoo, or her trousers an iron? The top she had on didn't help. As shapeless and unflattering as a pillowcase. And she was so pale. On closer inspection, I saw why. A thick mask of pan-stick make-up clogged her skin from hairline to neck, where it rubbed off onto the white of her billowing top. What was it concealing? The unflattering red lipstick didn't help.

Amanda was subdued, often not bothering to finish her sentences. Finally, finally, the endless two hours were up and I could escape. She insisted on coming to see me off the premises. The gate motors were on the blink, she said. She'd have to push them open for me. She looked so frail I said I could do that. Amanda was having none of it.

I drove up and she crunched across the gravel, head drooping, still a picture of misery. I waited in the Mini while she wrestled with the gates, rusty hinges complaining as she swung them open, first one side, then the other. As she struggled, I saw her wince. She stood aside to let me through. I drove past and she gave a wave. The loose neck of her pillowcase top slipped down. It was only a split second, before Amanda yanked it back up, but it was long enough. I caught a glimpse of bare shoulder. Admittedly, I was in the car and squinting into the sun but I saw – I'm almost certain I saw – purple marks, the sort you'd get if someone grabbed you by the shoulders really, really hard.

***

Can't sleep. Keep churning it over. The slap. LBK. The bruises. It's all adding up. Should I tell someone? Talk to Amanda? Confront Pavel again? Phone the police? What should I do? I know I need to pull myself together but I don't want to jump the gun. Or risk antagonising that man. That would only put Amanda in worse danger.

The sky is turning from inky black to underpants grey and I still haven't come to a decision, beyond keeping watch and writing everything down in this journal, which isn't a journal any more by the way. It's evidence, ready in case … well, just in case.

> *Made up her mind to do nothing, she means. Ain't she seen enough?*

Forty-Two

Flo is cheerful. Which is summat of a miracle, considering. She don't moan about her arse-numbingly boring job or aching legs. She don't snap when Trish fusses over her, blending up a kale smoothie and dishing out vitamin pills. She gets on with it. Or, at least, so Trish thinks.

She was singing as she let herself in. Humming under her breath. She walked through to the kitchen where I was chopping up a red pepper. Much to my surprise, she dumped her keys on the worktop, put her arms round me, and murmured into my hair, 'I do love you, you know, Mum.'

'If it's money you're after, Flo, you're out of luck. Your dad and his floozie have grabbed the lot,' I teased, aware it was her hormones talking but enjoying the attention all the same. 'Would you settle for a protein-rich tuna bake?'

'That'd be brill,' she replied, letting me go. 'I'll get showered and knock up one of my special everything-but-the-kitchen-sink salads, like I do for the guys at uni.'

195

'You missing them?'

'Not really,' she shrugged. 'Lazy buggers never wash up. You've got a dishwasher.'

After Flo went upstairs, I found myself reminiscing. I remembered how, in the early weeks of my pregnancy, I woke up most days uncertain about everything except that having a baby was absolutely the worst idea I'd ever had. As for the buy-one-get-one-free double whammy of twins, well, that news left me numb. In time, I got used to the idea and by the time I was thirty weeks gone, I couldn't wait for the babies' arrival.

I have to admit, damn him, Gregory was great, rubbing my back, traipsing round Mothercare, totally at ease that, not one, but two little disruptors were about to explode a bomb under our lives.

'Half the sleep. Twice the fun,' he'd said.

Have to keep reminding myself that Gregory was once quite a decent human being. I wonder how Flo will cope, given her circumstances? Which I am not allowed to mention, by the way. Like I'm not allowed to call her a single mother.

'All mothers are single,' she says. 'Everybody only has the one.'

I waited, tuna bake at the ready, but Flo didn't reappear. An hour had gone by. I went in search and found her curled up on her bed, sniffling into her pillow. As soon as she saw me, sniffles became tears. I plonked myself on the edge of the bed and gave her a hug, rocking her, repeating those empty, but somehow soothing, words, 'I know. I know.' But the thing is, I actually did.

'You seemed happy when you came in,' I said, when her tears subsided. 'You were singing a merry tune.'

'It's a front, Mum. The more miserable I am, the

196

more I sing. I've been feeling like shite all day. When I wasn't singing, I was crying in the bogs. Didn't want you to think I wasn't coping. But I'm not. I'm really not.' The tears started flowing once more.

'Listen to me,' I said, putting my hands on her shoulders. 'No new mother in the history of the human race has ever thought she was coping, Flo. None of us. The best we can hope for is to muddle through.'

She made a brave effort at a smile.

'It's true,' I told her. 'Every mum-to-be feels inadequate. I did. Granny did. Mrs. Cavewomen, weeping over her sabre-toothed tiger steaks did. It's a huge thing you're doing, growing a whole new person. It's normal to be anxious. It's natural to be frightened. It's fine to spend hours in the bogs, feeling shite.

'But you're not on your own. You have me and Nell. And, though it pains me to say so, you have your dad. No matter what crap the two of us are going through, we'll both always be on your side. And don't you forget it. And you will find it in yourself to cope. I know you will. Better?' Flo sniffed.

'Now,' I continued, thumbing away a lone tear on her cheek, 'what happened to this famous everything-but-the-kitchen-sink salad?'

Forty-Three

Lesson 16: Raising The Stakes

Today was all about upping the ante. A poker term, Amanda said. Or horse-racing. I'm not sure. I was distracted by how she looked, which was even worse than last time: ghostly pale, dark smudges under her eyes, and cheeks like she was permanently sucking on a clogged straw.

And she kept yawning. Open-mouthed and quite, I have to say, rude. 'Excuse me!' she said. 'Don't know why I'm so sleepy. I slept like a babe. Didn't come to until after nine. Yet now I feel I could go back to bed and sleep for another eight hours.' She yawned again. 'I'll get …'

She stood, swayed and would have fallen if she hadn't had the kitchen table to lean on. Alarmed, I grabbed her arm and steered her back to her seat.

'This isn't right,' I said. 'You look terrible. You need to see your GP.'

She waved me away. 'Don't fuss. It'll be the HRT. They changed my prescription.'

'What if it's not? What if it's your blood pressure? Or your heart. The menopause can make you more prone to heart attacks. I watched this documentary. You should get yourself checked out.'

'I'll be fine in a minute or two. Stop nagging, Trish.'

Call me suspicious but I saw the hand of that man in this. Was he slipping her something? She had deteriorated so quickly. You read of such things. Conmen who befriend lonely, well-off women, drug them and, when they're in a confused state, get them to change their wills or run off with their jewellery and Old Masters. Wouldn't put anything past that man. What I needed was proof.

I'm learning to be more devious. I faked a headache.

'I'll run to the bathroom and help myself to a couple of aspirin, if that's OK.' I was halfway up the stairs before Amanda had time to object.

Nothing obviously dodgy in the bathroom cabinet. Nothing with a skull and crossbones on it, at least, or a label saying, *Danger – may cause extreme drowsiness if administered by a wicked boyfriend.*

Was about to give it up when my eye was drawn to a Holland & Barrett multivitamin bottle. The screw top was askew, as if someone had replaced it hastily. Some guilty person, perhaps, almost caught in the act. It wasn't much but it was all I had to go on.

I removed the top and tipped a couple of pills onto my hand. Shiny red things they were, not unlike Smarties. They looked innocent enough, but who could tell?

Replacing the bottle, careful to put the top back as I had found it, I reached up to close the bathroom cabinet door. As I swung it shut, a beam of sunlight flashed across its mirrored surface, blinding me for a second.

'What you do, Trish?'

Him, Pavel. How long had he been standing in the doorway, spying on me?

As I spun to face him, I palmed the pills into my mouth and swallowed.

I think he bought my explanation. It's hard to tell with Pavel. The word 'inscrutable' could have been invented for him. Worried I might drop down unconscious – or worse – once the pills kicked in, using the headache as an excuse, I cut the lesson short and went home.

So here I am, curled up on the sofa, waiting. Waiting, wondering and worrying. Any minute now I'll either be bouncing off the walls like a gazelle with ADHD or ... maybe I won't put that down on paper.

***

The sun caresses my bare shoulders. Fingers of grass stroke the backs of my legs. I feel relaxed, at ease, as I stroll through the grass, arms outstretched. The land before me is flat and featureless. Grey clouds gather on the horizon. They roll overhead, like waves against the shore. I start to feel nervous.

Now it's raining. Spiteful drops sting my cheeks. A vicious wind lashes my hair. I'm cold. I'm stuck, ankle deep in mud. I crouch, hugging my knees, desolate and alone.

I look up. There's a figure on the horizon. A man. He looks familiar. I squint and see it's Gregory. I stand to greet him. As he gets closer, I see it's not Gregory. It's Pavel. He reaches me and rises, enormous, menacing and monstrous, into the dark sky above me. I try to free myself. Pavel soars higher, then sweeps down, enveloping me, choking me in his icy grip.

I jerk awake. It's five in the morning. I'm tangled up in a throw and freezing cold.

Forty-Four

There's news. Over in the US of A, happy-clappy accountant Jay has put aside his joss sticks and his Peruvian worry dolls, interrupted his Buddhist chanting, and devoted hisself unsparingly to examining Gregory's company books.

Peter arranges a video call to update Trish. They meet at his office. Partly cos he's that sort of friendly chap but mainly cos he suspects, with some reason, that Trish will make a total bish of it, if she tries to join in a three-way on her own.

Hard to believe Jay and Peter went to the same school. They are so different.

Peter was his usual, jovial, twitchy, untidy self: creased suit, collar up at all angles, papers scattered over the desk. Over in San Francisco, the handsome, heavy-eyed Jay had clearly gone native: curly, black hair scraped back in the nape of his neck, from where it sprang out like a chrysanthemum, silk shirt so bright, it was a wonder planets weren't orbiting it, and a slim electronic notepad, no bits of paper, before him.

'Blast to see you, *amigo,* even if it is only via the old Zoomerola,' Jay said in a slow, mid-Atlantic drawl, fist-bumping the screen. 'And you too, Mrs. Lightwoller.'

'Owler,' I corrected wearily.

'Sure,' he said. 'I'll go right ahead and dive in, shall I?'

He may have had the tan, the hair, and the sleepy eyes of a surfing stoner but Jay's brain was, let me tell you, razor sharp – though he, like so many others, had a blind spot when it came to my name. He quickly filled me in on the tricks used in some divorces. Though many splits, he explained, are resolved with spouses honestly declaring their finances, in a small minority of cases, one or sometimes both parties try to hide what they've got.

'It's the role of a forensic accountant, like yours truly, to call them out. Let me spell it out for you, 'matrimonial assets' means anything like property, possessions, pensions, investments, and savings acquired during the course of the marriage. You feel me? And in the case of Mr. Lightwoller –'

'It's … oh, forget it.'

'In the case of Mr. Lightwoller, there appear to be substantial assets unaccounted for. I applied for bank and tax documents, share certificates, and the rest and have gotten them. Right now, I'm elbow deep but I should have the full picture of your spouse's actual assets, as opposed to those he wants us to know about, real soon.'

'What if he starts shifting stuff about?'

'We can take steps through the courts back over there in dear old Blighty. A freezing injunction for example. Don't worry, you're in safe hands, Mrs. Lightwoller.'

The rest of the call passed in a whirl of statistics and legal terminology, with Jay detailing the trail of deception he was following, all leading back to one, Gregory Lightowler. Or Woller.

'Great work, Jay. Keep on it,' Peter encouraged. 'I've

got a good feeling about this. After we deliver our broadside, Mr. Lightowler won't know what's hit him.'

'Rrrrrrrrrright onnnnnnnn, maaaannnnnnn!' Jay stuttered, giving a wobbly thumbs up, before freezing, dissolving into juddering stripes and finally cutting abruptly to black.

'Don't look at me,' I pleaded. 'I didn't touch a thing.'

Forty-Five

Lesson 17: Fishy Goings-On

Aaaaaargh! She's going back to the madhouse again. I despair! What does she think she's playing at? Amanda is an ungrateful PITA who don't deserve Trish. But does she listen to me? Does she buggery. She returns to discover the situation at Woodview has changed. It's jumped from 'a bit off' to 'abso-fucking-lutely weird.'

OK. So I went back. So what? Shoot me, why don't you? What sort of friend would I be if I abandoned Amanda?

Checking the mailbox is one of the many little jobs I've slipped into doing for her. Not that I mind. She never locks or empties it. It irritates me seeing junk mail spilling out, blowing about on the drive, and out into the lane, where anyone could pick it up.

'What does it matter if someone nicks a bunch of pizza leaflets?' Amanda says. 'They're welcome.'

'Or your utility bills? Or your identity?'

But I was talking to myself.

This morning when I flipped open the box, I found, not junk mail, but something surprising: a brown paper package, tied up, as it happened, with string. It drooped in my hand when I picked it up, like one of those bean-bag hot water bottles. No stamp. No address. Must've been hand delivered. I took it into the house and left it on the hall table while I sorted out my stuff. Thought no more about it as I entered the kitchen, that old tune from *The Sound of Music,* still earworming round in my skull.

Today we were in the newly painted and, I'm pleased to say, un-smelly study. Amanda was a little less groggy, though still a bag of nerves. While I was unpacking, I dropped my pen on the floor. You'd have thought a bomb had gone off.

'What's given you the jitters?' I asked.

'Don't know what you mean,' she snapped, about as non-jittery as a tabby cat who's ended up in the middle of Crufts Dog Show.

'What you need is a break.' I offered. 'I don't have much on at the moment. How about we have a long weekend away? The two of us? The Peak District is nice. I know a nice bed and breakfast in Buxton. Buxton is *extremely* nice. We could do some nice walks.'

Silence.

'Amanda? Did you hear?'

'I heard,' Amanda said coolly. 'You and I? In a bed and breakfast in Buxton? Correction. A *nice* bed and breakfast in *nice* Buxton, where the walking is *nice*?' I didn't much care for her tone. 'I don't think so, Trish. We hardly know each other.'

That was a low blow. For almost five months we'd spent most Thursday mornings hanging out together. Didn't that add up to some kind of friendship?

'In any case,' Amanda continued, 'Pavel and I have only just got back from our engagement jolly. Life isn't all fun and frolics you know, Trish. Writing, despite the popular conception, is damned demanding work. I need to put in the hours on my next novel. A holiday at this stage of gestation is unthinkable. If you were any sort of a writer, you'd know that.'

I was smarting. How could I know? I didn't even know Amanda was working on anything. I'd seen no evidence. She hadn't said. But, in the interests of peace and quiet, I said nothing. Swallowing the remaining tatters of my pride – ouch! a tortured metaphor if ever I wrote one – I put my mind to the topic of the day: subplots.

Happy to say, after a slow start, Amanda threw herself into this one almost like the woman of old.

'It's never too late to inject new life into a tale that is in danger of flagging,' she explained. 'Get the reader to sit up and say, *Hmmm. I thought I knew where this one was heading. Now I'm totally discombobulated*'.

Discombobulated. I wrote that down, wondering, is anyone ever 'combobulated'?

'The trick is …' Suddenly Amanda twisted in her seat and announced to the half-open door. 'Come in if you're coming in, for God's sake. Don't hang about out there.'

Him, of course. That man.

He burst through the door. 'Talk, talk, talk. Books, books, books,' he jabbered, wringing his hands. 'Is all the times the same. All the times you with your bloody books. How can you talk about bloody books when there is big danger?'

Amanda smiled. 'Take no notice, Trish. Such a drama queen. Do calm down, darling. You're upsetting Trish.'

Pavel wasn't inclined to calm down. 'Trish is upset. I am upset also. You should be upset, Mandy.'

Was that a little tic of contempt I saw tugging at the corner of her mouth? There certainly was a sigh of what seemed like irritation.

'I'm telling you, it's nothing,' she said.

'Has something happened?' I asked, wanting, and at the same time *not* wanting, to know.

'It's hardly worth talking about. Pavel had a couple of strange phone calls, that's all, yesterday while I was out. Clearly a misunderstanding. Or a wrong number. Or simply a nutter. I wasn't here, as I say. I'd run into town for emergency vaping supplies. When I got back I found him like this. He hasn't stopped ranting on about it ever since.'

'I tell you, Mandy,' he said, clutching his head, 'is no wrong number. Is no nutter. Is them. My father warn me before I come to this bloody country. He say be careful, Pasha. He say, without my protection, things can happen. The brothers they have ...' He stopped. 'What you call them?' He wriggled his fingers at her.

'Spiders?' Amanda suggested, with a sly wink at me.

'Is not funny, Mandy. They have legs of ... I forget the bloody word.' Pavel wriggled his fingers again.

'I think he means tentacles,' I said.

'Yes. Yes. This is it,' he said, excitedly looking from me to Amanda. 'They have testicles everywhere.'

Amanda let out a snort.

Pavel gave her his Easter Island stare. 'You not find it funny if they come, I tell you. They are bad men. My father, they cannot get. But me, I am sitting on the duck.'

She stifled another snort. 'Sorry, darling. But honestly!'

'Who's he on about?' I asked.

Amanda wiped her eyes. 'Some thugs from his country. The Kaminski ... Kolinski brothers. Something like that. He's convinced himself they're after him. Some sort of ridiculous family feud apparently.'

'Kandinski!' Pavel shouted. 'Is Kandinski brothers! If

you are from my country, you will know this name. Everyone knows the Kandinskis. Everyone is scared. They kill many, many people. Killing is … how I say this? Killing is their work. What I do, Mandy? You must help me,' he pleaded. 'What I do?'

Amanda was unmoved. 'Darling, nothing is going to happen to you. People here don't get attacked in the street by foreign gangsters. We simply do not allow it.'

'What about that man and the poisoned teapot,' I said. 'And those poor people in Salisbury?'

Pavel's eyes widened. 'What she say?'

Amanda glared. 'You're not helping, Trish. Tell me, darling, what exactly did this person say on the phone?'

Pavel rubbed the back of his neck. 'She say… I don't remember word. She speak English in funny accent but I get message: the Kandinskis, they come to get me.'

'*She*? A woman! Are you sure you haven't got your wires crossed?' Amanda said.

'Wires?' he repeated. 'You say they hurt me with electricity wires?'

'No, no, no.' Amanda patted the seat beside her. 'Here, come and sit down. Tell your Mandy all about those nasty Kandinskis.' Behind his back, she rolled her eyes. 'You don't mind taking five, do you, Trish?'

What choice did I have? I picked up my stuff and went and sat in the custard drawing room to read my book, an addictive Victorian detective mystery. When I poked my head round the door half an hour later, the two of them were still in a huddle. Amanda had her arm round his shoulder and I'm pretty sure Pavel had been weeping. Like most bullies, the man was obviously a coward.

Clearly, there would be no more teaching that day. I was in the hall preparing to leave when I remembered the parcel. Dark stains were soaking through the brown paper. I could have left it there to ruin her table but that would have been petty, and unfair on the furniture. I scooped up the soggy bundle and went back to the study.

'Where's this come from?' Amanda demanded, as I dumped the package on her desk.

'The post box. Found it when I got here, then forgot all about it.'

'Pavel, be a love and see what's in it.'

Red-eyed and looking even more miserable than usual, Pavel warily approached the package. He started pulling at the wet brown paper, not attempting to tackle the knots. I was about to suggest he cut the string when, grunting in frustration, he picked the whole squelchy mess up. It fell to pieces in his hands. Something– I couldn't see what – slid through his fingers and flopped off the desk and onto the floor. Pavel gave a short – and I'd have to say, girlish – scream, and took several paces back.

'Let me see,' Amanda said, elbowing past. When she straightened up, she was smiling. 'Silly boy. It can't hurt you. It's quite dead. It's a delivery gone wrong, darling. Or someone's idea of a practical joke.'

Pavel shook his head. 'Is no joke. Is them. I know. They are already here.' His voice was flat, defeated. His eyes darted around the room, as if his enemies were already in the house.

'You're over-reacting, darling. Throw that thing in the bin and forget about it.'

'I not touch it,' Pavel said, recoiling even further. 'Is evil.'

Amanda looked at me. I looked at the thing, spreading a pool of its juices across the floorboards. With no-one else volunteering, I said, 'I'll get the mop and bucket then, shall I?'

Scatterbrain Trish ain't said what it is, has she? You'll wanna know. It's a fish. Trout, I think. Or seabass. I'm not good on fish unless it's haddock or cod and coated in batter. Whatever it is, judging by the pong, it's on the turn. And it ain't a mistaken delivery. Pavel is right. It's a warning. How do I know? Cos of the red rose jammed in its gaping mouth. Like I said, abso-fucking-lutely weird.

Forty-Six

Lesson 18: Traits, Foibles, And Quirks

Mannerisms, today's farce was supposed to be about. The way characters talk and walk, and stuff. But Amanda was having another one of her off days. From the start I could tell her heart wasn't in it and neither was mine. I missed the old Amanda, the one who had ripped the pee out of me. At least she held my attention. This washed-out version was in danger of sending me to sleep.

Didn't take long before she'd run out of things to say about stuttering, twitching, scratching, nail chewing, eyebrow raising and the like. Silence descended, which of course I felt I had to fill.

'Isn't that lazy?' I asked. 'You know, the dark-haired, scowling baddie. The blond, crinkly-eyed goodie? No better than the white hats and black hats in those old westerns.'

Amanda stirred in her seat. Think I'd touched a nerve. Good. At least now she might buck her ideas up.

'Do not underestimate the power of mannerisms as a short cut to character,' she said. 'Take, for instance, I

212

don't know, a simple thing like eating. One person might trowel butter and jam onto their crusty, homemade slice, hot from the toaster, before crunching into it, melted butter dripping down their chin, sharp teeth leaving feral bite marks in the toast.' She bared her teeth.

'Feral?' I queried.

'Nothing wrong with an unexpected adjective every now and then. While another character might cut their thin, lightly toasted sliced white into eight postage stamps, spooning a half-teaspoon of jam onto each and posting them neatly into their mouth.' She mimed that, lifting a pinkie and pursing her lips to receive the imaginary little squares.

'The cruncher and the spooner. Two very different and, I would suggest, incompatible characters. Put them at opposite ends of a breakfast table and you have the perfect set-up for conflict. And conflict, need I remind you, is the meat and gravy of drama. Are you OK? You've gone quite pale.'

'I'm fine,' I lied.

I wasn't. I was stunned. She had done it again. Described a piece of my life she couldn't have known about. I was certain me the cruncher and Gregory the spooner had never come up in conversation.

We spent the rest of the two hours talking about Sherlock Holmes, or rather his violin, his stupid hat, and his partiality for Class A drugs. Still troubled by Amanda's uncannily accurate description of me and Gregory, I was halfway to the car before I remembered I hadn't had what me and the girls call a 'pre-emptive wee'. *Always start a journey with an empty bladder*, that's the Lightowler family motto. I went back inside to the downstairs loo, which meant passing the study. Amanda and Pavel were still in there. The door was shut but they spoke so loudly, I couldn't help but overhear.

'His family is from my village.' Pavel said, speaking quickly. 'He moved to this country to a place called Bristol. He knows about such things. He helped me before. He will know what to do.'

'You're sure we can trust him, this man from Bristol?' Amanda said.

'Sergei? Of course. He is son to old friend to my father.'

'Sergei?' Amanda said, amused. 'Like the meerkat?'

'No more of jokes, Mandy. I call him. Sergei will get us what we need.'

'Let me handle that for you, darling,' Amanda said. 'I'll charm a better price out of him.'

Pavel grunted agreement.

'Where would we be,' she said, 'without your Daddy's mafia connections?'

'How many times I tell you?' Pavel sounded angry. 'My father is no mafia. He is legit businessman.' It sounded like a phrase he'd learnt off by heart. 'Sergei, he will want cash money.'

'Understood,' Amanda said. 'I'll arrange a meeting and go to the bank. I don't imagine such things come cheap.'

Forty-Seven

Lesson 19: Cut To The Chase

> *How does Trish find out the wheres and whens of the*
> *rendezvous with Sergei? By doing what she's getting good*
> *at: earflapping. After today's lesson, she hangs about at*
> *the foot of the stairs, pretending to search for her keys.*
> *Pavel and Amanda are so keen to head for the bedroom*
> *they don't bother making sure she has actually left the*
> *building.*
>
> *'Nine o'clock, Monday night,' she hears Amanda*
> *say. 'The White Hart.'*
>
> *'Thank you, Mandy,' Pavel says. 'This makes me so*
> *happy.'*
>
> *Trish takes the sounds of slobbering as her cue to get*
> *off home.*

Have you got any idea how many White Harts there are within spitting distance of Oxford? Six. The only way to be sure I pick the right one is for me to follow Amanda. Like they do in *Line of Duty*. I'm terrified but a little bit excited at the same time. Terricited, you could say.

Hey, look at me now, making up my own words, like a real writer?

Arrived at Woodview on Monday evening a little after seven-thirty, well before the appointed hour. Parked down a side lane, Gregory's second-best birding binoculars at the ready. It was still light and through the trees, I had a clear view of the gates – an eyeball, I should probably call it.

As the light began to fade, the gates squealed open and the BMW drove out, Amanda at the wheel. She turned into the lane, headlights sweeping across the sky. I waited a couple of minutes, then set off after.

Ever tried tailing a car? Not as easy as it looks on TV. Too close and they spot you. Too far away and you'll lose them. It wasn't so bad in the lanes by the country park. I could follow Amanda's headlights. It was a different matter when she joined the ring road and hit the Oxford evening traffic.

I'm a careful driver. Amanda less so. She soon left me behind. Then we hit the usual roadworks clag-up. The traffic slowed to walking pace. Up ahead, I saw Amanda's BMW swing sharply across into another lane. Taking evasive action? My heart pounded. No, she was dodging the jam. My lane cleared. I put my foot down, starting to enjoy the thrill of the chase.

That didn't last long. Up ahead, Amanda's line of traffic slowed, then stopped. Mine crawled forward. Too late, I twigged what was about to happen: my car would pull up alongside hers. We'd be only feet apart. Hemmed in as I was, there was nothing I could do about it. Amanda was bound to glance across. How could she miss me, gliding past looking shamefaced in the neighbouring lane?

The gap narrowed. I inched forward, sliding down in my seat until my eyes were level with the dashboard. If I couldn't see her, I reasoned with the logic of a three-year-old, she couldn't see me. When I thought the coast was clear, I poked my head up. No sign of the BMW. Her hold-up must have untangled itself and she'd shot ahead. Out of the corner of my eye, I noticed the driver on my left had been watching my performance. He made a wanker sign at me. Flicking him a brisk V, I accelerated away.

A few minutes later, the mystery of the White Hart was solved. Amanda took the turning to the village of East Frayling. I parked outside the church and walked towards the White Hart. Rounding the corner, I almost bumped into Amanda and Pavel. Just had time to duck behind a skip in the pub car park. Creeping round to the side of the building, I pressed myself against the whitewashed cob wall and peered in through a window. The bar was brightly lit and half-full.

Amanda and Pavel were sat at a table. Across from them was a small man with a big moustache and an almost full pint of beer. Sergei. Had to be. Amanda and Pavel hadn't got any drinks. The night was warm and, luckily for me, the window was open, though I could make out only the occasional word over the thump, thump, thump of the background music.

Sergei, taking sips of his beer, was dominating the conversation. Amanda was paying close attention. Pavel, head twisting back and forth, was struggling to follow. Sergei was going on at some length about something, trying to reassure Amanda, it looked like. Though I put my ear as close as I dared to the open window, all I heard him clearly say was, 'Made in Bolton.'

Thankfully, then there was a lull in the music and I heard Amanda say, 'And the technical side. That was all sorted?'

'Of course.'

'In that case, I'm happy,' Amanda said. 'As long as you got the spelling right.'

The two of them shared an uneasy laugh at this, while Pavel looked on vacantly, and the music thumped back into life.

Evidently satisfied, Amanda took a thickish envelope from a bag and slid it towards the centre of the table, keeping a hand on it. Sergei took his time downing the last of his beer. Then, almost casually, he reached into his pocket and took out a jiffy bag. He pushed it across the table, his hairy hand still on it.

There was a brief exchange of words, which I couldn't make out, and in one smooth movement, they swapped packages. Sergei took the envelope, Amanda the jiffy bag.

Not much to go on but, with what I already knew, it was enough. They were buying a black-market passport for Pavel, in case he needed to make a quick exit.

They stood, shook hands, and Amanda and Pavel headed for the door.

I got a terrible stitch sprinting ahead of them to the car.

Forty-Eight

He rang the bell this time, like a civilised person. And, like a civilised person, I answered the door.

'Mrs. Patricia Gertrude Lightowler?' he said in his best Daniel Craig rasp, getting my name right this time, I noted.

'As the process server authorised to serve papers pertaining to your divorce from Mr. Gregory Alan Lightowler ...'

I didn't listen any further. I held out my hand.

He finished his little spiel and offered – proffered, should that be? – the dreaded envelope. I took it. And it was done. Just like that. The divorce application was served.

He made to leave.

'Not so fast,' I said. He paused, no doubt expecting an earful. He looked apprehensive but waited politely. I expect that's part of the training.

'I wanted to say ... thank you.'

His eyebrows – emphatic without being at all bushy – shot up. Don't imagine, in his line of business, he got many thanks.

'For not stepping on my flowers,' I went on. 'Last time you were here. That was thoughtful.'

He recovered quickly. I expect that's part of the training too. 'No problem, madam. I'm a gardener myself. All part of the service.'

It seemed to me, if he'd been wearing a cap, he'd have doffed it.

So I've accepted the application. I'll sign it and put it in the post tomorrow. That's the Conditional Order sorted. Final Order here we come! Everything should be plain sailing from now on, to borrow a Peter Bungle phrase.

Forty-Nine

Peter asked me in for another meeting. I went expecting a calm sea but encountered nothing but choppy waters.

'It's brilliant,' Peter said. 'And brilliance is to be appreciated wherever it's to be found, even here. Appreciated, if not approved of,' he added quickly. He tapped the laptop screen. 'And this is undeniably brilliant. Allow me to demonstrate.'

Did he have to be quite so impressed by my ex's attempts to defraud me? I thought.

Peter indicated I should shuffle round to his side of the desk. Stepping over an overflowing bin, I leant in. At first the figures scrolling up the screen made no sense, but with Peter's patient commentary, they eventually led me to the truth. Gregory was pulling a fast one. Or trying to.

'These figures indicate a multi-million-dollar investment portfolio,' Peter said, 'owned by an offshore company and registered with the Jersey Financial Services Commission in 2017.' Peter flicked between displays.

'So?'

'Look at the name of the company.'

'MRH Holdings. What of it? Oh, flaming Nora! MRH. Madison-Rose Harrington.'

'"Fraid so. The directors are one Gregory Alan Lightowler and William J Harrington.'

'Madison-Rose's father. Hang on! 2017? Did you say 2017?'

'Maybe you should sit down,' Peter said.

'Thank you. I'll stand.'

I soon wished I had accepted his offer. What Peter had to say was shocking. It hit me right in the back of the knees. Gregory hadn't worked for Vanstone International, he explained, for more than five years. Five years! In that time he'd founded MRH Holdings, and him and his co-director had squirreled away a fortune in a Russian-doll of companies – offshores and shells, Peter called them – to hide it. And I knew nothing of any of this.

'It appears,' Peter said, 'Mr. Lightowler has been reorganising his affairs in anticipation of divorce for quite some time. Financial infidelity, we call it. Every bit as vile as the other kind but, sadly, not uncommon in cases like this, where the potential pickings are good.'

The awful truth was sinking in. This was no sudden rush of blood to the groin, as Gregory had suggested. The affair with Madison Rose had been going on for at least five years, probably longer.

I felt the heat rising, ready for another menopausal display.

'I'll take that chair now, please,' I said weakly.

'You all right?' Peter said, sliding it under me. 'Should I go on?'

I nodded, sinking onto it. This was too important to be interrupted by my out-of-whack hormones.

While Peter explained, I fanned my face, mind straying to the recent years of my marriage. No wonder

Gregory had been so dog-tired! Too pooped to go to the cinema or out to dinner. Too busy to make it to school concerts or university open days. Too knackered to have sex with his wife. It must've been so difficult for him, running two families.

'It's not legal is it, what he's up to?' I said, back in the room.

Peter leant back, grabbing his lapels and giving me a glimpse of his courtroom manner. 'Legally, a spouse cannot evade their financial responsibilities by using the corporate structure. Should they, however, decide to give it a try, they could find themselves facing a painful pay out, or even a custodial sentence.'

'Prison, you mean? Fabulous,' I said, allowing myself a few seconds to picture Gregory in grey prison sweatpants, sewing mailbags.

'However, and I take no pleasure in telling you this, Trish, Mr. Lightowler has a further trick up his sleeve. One that could prove problematic.' Peter rubbed his chin. 'There's no easy way to say this. Mr. Lightowler claims your marriage was over long before MRH was founded. That you and he have been, *de facto*, separated for years.'

'I think I might've noticed, if that was the case,' I laughed. 'I'd have had to sign something, surely?'

'Not true. Informal separations can, if both parties agree, be arranged verbally without any formal legalities.'

'There! You said it. *If* both parties agree. I never agreed to any such thing.'

'Mr. Lightowler says otherwise.'

I was lost for words. Then they came in a torrent. 'That's ludicrous. Where's his proof? He can't just say that?' I took a breath. 'Can he?'

Peter fixed me with a look. 'Tell me about your marriage, Trish. How much time did you and Mr.

Lightowler spend together?'

I tried to explain but the longer I spoke, the flakier everything sounded.

Yes, Gregory spent weeks, sometimes months, away travelling for work, I said. But he always returned to the family home. To me. Except when he went to a little boutique hotel near Heathrow for a few days after he landed. To get over the jetlag. They had superfast broadband, I said, like I was writing a TripAdvisor review for the place, and did his eggs the way he liked them. Yes, I paid the utility bills That was only because Gregory always forgot. Yes, Gregory had visited me recently but no, he didn't stay over.

'And how are things …' Peter cleared his throat, 'sexually? Are you and Mr. Lightowler …' He cleared his throat again, 'regularly intimate?'

'If you count twice a year – his birthday and our anniversary – as regular.' Me and my nervous humour!

Peter was not amused. 'Mr. Lightowler's birthday is in August and your anniversary, October? Correct?' He was frighteningly well informed. 'That would make the last time – what? – getting on for nine months ago?' He glanced at his screen. 'Whereas Mr. Lightowler maintains you two haven't had sexual relations since March 2015. He further claims, since that date his primary place of residence in the UK has been The Garden Boutique Hotel, Hounslow.'

'Wha-at?' I shot bolt upright.

'A Mr. Joseph Gardner, owner of the hotel, corroborates the claim. See?' He swung the screen to face me.

'That's a pack of lies!'

'Maybe so. It wouldn't be difficult to arrange. Spin the hotel owner some sob story about an unreasonable spouse and slip him a discreet cash sweetener. Some

224

people will say anything if the price is right. Sign of the times, I'm sorry to say.' Peter pulled a face. 'To summarise, Mr. Lightowler says the separation is consensual and goes back some eight years, offering as evidence the testimony of the hotel owner, the household bills in your name, and the long-standing lack of intimacy.'

'Why is he doing this to me?' I wailed.

'Money. Not so pure and not so simple.' Peter clasped his hands across his belly. 'If the separation pre-dates the founding of the company, you won't be entitled to a cent of his American fortune. It would be classed as 'post separation accrual' and not part of your settlement.'

'Can he get away with that?' I said, my voice small and wobbly.

Peter hitched up his glasses. 'Not while I'm at the helm.' He passed me a crumpled hanky.

'Well, then,' I said, blowing my nose with a loud honk. 'Let's go get the bastard.'

Fifty

Lesson 20: Don't Overwork The Pastry

Here's one for you: are so-called nice people just nasty people without the courage of their convictions? I mean, we've all got a bitchy side, right? But we don't all show it. Bet even the Dalai Lama and Tom Hanks must get cranky sometimes.

Most people would say Trish is a nice woman. Never has a bad word to say about anyone, and all that. Even Stephen called her 'A good sort', as he shoved her P45 into her hand and pushed her out the door. But is she? Is she really? Hasn't she just been holding back these last forty-nine years, smiling and nodding, keeping her dark thoughts locked inside, secretly longing to give the odd person the occasional kick up the jacksie.

That's how it seems to me, at any rate, though I'm probably biased, being as how I'm the one who gets to hear her inner bitchings and see her fantasy boots up the bum.

Please Gawd, that's all behind her. Leastways, I hope so. Trish has at last grasped that putting on a nice front ain't always the best way. From now on she's gonna do her best to be one of them people known as 'difficult', who 'don't suffer fools gladly'. An awkward bugger, in other words

Amanda had a face on her from the start. And she looked a right mess, hair all over the place, make-up inch thick. We were in the summerhouse within sight of LBK's final resting place. The small mound of bare earth kept tugging my gaze away from the book we were studying.

'Gazing vacantly into space won't make you an author,' Amanda said sharply. 'Is it still that wretched stray?'

'He was not a stray, Amanda. He was a sweet little kitten who didn't deserve his fate,' I sniffed. 'I'll never forgive that man for what he did and I'm surprised you can. Think of it, little LBK is laying under that earth over there, never more to laze in the sun or have his pink pot-belly tickled.'

'Dear God! What twaddle you come out with. He was a stinking stray whose nine lives ran out. And it's "lying", not "laying" by the way. Such basic syntactic errors – and you make quite a few – let you down, Trish, show you up for what you really are.'

Aaaaargh! She was so annoying! But I would not be diverted from my point, no matter how much she provoked me. Bracing myself, I launched in. 'I wasn't actually thinking about him in any case. I was thinking about you. And Pavel. Psychopaths, did you know, are into animal torture and killing? For them it's like entry level serial murder.'

'I beg your pardon!'

'I worry about you Amanda, all alone here in the woods with that man,' I said. 'He killed LBK. Who's to say he won't show *you* his violent side one day? Who's to say he hasn't already?'

'How dare you! What gives you the right?'

'The right of one mate to look out for another. You're not alone, Amanda. You have me. He's been knocking you about, hasn't he? I've known for ages. The camouflage makeup and the long sleeves, they're a giveaway.' She said nothing. 'Now he's got you involved in … ' I stopped. I didn't want to let on I'd followed them to the White Hart, so I said, 'I worry he's dragging you into something illegal. He doesn't even make you happy, Amanda. Anyone can see you're depressed. The state of you.'

Amanda made a choking sound. 'Me? That's rich, coming from a woman who wears her kids' school castoffs and thinks it's acceptable to appear for a mentoring session in clothes she's slept in.'

Nothing escapes those sharp steely eyes.

Was I going to sit back and take it? No, I was not. Time to put on the hat with the *Awkward Bugger* logo – the metaphorical hat, that is – and unleash new, improved Trish.

'Call them mentoring sessions?' I said, anger mounting. 'More like chances for you to show off and make a bit of easy money. What's more, I'll have you know, I ironed this shirt and these chinos are brand new.' I could have added, *they don't dig in, because for once I bought a size that fits.*

'You can take it out on me all you like,' I continued. 'But I have to speak up. I can see that man for what he is: a chancer taking advantage of a lonely and vulnerable older woman. It's got several names: rom-conning, love-bombing, or plain romance fraud. All comes down to the same thing: men pretending to fall for an older woman, so they can cheat them out of their savings. Isn't it obvious, that's what Pavel's up to. Dump him, Amanda,'

I pleaded. 'Dump him now, before something terrible happens.'

There was a long silence before Amanda said, 'Have I got this right? According to you, he's a gold-digger ... what was it? ... rom-conning me. And I'm a pathetic old hag desperate for a man, any man. Little better than an aged whore.'

'I never said *that*. I said *lonely* and *vulnerable*.'

Amanda gave a disapproving sniff. 'Since we're talking straight, how about this? It's not me who's blind, Trish. It's you. With your own love-life nothing but a shrivelled husk, you can't stand to see anyone else enjoying a scrap of happiness.

'And for the record, you are not my 'mate'. The very thought of the two of us going on holiday together,' she sneered. 'Or me kipping in your spare bed, even if it does have a nice, new mattress topper from John Lewis. No, Trish Lightowler, face it, you're a washed-up *hausfrau* on whom I took pity. A woman so devoid of creativity you have to pay me a hundred quid a week to squeeze what little there is out of you. How *is* the novel coming along, by the way? Still stuck on those first three chapters?'

I gaped. 'How on earth ...?'

'... did I know you've only written three chapters?' Amanda said. 'Because that's what you do, isn't it, you amateurs. You pick over the same few thousand words, thinking the more you rewrite them, the better they'll get. I've got news for you. Writing is like pastry: overwork it and it turns indigestible. You do all that,' she was shouting now, quite loudly, 'but what you never, ever do, is finish the fucking thing!'

'I promise you this, Amanda. I *will* write a book and I *will* finish the fucking thing.'

'I very much doubt it. Do you know why? Because, underneath all that earnestness, that niceness, you have the creative ability of an illiterate sea slug. You like the idea of being a writer but you don't have the ability, the personality, or the sheer grit to be one.'

I took a deep breath, unable to contain any longer the rage I'd been holding in, a rage not only with Amanda, but also with cheating Gregory, lizard-eyed Stephen, entitled Nell and even contraceptively-careless Flo.

I let it out. Not shouting, not screeching but strong and firm. 'I'm fed up to the back teeth, Amanda, of being taken for granted. "Oh Trish won't mind. Trish won't notice. Trish will suck it up." Well I do mind, I do notice and I'm not going to suck it up a minute longer. As for being an illiterate sea slug? A sea slug, I'd like to remind you, you were only too happy to string along for weeks on end and rip off to the tune of a thousand quid. A sea slug who's done her best to be a good friend to you. A sea slug, God help me, who's sat through your useless so-called lessons and never uttered a word of complaint. I don't know how you've got the bare-faced gall, Amanda.'

But it was water off a duck's proverbial. 'I thought you might have a spark,' she shrugged, unperturbed. 'I was wrong. You'll never make a writer.'

I made one last attempt at the role of peacemaker, albeit a severely pissed-off one. 'I get what's happening here. You're protecting him by having a go at me. But that won't save you, Amanda. As long as you share this house with him, you're in danger. I know it and, in your heart of hearts, you know it as well.'

'In your heart of hearts, you know it as well,' she parroted. 'What is this? Cliché Corner? Get this through your skull, I don't need help from anyone, least of all you, Patricia Lightowler.'

The scales fell from my eyes. As she smirked and sneered, I saw Amanda for what she really was: a grasping, greedy, big-headed opportunist. I understood for the first time that the classes I'd put so much trust in, were for her nothing more than a nice little earner; a business arrangement she'd got bored with. I couldn't save her from Pavel. In that moment, I was so furious with her I wasn't even sure I wanted to. They deserved each other. I was done with the pair of them. Let them fight it out between them.

'Right' I said, rising and packing up my things. 'I quit. And I'll be expecting a refund for today's farce.'

'Expect all you like. You won't be getting one.'

I paused, my hand on the summerhouse door. 'Know what, Amanda, this whole thing has been like that film of *Cats*: one huge mistake from beginning to end.'

Amanda gave one of her amused snorts. 'On that at least,' she said, 'we can agree.'

Fifty-One

They never say, do they, Jo Rowling, Philip Pullman, Marian Keyes, Ian Rankin, Kate Atkinson, Nina Stibbe and the rest, what it's really like.

Never let on they spend three days writing a description of a trip to Istanbul, Googling images, checking the weather, tides, trains and airports, before slapping their foreheads, remembering the plot demands their character is in Ipswich. Never admit that pithy sentence that trips so lightly across the page took four hours and thirteen rewrites to get right. Never tell you about the time they woke in a cold sweat, realising they'd killed off Great Aunt Maud at the beginning of Chapter 4, forgetting she needs to be alive in Chapter 62 to poison her wicked husband with a cup of oleander leaf tea. Never reveal writing is like childbirth: exhausting, painful, exposing, long drawn out and relentless with, you can only pray, the promise of something amazing at the end of it.

As you might've sussed, Trish is writing. She applies bum to seat in time-honoured fashion and, pushing to the back of her mind all comments re sea slugs, wills inspiration to come her way, hoping, if she wants it hard enough, it will arrive.

Words do come but they ain't the right ones. Her finger hovers over the delete button. Should she? She knows she has to be ruthless, so she does. Straight off she regrets it. One or two phrases was OK, she thinks. Are they still hiding in the trash bin? Hooray, they are. She drags them out, only to find they wasn't so much Simon Armitage as Simon Cowell. She empties the trash bin, grits her teeth and starts over.

It ain't the instant breakthrough she's looking for but summat is stirring deep in that brain of hers. Synapses are firing, molecules changing track, new neural-whatsits being formed. She is yet to find, as Amanda would say, her voice, but she ain't giving up neither. She's sticking at it. You go, girl!

I like this new, improved Trish.

Fifty-Two

She's a quiet one, Felicity, but persistent. And she quietly and persistently insisted we had to go out to celebrate my coming granny-hood. Felicity, by the way, is the only one outside of close family who knows about Flo and the baby.

Ironically, though Nell and Gregory had been lukewarm when I told them the news, Felicity was thrilled to bits. I didn't have her down as the demonstrative sort but, next to books, children are her soft spot. She'd have been a primary school teacher, she told me, if nerves hadn't messed up her A levels.

Me and her ... she and I ... were in the library when I told her. I was taken by surprise when she did no more than drag me down the Local Authors stacks – no-one hardly ever goes there – threw her arms around my neck and bounced me round in a silent jig.

'No argument,' she said. 'We're going on the town.'

That sounds a lot racier than what it will be. This is Felicity we're talking about, the Felicity whose neck goes scarlet if you say the word 'bum' in her presence. OK, so we were standing in the Theology section next to a young man in a dog-collar and a knitted tank top, but I mean, who's shocked by the occasional 'bum' these days, even in a library?

Felicity has the evening planned out. We start with a Pizza Express voucher meal in the market square, moving onto a jug of Margarita in the new bar in the old post office building, then home in time for cocoa with Graham Norton. Not exactly painting the town carmine. I don't mind. With all that's going on, I'm not in the mood for a rave up and neither one of us can afford to push the boat out too far from shore.

I showed willing and ordered a dress in an online sale. When it came, I saw why it had been reduced. The yellow is a lot more hi-vis than I was expecting and the skirt a lot more voluminous. I felt as if it was wearing me, and not, as it should be, the other way around. But, embracing my new, more daring attitude to life, I didn't send it back.

***

Well, that was more eventful than I thought it would be!

Felicity and I walked into the bar, arm in arm, each already a prosecco and two large glasses of house white up. She led the way. I took in the group of men at the bar, swung around and walked right back out. A baffled Felicity scurried behind.

'Did you see him?' I said, all of a dither. 'At the bar. Big bloke, no hair and no discernible neck? It's him I told you about. The bailiff. Ross Kemp.'

Felicity pushed the door open a crack. 'Looks more like a Mark Strong to me. Come on. Don't let him spoil our evening. He probably won't even remember you.'

Bit of a backhander, Felicity, I thought, but I let her bundle me back inside. We claimed tall stools in a dark corner, me holding up my hem, like one of the Bennet sisters, as I climbed aboard. Couldn't stop myself glancing over at the bar every few minutes. Half a jug of weak Margarita later, No-Neck still hadn't turned round. That was irritating.

'I can't be doing with this,' I told Felicity, pulling down firmly on the peak of that invisible *Awkward Bugger* baseball cap. 'I'm going to have to go over and have a word.'

'You sure you've thought this through?'

'Course not,' I said, slipping unsteadily from my perch. 'If I'd thought it through, I wouldn't be doing it.'

''Scuse me.' I tapped him on the shoulder. He swung round and his eyes crinkled with amusement. 'Wanted to clear the air. About the other day. Sorry, I was a complete arse. My solicitor confirmed to me I was being an arse – that's the legal term, apparently. That's why when you came round the second time, I wasn't quite so much of an arse.'

Why in heaven's name couldn't I stop saying 'arse'?

'That was you, was it? Hardly an arse at all, as I recall,' he said, taking up the theme. 'You'd be amazed what daft things people do when they spy a process server at the door. That was nothing.'

'Well,' I said. 'Just wanted to clear the air.'

'You already said that,' he replied, his back to me as he took a sip from his pint.

Obviously, it was time for me to go but I didn't. 'One more thing. Thank you, for not flattening my petunias.'

'You already said that, too.' He was facing me now, smiling. 'At the time.'

So you do remember me! I thought, and this time did say out loud.

'Well, yes. You're pretty hard to forget,' he said, smile

broadening.

'Anyhow,' I said, 'better let you get back to your mates.'

'They're not my mates. I'm here on my own. Quick after-process-serving pint.'

'In that case, enjoy your sad, solitary beer,' I said and, spinning on my heel, still feeling reckless, warbled over my shoulder, 'Toodle-oo!'

This performance didn't go unnoticed.

'You dirty flirt!' Felicity said when I got back to my seat, feeling quite proud of myself.

A while, and quite a few more Margaritas, later I was letting Felicity into the secrets of baby travel systems. 'Never call them pushchairs,' I told her, waving my glass in her face. 'Buggy is acceptable.'

I felt a presence at my elbow. It was him. Mark Strong, with two large gin and tonics and a pint on a tray.

'Can't tell you how much out of my comfort zone I am right this minute,' he said, his whole head turning a fetching shade of cerise. 'But drinking alone isn't my style and I thought you ladies might like a proper drink. Them cocktails are mostly ice and lime juice.'

'Would you care to join us?' Felicity said, jumping into the social breach once more, as I seemed incapable of speech. 'I'm Felicity and this is –.'

'I know,' he said, eyes never leaving mine. 'Patricia Gertrude Lightowler.'

'Trish, please!' I said, giggling rather too girlishly.

He dragged a stool over and the three of us sat and sipped self-consciously.

'Like your dress,' he said. 'The colour of sunshine.'

'Why, thank you kindly, sir,' I said in the accent of a Southern belle, wondering why I was behaving so weirdly.

We lapsed into another strained silence.

'Anywhoo,' Felicity said, clonking a half-full gin goblet onto the table. 'This has been fun but it's time for me to call it a night.' She stood and yawned. 'Got a very early shift in the morning.'

An early shift! The library never opens before nine.

'Do you have to go?' I said, eyes widening to signal *Don't leave me alone with him!*

'Yes,' she said firmly. 'I do. You two stay and have a nice long chat.'

She paused when she reached the door and, out of Mark Strong's eyeline, gave me a double thumbs up. I managed a feeble wave.

We sipped our drinks.

'Have you been watching …?' I began, then stopped. 'You know that thing when you begin to say a thing and while you're speaking, you realise you can't remember the name of the thing you were going to say the thing about?'

'Think so,' he said cautiously.

'Well that's me. I mean, that's what I did just then. Wanted to ask if you'd watched something and then completely forgot the name of the thing I wanted to ask you about.'

'I see,' he said, clearly not.

Get him talking about himself. Isn't that what you're supposed to do? At least it was when I was a teenager and getting dating tips from *Jackie* magazine. I racked my brains. Then had a stroke of inspiration.

'What sort of daft stuff do people get up to when they see you coming?' I asked.

'All sorts,' he said, launching into what were obviously a few well-polished anecdotes. But good stories, told well. We shared a laugh over the time a woman had climbed into a wheelie bin to hide from him. 'I heard a sound, tipped the bin up and out she slid, covered in garden muck. The state of her when she stood up!'

He had plenty like that. Before he worked for the courts, he told me, he'd been a police officer. A sergeant. He came up with some funny stories about that, though, he said, serious for a moment, most of the time it wasn't all that funny. 'A lot of runaway kids and drug-addled sex workers. What about you?'

'Oh no,' I said. 'I'm not a drug-addled sex worker.'

That got him pink-headed once again. I grinned to show it was a wind-up. Then I did it again. Said it. 'I'm writing a novel.'

'A novel, eh?' He made as if to climb from his seat. 'I'm off in that case, before you get any ideas about putting me in it. Gotta shampoo my tresses.' He put a hand to his shiny dome to show now he was winding *me* up.

We relaxed after that. I told him more about the novel I'm struggling to write and the creative writing classes I'm no longer taking. He didn't crack a terrible joke and say I could use it in my book, for a percentage of the profits, mind. Ha ha! He didn't say he was sure he had a book in him, if only he had the time to write it. He did good. Neither bastard nor bore, as far as I could tell.

I did pretty good, too, once I'd got over the nerves. Didn't talk about Gregory. Or the girls. Didn't even mention the baby. Told him about me and my shit life, making it sound a lot more amusing than it actually was. Grace and the drunken funeral. The bike crash. The Ozzie doctor in A&E. How I took my revenge on Stephen's Swedish flooring.

He didn't try to change the subject or top my story with one of his. He listened, leaning in, smiling. Before I knew it, we were the only customers left in the bar. We paused on the steps outside, embarrassed once more, as the bartender slid the bolts behind us.

'Feel like I'm sixteen all over again, but here goes,' he said. 'Can I see you home?'

'Yes,' new, brazen Trish replied. 'That would be delightful.'

And it was. We walked. It's not far. Twenty minutes. Mostly in silence. An easy silence, not like earlier. Close but not touching. I hadn't realised how tall he was. It's not often I can look up to anyone, even men. I liked the feeling. I felt protected. Would have been perfect, if it hadn't been for the big fat elephant that hung in the star-filled sky above our heads. That's a jumbled mess of a sentence that would have enraged Amanda but you know what I mean. What I was thinking, and I bet he was too, was, what's going to happen once we reach my door?

In the end it couldn't have been simpler.

'Do you want to come in for coffee?' I asked.

'Erm, do you actually mean coffee?'

'Most definitely.'

'Wow. That's a relief,' he said, blowing out his cheeks. 'In that case ...'

And in he came. We had to be quiet because of Flo but that wasn't a problem. Despite his size, he's light-footed and softly spoken. We sat in the kitchen. I had cocoa. He had black coffee. Caffeinated. Two cups. What a man! Gregory lets no coffee pass his lips after mid-day.

I saw him to the front door. He hesitated, hand on the catch. Then he kissed me. Not a slobbery, face-chewing kiss like they do in telly dramas. A peck. On the cheek. I pecked back. We were like two shy chickens.

'I should go,' he whispered, bending to rest his forehead against mine. 'We sixteen-year-olds need our beauty sleep. To be continued.'

'Most definitely,' I said again.

***

I'm in bed, replaying the highlights in my head, a stupid grin plastered across my face, feeling more positive than I have in a long, long time. I'm thinking I could get used to this new me. I'm also thinking he's too slim to be a Ross Kemp and too stocky to be a Mark Strong. And he *has* got a neck, though it tends to hide itself between muscly shoulders. Jason Statham, perhaps.

His actual name is Bernard, by the way.

A final thought before I put out the light. The whole time I was with Bernard, I didn't have a single hot flush. Even when I told him about being a writer, even when he kissed me. Could the worst be over?

Fifty-Three

Did that romantic stuff make you go all gooey? Well, hard luck. Cos, now comes the bad news. 'To be continued' don't continue. That is to say, Bernard don't phone. For a week. Unfortunately, Gregory does.

'What is it with you, Pats?' Gregory said, phone so close to his mouth I heard his breath popping. 'It's not enough I've got your chinless Brit solicitor hassling me, now some hippy from San Fran is having a go. We've had to let him see bank statements, tax returns and all sorts. What business is it of his, I'd like to know?

'I've been patient, God knows, but even my patience isn't limitless. Look, I understand the world of finance. I've been operating in it long enough. You – and I don't mean this as a criticism, Trish – you don't. I mean, I couldn't make a cheese and onion quiche to save my life. You're no good with figures. That's how it is. Do the sensible thing, please, and pack in the meddling. Leave it to me and my team. After all,' he gave a nervous titter, 'if you can't trust me to play fair, who can you trust?'

'Who, indeed?' I said, adding under my breath,

'Cheese and onion quiche! Patronising git.'

'So, you'll call off the Eton Mess and the Californian Flowerchild?'

How I was enjoying this! I'd never been able to rattle Gregory on a scale like this before.

'What? Just when things are getting interesting? Not on your life.'

Yay! I've pissed Gregory off. That almost made up for Bernard not ringing. Then I thought, why wait for him to ring? That's the old, passive Trish. What would new Trish do?

***

You'll never guess. I've got a date. Yes! A proper *wash my hair, wear a dress, scrounge a pair of Flo's three-inch espadrilles* kind of date.

What happened was, Bernard didn't ring. After a period of pacing and nail-chewing, I grasped the whatsit by the thingies and decided to phone him. My finger was actually on the little green button, when 'ping', in came a text.

Good time to call? Soz. Been OOT. Work.

Him. Bernard from the Bar. That's how I'd saved his number.

Took a moment to work out OOT. Out of town.

I texted back. *Weird. Was about to phone U.*

Pressed 'send', then regretted that 'weird'.

When he didn't immediately answer, I panicked, sure that my poor adjectival choice had put him off. I composed an involved and apologetic explanation but didn't send it. That was what old Trish would have done. 'Stuff this,' I said out loud and dialled his number. Got, *the person you are calling is not available.*

Aaaaargh! Back to texting. *UR busy today!*

U2! he texted back, with a tennis racket and a winking face emoji. We were playing text tennis! I waited and after about thirty seconds my phone rang. Bernard, of course.

'What are we like?' we said over each other, which gave us both the giggles. When we'd calmed down, he asked me out and I said, 'If you like'. And that was it. Who needs dating websites?

We went to the cinema. I let him choose. Ironically, we ended up watching Jason Statham. One of the *Fast and Furiouses*. I forget which number. He ate most of the popcorn. I lost track of the heist-y goings-on on screen, as I kept sneaking sideways glances to check he wasn't a figment of my imagination. And to look for signs of stubble. Call me bald-ist if you like, but I don't think I could do *bald bald* but I think I could accept *shaven bald*. In the dark and without actually touching his scalp – and I wasn't going to do *that* on a first date – I wasn't sure.

With the jury out on the state of Bernard's bonce, I tried to pick up the plot of what was left of the film. Not much luck there. The louder and more spectacular the action, the heavier my eyelids grew. Seconds later, or so it seemed, the end credits were rolling and Bernard was leaning over, grinning into my face and saying, 'Wake up, Sleeping Beauty.'

He joked, as we shuffled towards the exit with the rest of the crowd that I was the only woman he'd ever met who could nod off during a F&F car chase. Just good-natured joshing but, nevertheless, I found myself a little sad at the thought I wasn't the first date he'd ever taken to an action film. Ridiculous. I hardly know the man.

'Pizza?' he asked on the pavement outside.

'Tapas?' I countered. 'Not a pizza fan. Too much pastry and stuff.'

'I'm not keen on tapas. Too many tiddly dishes and stuff.'

We compromised on Mexican.

He teased me when I took a long time deciding on what red to have with my extra hot burritos. 'What does it matter? Your taste buds will be burnt to charcoal,' he said, taking a long draught of his lager. I had the last laugh. After another beer, he challenged me to a jalapeno-eating contest. How was he to know several holidays in Cancun – handy for Gregory – had given me a fire-proof throat and an asbestos stomach? The sight of him not knowing which to mop first, his sweaty head or his dripping nose, will stay with me for a long time.

Was it a good first date? I'm unable to judge due to a lack of recent comparable data. We laughed a lot, that's for sure. As for the issue of his head, I did get close enough, when we repeated our shy chicken impersonations, to detect a fuzz of grey stubble.

So far, so good. That's all I'm saying.

I've done a stupid thing. In my new, perky state I told Flo about the goings-on at Woodview. My timing was all wrong. She'd not long come in from work, tired and, as I quickly found out, feeling prickly. With both of us at the mercy of unpredictable hormones, I guess it wasn't surprising we'd clash.

'Thought you were done with this woman, Mum,' she frowned. 'Let it go.'

'I'm worried. If you'd listen, Flo.'

'So, tell me,' she said.

I did. Told her everything. About the bruises, the dead fish, LBK, the pills. Everything. All in a mad muddle. Even Sergei from Bristol.

'Sergei?' She chuckled. 'Like the meerkat?'

'Flo,' I said, exasperated. 'He hit her!'

'That's a serious accusation. Are you sure?'

'Well, no. I wasn't in the room. But I heard her cry out, and the sound of a slap.'

'Cry out what exactly?'

Now I was getting really pissed off. 'Something like, *You bastard! That hurt!* What does it matter? Should I go to the police? I'd never forgive myself if something terrible happened. I should phone 999, shouldn't I? Or contact her son in Cardiff. Louis, he's called.'

I clapped my hand to my mouth, realising how little I knew about Amanda's family. 'Except, I don't even know if Turner's his surname! Probably not. No, better to phone the police and let them take it from there. I can't forget it, Flo. My blood runs cold at the thought of what that man is capable of. Here, feel my hands, they're frozen.' I held them out but Flo didn't grasp them or meet my gaze. That was unsettling. What was so fascinating about the way the afternoon sunlight played through the kitchen blinds, I wondered? Then I realised. Flo was humouring me, waiting for me to talk myself to a standstill. Soon afterwards I did.

'What do you think?' I said when Flo didn't immediately respond.

'I think, you're going through a tough time, Mum,' she said, still staring at the flickering sunbeams. 'A nasty divorce. It's not long since Granny died. You've lost your job. And one of your daughters has gone and got herself pregnant. To top it all, you've been spending more time than is healthy with a woman who, from the sound of her, is a grade A drama queen.'

'You think I'm imagining it,' I said, jumping to my feet. 'I'm not, Flo. I've seen things. Heard things. Come on, you're the MeToo generation! You don't take shit from anyone. Surely you can see…' But when I looked into her face, all I saw was weariness.

'Look, the last thing I want to do is upset you, Mum, but think about it.' And one by one she demolished my arguments.

The long sleeves: Amanda was one of those skinny women who feels the cold. The bruises: she'd bumped herself, or else I imagined them. 'You said yourself you only caught a glimpse.' The pills: I'd swallowed some pills and had a nightmare but the one thing did not necessarily follow the other. 'Correlation does not imply causation,' she said, with the know-it-all confidence of youth.

'And the fainting? That was real enough.'

'Not eating proper meals? Anaemia? Menopause? She's at a funny age.'

'She's almost exactly the same age as me.'

Flo shot me a *that's what I mean* look. 'Face it, Mum, when you examine the evidence, there's nothing there.'

'But the rows?'

'What couple doesn't have the odd argument? You and Dad were at each other's throats all the time.'

'I thought we'd managed to hide that from you.'

'Uh-uh. You thought wrong.'

Another illusion shattered.

'And Sergei?' I said, not giving up. 'What about the cloak and dagger meeting? I didn't invent that.'

'What did you see, Mum? A dodgy-looking bloke sold them something. People buy all sorts of things in pubs. Weed, bootleg booze, fake phones, cheap foreign cigarettes, French bulldog puppies.'

'Do they?' I said, momentarily distracted by the puppy reference. 'No, it was a passport. I know it was. It was the right size and shape. Anyway, I heard Amanda say they needed cash to pay Sergei because fake passports don't come cheap.'

Even as I said it, I doubted. *Was* that what Amanda had said? And what about that puzzling reference to

Bolton? Could I have got the passport idea fixed in my head and back-projected? Made it up, is the less kind way of putting it.

The more I doubted myself, the more I blustered on. 'And LBK? I saw his grave with my own eyes. A man who can do that to a kitten is dangerous.'

'Foreigners aren't sentimental about animals like us Brits.'

'I still think something's going on. Amanda can't see it. And you obviously can't, apparently,' I fumed. 'I'll get to the bottom of it, with or without your help.'

Flo cupped her head in her hands. 'I want to believe you, mum, really I do. Violence against women and girls is disgusting. And I would, if only I didn't think ...' She gave a wince of apology. I knew what she wanted to say but, dear, sweet girl that she is, she didn't want to stick the knife in. So I said it for her.

'You think I'm making a fuss over nothing? Losing it? Turning into granny? Becoming a properly bonkers old biddy?'

'Granny wasn't bonkers,' Flo protested. 'She was a kick-ass old lady who'd camped at Greenham Common and got arrested in the poll tax riots. I loved that about her. And I understand. Really I do. Your life's in meltdown. Rather than face that, you've got fixated on this Amanda Turner woman. It's a classic coping mechanism.' Flo patted my arm. 'You're letting your emotional, impulsive brain take over from your rational one.'

I exploded. 'Thanks a bunch for the first-year psychology lecture,' I said, brushing her hand off. 'I don't get it, Flo. You defend your father when he walks out on twenty-one years of marriage. You roll your eyes when I try to make something of my life. And when I ask for your advice on a friend in trouble, you tell me to forget it,

I'm over-reacting. Frankly, I'm disappointed.'

Flo's face was stony. 'Before long, Mum, you'll be a grandmother. Why don't you think about that? Not about a woman you hardly know. What is it? What's behind this? Do you fancy her or something? If you do, that's no biggie. It's never too late to explore your sexuality. As long as you understand why you're behaving like this. You're jealous.'

I gasped. 'That's a shitty thing to say.'

'The truth is sometimes shitty.'

***

Neither of us felt like eating after that. Flo went to her room. Though it was still early, I had a bath and lay on my bed, stiff as a board despite the warm soak. I could hear Flo on her phone. She'd be talking to Nell. Griping about me, no doubt. *You'll never guess what the old bat is on about now,* I imagined her saying. I didn't hear any actual laughter, which was something I suppose.

Fifty-Four

It's getting dark. The murmuring from Flo's room has...

Shut up, Ivy! I don't need you Ivy-splaining every move I make. Flipping well give it a rest, can't you? I've had enough of you giving a running commentary and filling my head with your chaff. There was a time when it comforted me, hearing the echoes of Grace in your voice. But you've become irritating of late. And you are, after all, only a sound I make inside my own head, a sound I can switch off whenever I want. Like now.

The murmuring from Flo's room had subsided into gentle snoring. It was too early for me to sleep and, anyway, I had too much on my mind. Not only the row with Flo. I'd cut my ties with Amanda but that didn't stop me fretting about what was going on at Woodview and if she was safe. Soft touch that I still was somewhere underneath, I felt responsible.

I turned over, punched the pillow and tried one last time for rest. It wasn't happening. So I got up and quickly dressed. Time to show Ivy. Time to show Flo. Time to show them all. New Trish was on the warpath!

It was just past nine when I got to Oaker Wood. Twilight.

I've always liked twilight. As newlyweds, Gregory and I would take a short evening walk before bedtime. I loved the way, as the sun dipped, the birds fell silent and the light changed. Everything was sort of wrapped in a blue velvet cloak. Dark colours pushed back, lighter ones given an added ... I don't know the word. Is it luminousness? Luminosity, perhaps?

Then one evening Gregory took it upon himself to explain. Tried to tell him I knew all about the red, blue, and green cones in our eyes from my dear old dad. That I wasn't interested in what caused the effect, only in how it made me feel. Gregory didn't let that stop him. I took my twilight strolls alone from then on.

There was something different about twilight in Oaker Wood, something sinister. Shaking off the feeling, I parked the Mini down the lane, close enough to see there was a light on in Woodview. Someone was at home.

I sat for a while, drinking coffee from a flask, scoffing an energy bar and wondering what to do for the best. It was a stake out, you see, like you see in the films. Only in films people don't have overactive bladders and have to squat down on the grass verge, or spill coffee down their shirt fronts, or fall asleep and wake up with their necks at an odd angle. In films stuff happens: a car headlight sweeps across the night sky, a shot rings out or a security light blazes on. Nothing was happening here, as far as I could see. No shouting. No screaming. No drama. No sign of life except that weak light in the bay window of the living room. Other than that, not even the hoot of an owl or the screech of a fox to keep me company.

I yawned and checked my watch. Coming up for ten. Flo could wake at any moment for a pregnancy pee and the jig would be up. Perhaps if I moved closer … I got out of the car and, hugging the shadow of the hedge, crept forward. One quick check, I told myself, and in twenty minutes I could be back home to a flushing toilet and a warm bed. Flo would never have to know I'd been out chasing wild geese.

***

I didn't make it home.

I reached the gates and peered through. Still nothing untoward. That's another strange one. Nothing is ever 'toward' is it? Now I was nearer, it was clear the light I'd seen was the flickering of a television. Great! Here I was, staggering about in the dark, worried sick, imagining all sorts of mayhem, when all the time they'd been cuddled up nice and cosy on the horrid green sofa, watching *Gogglebox*.

Reassured that Amanda was safe, I could end my vigil and go home. Then I did a double take. Was that? Surely not? No longer bothering to hide myself, I went through the gate and ran the short distance across the gravel to the house.

Fifty-Five

You idiot, Trish! How could you have missed it? Almost an hour I'd hung about outside Woodview, supposedly observing, when all the time the front door, half hidden in the shadow of the porch, had been gaping wide open. That was careless, even for Amanda. And suspicious.

'Anybody there?' I shouted, poking my head round the door. 'Amanda?'

No response. Expecting at any moment an outraged Amanda, or worse still, an irate Pavel, to burst through the door, I made my way cautiously towards the living room.

'Hello,' I called out. 'Amanda, did you know, your front door's …?'

But there was no-one there. No television on and no cosy couple canoodling on the sofa. A bulb in one of the floor lamps was flickering, that was all. I crossed the room and turned it off, then went through to the kitchen, still calling as I went. The table had been cleared and the dishwasher stacked. I checked the other rooms downstairs. Nothing out of place. Nothing out of the ordinary. Except that worrying open door.

And that warm bed was calling.

Except … I lifted my head and sniffed, like a pointer on a pheasant shoot. There it was again. Nothing like the off-paint pong of before. This was unpleasantly sweet and heavy, and seemed to be coming from upstairs.

The higher I climbed, the stronger the smell. By the time I reached Amanda's bedroom door, I had to pull my cardy over my nose to block it out.

'You in there, Amanda?' I whispered through the woolly. 'It's me. Trish.' Nothing.

I leant against the doorframe, a flutter of panic rising in my chest. It had been a fortnight since I'd last seen Amanda. The inside of my mouth turned to cotton wool. A fortnight when anything could have happened. I'd watched enough police procedurals to know what that cloying, sickening sweetness could mean.

What horror would greet me inside that room? Yet I had to go in. I was the one who'd abandoned her. This was my punishment. I shouldn't have let her push me away. Hitching the cardy over my nose once more, I twisted the handle. The rancid smell flooded my nostrils. Yet I forced myself to go in. I owed it to Amanda.

It took me several seconds, coughing, eyes watering, before I could register the scene before me. There on the floor, a large stain spread around it, lay, not Amanda's body, but the huge bottle of perfume I'd noticed before. The *Ce Que Tu Sais*, knocked from the bedside cabinet, judging by the trail of bleached varnish, its contents spilling out onto the rucked-up Chinese rug.

For a moment, I was relieved. Boy, was I relieved! It was scent, gone off and left to fester in the heat, not a body. I sank to my knees on the ruined rug, uttering a prayer of thanks at having been spared the sight of Amanda's less-than-fresh corpse. Then I looked round and my anxiety levels spiked once more. The room was a wreck, furniture upturned, a mirror smashed, broken glass scattered over the floor. I was looking at the classic signs of a struggle.

My stomach heaved and, quite suddenly, I had to get out of that room. Donning the cardy mask once more, I staggered down to the fresher air of the kitchen. Heart hammering, I forced myself to make a calming cup of herbal tea and sat in Amanda's Windsor chair to have a damn good think.

Though the night was warm and the tea hot, I shivered. Even with the hairy blanket round my shoulders, I was cold. It was as if the heat was being sucked out of me by the house. I wished – oh, how I wished! – that I'd never set foot in the blasted place. Throwing the blanket aside, I wandered the rooms, cradling my tea, trying to focus. Now I was over the shock of not discovering Amanda's lifeless body, I needed to figure out what exactly was going on at Woodview.

My search for clues took me to the hall. Jeepers creepers! What was wrong with me? For the second time that night I'd failed to notice something important; first the front door, now this. On the side table with the curvy legs, where she always left it, lay Amanda's little black handbag. My fingers fumbled to open the clasp. I tipped out the contents. There among the tissues, combs, and lipsticks were her wallet and mobile phone. That clinched it! Amanda was in trouble.

I dashed back upstairs to hold my nose and do a more methodical search. Amanda's empty suitcases were in the spare room. Her wardrobe was full of clothes. Her tatty underwear filled the chest of drawers, and her bikinis were in the bottom drawer, including the hideous lime green number and, laying... lying beneath it, was her passport.

I racked my brains. Was there an innocent explanation? Her BMW was still on the drive. Had they simply taken a taxi into the city for a night out? Why the ransacked room, in that case? Were they off walking in the woods? At this time of night? In the dark? Unlikely. I checked my phone. Half ten. The more I thought, the more I became convinced they must have argued, it had got physical and Amanda had run off, with Pavel chasing after.

Having worked out a likely explanation, the big question now was, what was I, the new badass Trish, going to do about it?

I think I've mentioned before, I'm not the best with decisions. I was learning to be more strong-minded but it wasn't easy after a lifetime of people-pleasing. I was scared for Amanda but another fear, as strong, was holding me back: the fear of making a monumental tit of myself. What if I'd got it wrong and Amanda was safe? Could I take that risk? Was it worth the embarrassment? I took out my phone and stared at the screen for what seemed like a long time. Then, gritting my teeth and muttering 'Fuck, fuck, fuck', I punched in the numbers.

Hugging my knees, I sat on Amanda's front step and waited. What was I expecting? The flash of headlights, the screech of brakes, the slam of a car door? Hooray, the cavalry is here! It took quite a while for the truth to dawn. There would be no headlights. No cavalry. No-one was coming. I was on my own. So be it. I lifted my head.

I've never thought I was anyone special. Didn't do that well at school. Was a willing but unexceptional workhorse in the office. Thought I'd broken the mould when I made what they used to call a 'good marriage'.

Look how that worked out! Thought I'd made a decent fist of being a mother. Seems I was no great shakes there either. Now I was being tested like never before. How would I react? Slink off home or join the vertebrates and do something?

I heard a sound, coming from the direction of the woods. Not loud but it carried on the night air. I stood, squinting into the darkness. Was someone up there? In that moment, I knew what I had to do. It seemed obvious, inevitable really, since the first day I'd walked under the Virginia creeper and into Woodview. Straightening my shoulders, I let myself out through the gate, and strode up to the Old East London Road and into the woods, heading for the ochre pit.

***

I'd almost reached the workings, when a rustling stopped me in my tracks. I crept from the path and hid. A shape was moving in my direction. A silhouette, passing in and out of the shadows. As it grew closer, the shape resolved into a human figure. It appeared and disappeared between the trees, bent over, groaning and puffing, pulling something along the ground. I inched forward, risking another look. The figure was dragging a large and evidently heavy holdall by its end handle. When I say large, I mean large enough to contain a human body.

Fifty-Six

He'd done it! He'd actually done it! I wasn't letting my imagination run riot. I wasn't acting like a bonkers old biddy. Pavel had moved on from cats to people. To a person. To Amanda. He'd killed her and stuffed her body in the holdall.

Silently, I cried to the heavens. *Why wouldn't you listen to me? Why did you poo-poo my fears?* Or perhaps not so silently, because the figure stopped, straightened up and faced in my direction. I shrank back, not knowing if I could be seen.

'Who's there?' a voice called out, hesitant at first, then more confident. A familiar voice. 'Is that ...? Of course it is. Who else would it be? I can see you, you know, crouched behind the gorse. Come on out.' Dropping the handle, Amanda Turner put her hands on her hips, tipped her head sideways and said, cool as you like, 'Are you stalking me, Patricia Lightowler?'

I stepped out into the open. 'Am I glad to see you, Amanda. I thought ...' But what I'd thought seemed too ridiculous to say out loud. 'Anyway, I'm happy to find you alive and well.'

Amanda breathed in the night air. 'Don't you love that pungent, woody bouquet?' she said. 'What does it say to you?' I opened my mouth to suggest 'compost' but she didn't give me the chance. 'One senses eons of timeless evolution, damp decay, and fresh shoots. The ever-turning circle of life.' She took another lungful. 'Mind you,' she said, bending to scratch her leg, 'I could do without these sodding nettles!'

Amanda was talking as if it was perfectly normal for us to be chatting like this, in the middle of a wood, in the middle of the night. What was she doing there? Come to that, why was she dressed in a very un-Amanda-like get-up of walking boots, camo jacket and trousers? Why was she wearing a pair of blue plastic gloves? And most of all, what the heck was in that worrying bag at her feet?

'What's going on, Amanda?' I said. A straightforward question with, you'd think, a straightforward answer. Should have known. Nothing is straightforward where Amanda's concerned.

'Did I ever mention I was a sixer in the Brownies?' she said, true to form, avoiding an answer. 'Oh yes, I can do outdoorsy. If pushed, I could probably rustle up a passable fry-up over a campfire.'

'You're camping?' The idea seemed outlandish.

'Yes. Over yonder.' Amanda pointed towards a thick spinney.

'But why? I don't get it.'

'No. I don't suppose you do.' She dug into one of her many pockets and taking out an e-ciggie said, 'You never were that quick on the uptake, Trish. I suppose, I'll have to spell it out for you. Follow me.'

Lugging the holdall one-handed and with some effort, puffing out clouds of fruity condensation, she headed off across the field. I followed. Reaching the spinney, I found my way blocked by a rusty barbed wire fence. Signs were attached to the posts. "Keep out. Unstable Ground!" and "Danger to Life. Open Pit."

'Come on!' Amanda yelled from the other side of the fence. 'We haven't got all night.'

'There's barbed wire!'

'You wimp! Climb over the sacking.'

I searched about and found where she'd thrown an old sack over the fence. With some difficulty, and no dignity whatsoever, I clambered over.

'Down here!' Amanda shouted. I followed her voice to a clearing and stopped in amazement. Below me, descending into the darkness was an ochre pit. Not the piddling little dimple Amanda had shown me before. *The* pit. The one Turner had painted. The big one. By the light of the moon, I could just about make out its crumbling cliff walls and the sandy floor where Amanda stood.

'Stop gawping and get yourself down here,' she shouted. 'See, where there's a bit of a landslide.'

Sure enough, in one place the ochre face had collapsed, forming a rough ramp. I made my unsteady way down, slipping and sliding.

'You never mentioned this pit,' I said, dusting off my jeans. 'Bit more to see here than at the other one.'

'It suited me to keep it as my little secret. Luckily no-one ever comes here. Put off by the lurid signs I suppose.' She gave a humourless chortle. 'That's the Nanny State for you! A crucial part of our industrial heritage barred to the public, because some snotty-nosed toddler or precious cockerpoo might take a tumble and break their foolish necks. Still, it makes a great location for my *denouement*. Behold!' She was indicating a makeshift camp: a scuffed patch of earth, a little gas stove and a tiny folding stool, arranged around the glowing embers of a fire. 'What do you think?'

'Brown Owl would not be impressed.'

Amanda was in the mood for talking. For showing off, I should say. I let her ramble on. There were, after all, questions I needed answers to. We sat, Amanda on a log, puffing on her fake fag, excitedly spouting nonsense, and me balanced on the stool, knees almost under my chin, trying to work her out.

As the night wore on, I got more and more confused, but about one thing I was certain: all was not well at the old ochre pit.

'Must say, I'm disappointed,' Amanda said between puffs. 'After all my expert tuition I thought you'd have untangled my plot by now. Let me nudge you in the right direction. What was your first thought when you found the house unlocked and abandoned, the bedroom in disarray, and me nowhere to be found.'

I squirmed. 'That Pavel might have … Amanda, this is stupid!'

'No. Go on. I'm interested. What did you think?'

'That Pavel had maybe kidnapped you or … when I saw someone dragging a bag, I thought it was him and I was afraid he'd …' I stopped, courage failing.

'What? Pity's sake, Trish! Stop pussyfooting about – love that word, by the way. You thought it was me in the holdall, didn't you? You thought Pavel had bumped me off and was about to plant me under the leaf litter and run off with my cash. Am I right?'

"Yes, well,' I said, dropping my gaze, 'Seems I got that wrong.'

'No, that's what you were *intended* to think, according to Plan A. Such a pity I'll have to dump most of it now. Can't be helped. Right, think Trish. Here I am, hale and hearty. So, as I'm not the *late* Amanda Turner, then what?'

'Oh … I don't know.'

Amanda inhaled deeply and puffed out a plume of fruity exasperation. 'Would it help if I told you Pavel's name isn't Kuznetsov? That was an alias. It's Dobransky. Pavel Dobransky, only son of Janek Dobransky? Boss of Dobranoil?' she prompted. 'Ringing bells?'

'Ah!' I said, a glimmer of understanding beginning to break through the clouds of my ignorance. 'Pavel's dad is that rich oligarch.'

'Bravo, Hetty Wainthrop. Fabulously rich. Whereas, I'm a cash-strapped scribbler. *Ergo*, if Pavel hasn't done away with me and scuttled back to Nowhere-istan on a false passport with my cash, then …?' She raised an eyebrow. 'Come on. Come on.'

'Can't you just tell me?' I wailed, though somewhere in the back of my mind I was beginning to think – to fear – that I knew.

'You weren't entirely barking up the wrong horse chestnut, Trish. Instinct told you there were dodgy goings-on at Woodview.' She gave a chuckle. 'And there were. Only not what you thought.'

As she spoke, I had the strangest feeling. The pieces of the jigsaw I'd been juggling in my head flew into the air. As they fell, they slotted themselves one by one into a new pattern. And at last I understood. I'd got it back to front. Upside down. Arsey-versy, as my bonkers mum would say.

'Pavel wasn't love-bombing you? You were …' I was unable to make myself finish the sentence.

Amanda was ecstatic. 'I was love-bombing him!' she cried, punching the air in an unladylike fashion. 'Took a while, but you got there.'

'So, Pavel?' I asked, still in a daze. My glance dropped to the holdall at Amanda's feet. I clutched my head. 'Oh my giddy aunt! Pavel! What have you done, Amanda?' I said, leaping to my feet, knocking over the stool. As it fell, it tangled my legs in its metal frame. Next thing, I was on my hands and knees.

Amanda's face appeared above me. 'You all right?'

'Fine. Thank you for asking,' I said, for some bizarre reason feeling it necessary to maintain the niceties, before adding, 'Have you gone insane, Amanda?'

'Far from it. Transferable skills, that's the name of the game. I've used my talent as a creator of fictional plots to devise a real-life drama. Plotting always was my *forte*, as you'll recall.'

'But to go this far,' I said, damp soaking through the knees of my jeans. 'It doesn't matter how rich he is or how desperate you are,' I shook my head, 'you shouldn't have killed Pavel.'

For a moment, Amanda's expression could have gone either way. Then she broke into helpless laughter. 'Trish Lightowler,' she gasped. 'Maybe you *do* have an imagination after all.'

***

When she'd stopped splitting her sides, Amanda put me right.

It wasn't Pavel's corpse in the holdall, she explained, unzipping the bag with a flourish to prove it. It wasn't anyone's corpse. It was the tent that had been her temporary home.

'So where is Pavel? What have you done with him?'

'Heptathlon,' she said, ignoring the question. 'You know, the sports shop. Got it there. Only a cheap pop-up job but surprisingly cosy. I've quite enjoyed going back to nature.' She grinned. 'Though I'll never be able to look another Pot Noodle in the face again.'

She'd been preparing for weeks, she told me gleefully,

buying and hiding food and equipment in the woods. 'I reckoned two weeks should do it. As luck would have it, those two weeks were up this very night.' She'd been packing up the camp, when I stumbled upon her. Half an hour later, and she'd have been gone. 'And there would have been no need for any of this tomfoolery. Still, we are where we are.'

'And where exactly is that?' I asked.

'Isn't this like old times?' Amanda gave a wriggle of pleasure. 'Though I've a feeling this lesson's going to be somewhat different from the others.'

As she told her tale, her smile widened. I did my best to respond, only achieving, I suspect, the sort of grimace you see on the faces of chimpanzees about to be shot into space on a one-way ticket.

'Had to make myself scarce. The whole plan depended on it. Running straight to the airport would have been the sort of rookie error someone like you would make. No, a couple of weeks in hiding under canvas it had to be. You must see that.'

I didn't but I let her talk on.

'You asked about Pavel,' she said, ditching the fake fag and retrieving a metal water bottle from the backpack. Not offering it to me, she took a swig. 'Are you sitting comfortably?' she asked. 'Then I'll begin.'

Fifty-Seven

Lesson 21: A Somewhat Different Kind

Looking down her nose, using the same *full of herself* tone as when she was, supposedly, teaching me how to bag that Booker, Amanda filled me in on the dastardly Dobranskys.

Daddy Dobransky, she explained, was one of those oligarchs who hoovered up vast quantities of cash in the Eastern European chaos of the 1990s. Unbelievably rich though he is, like many a moneyed bastard, Dobransky Senior doesn't believe in mollycoddling his offspring. Only son Pavel had to prove himself before he could inherit. Daddy arranged a test. He shoved Pavel on a plane to London with a big backpack and a small bundle of pounds sterling, telling him if he could survive to his thirtieth birthday, he'd cop for his cut of the family fortune.

'Unfortunately, Daddy Dobransky had overlooked one tiny detail: Pavel, bless him, had none of his father's cunning. He took after his mother – God rest her soul! – in that respect.' Amanda crossed herself.

'Naïve?' I suggested.

Amanda tipped back her head. 'I prefer plainer language. Pavel is a dimwit.'

Dim Pavel, alone in London, was soon out of his depth and out of money. It was then he happened upon the whydoityourself.com website.

'As a bored and lonely little rich boy,' Amanda told me, 'he'd often hang out with the workers on the family estate. They indulged him and he picked up enough practical skills to get by as an odd job man, and one of his jobs brought him to Oxford.'

'Where you met.'

She nodded, taking another sip from the water bottle.

'Had him marked down as a target more or less from day one, after he let slip about his coming inheritance, trying to impress me I suppose,' she went on without embarrassment. 'A plan began to form and who could blame me? It was hard to resist. I mean, taking sweets from a baby would have been more challenging. Babies have surprisingly strong grips,' she said thoughtfully, making me wonder if she had experience of nicking toddlers' treats. 'And the sex, when it came along, was a nice bonus, thank you very much. It had been a while and he was young, athletic, and not unattractive.'

She held up a hand. 'And before you ask, I don't feel guilty. There are literally billions to go round and I figure I have as much right to them as any of the Dobranskys. As I see it, stealing from a thief is not theft.'

'Why get engaged to the man?'

'To keep him onside, of course,' Amanda said. 'I sensed he might grow restless, as young men do. That nonsense at the Tennis Club was a red flag. I couldn't risk having him walk out on me before his thirtieth. Luckily, he lapped up my *down on one knee* performance, though, of course I never had any intention of going through with it. Imagine waking up to that miserable mush every morning!'

She took another long drink.

I licked my dry lips. 'Why was Pavel so miserable? I don't think I ever saw him smile.'

'*Burunduk!*'

'What?'

'It means chipmunk. Apparently, Pavel's pa told him on his sixteenth birthday that when he smiled he looked like a chipmunk. Hasn't shown his teeth from that day to this. But we were talking about my plan. Such a clever plan. And I haven't even reached the best part yet. This is where you come in. Or rather, your funny little journal.'

I blinked. 'My journal?'

'Yes, you *dumkopf.* For weeks I've been drip-feeding you information, dropping hints, encouraging you to commit your suspicions to paper. Surely you've noticed? I see by your face you haven't.' She gave me another of her smug looks. 'Anyone reading your journal couldn't fail to conclude that Pavel is a violent man scheming to get his hands on my lolly. His guilt is obvious, set down in black and white in your own clumsy words. Who could doubt the evidence of an ordinary, decent suburban housewife?'

My knuckles turned white, as I gripped the sides of the stool. Amanda had been playing me for a sucker. Not only taking money for useless lessons, but lying to me, week in and week out, using me.

Puffed up with pride, Amanda kept talking. Her plan was to clear out Pavel's now fat bank account, scare him into fleeing back to his own country, then disappear abroad herself. With no trace of either of them, and after reading my anti-Pavel journal, the police would conclude something dire had happened to Amanda, with Pavel the prime suspect. After searching the woods, unsuccessfully, for her body, the coppers would give up, the case would be filed away, marked 'Missing. Unexplained' and Amanda would be home free.

'Genius, you have to agree,' she said.

I roused myself. 'What if I'd gone to the police with my fears? What if they'd investigated and discovered your little camp? How would you have explained that?'

'You? Go to the police?' Amanda chuckled. 'No. I was on fairly safe ground there. I knew you'd dither. By the time you'd got around to dialling 999 and convincing the cops you weren't a mad woman – which might have taken a while – I'd be long gone.' She wrinkled her nose. 'You're too predictable, Patricia Lightowler.'

'You know me too well,' I said, thinking precisely the opposite. 'Tell me. Was Pavel violent?'

'Pavel? Pavel wouldn't squash a grape.' Again that smug look. 'But he was passionate and easy to provoke. And I had the signal of those rusty gates to warn me someone was approaching. All it took was a bit of provocation and stage management whenever I heard you come to the house – and bingo!'

'And LBK? Did he kill him?' I asked. 'I saw him digging the grave.'

'After all your emotive tosh about the cat, what's hilarious is, the wretched thing isn't even dead.'

'Not dead?'

'I'm not a monster, Trish. True, I did consider getting Pavel to give it the Ann Boleyn treatment but I knew he wouldn't have gone through with it. Too soft by half, that boy. And I certainly wasn't going to bloody my hands. I put it in a cardboard box, very much alive, all snuggled up in a cosy blanket, and left it outside the animal rescue centre.

'Pavel was in the dark. I let him think I'd dispatched it. He was quite upset with me, actually. For about five minutes. What he buried that afternoon was a rolled up towel. Your LBK – stupid name! – is currently probably having the time of his little life in the Furry Friends Animal Shelter.'

'In other words, the whole performance was another one of your mean charades.'

'That's about the size of it.'

'And the slap?'

'Which one? Actually there *was* only one. The one after the tennis match was imaginary, *ad libbed* to reel you in. The one you heard, or thought you heard. That one...'

As she spoke, the scene replayed itself in my head. This time, with the benefit of what I now knew about Amanda, I heard it differently.

'You bastard! That hurt!' I'd heard Amanda call out, apparently in distress. Now, with hindsight, I picked up a new emphasis. Not a cry of shock and pain. *Ouch, that hurt!* Quite the reverse in fact. A questioning taunt. *Did that hurt you?*

'I get it,' I said dully. 'You slapped him.'

'Precisely. He was being more than usually obtuse and for once I lost my cool and smacked him one. Could have ruined everything. Luckily, Pavel being the proud man he was, didn't grass me up.'

I shook my head. How could she be so callous? 'And the bruises?'

'Courtesy of a YouTube tutorial by a *Walking Dead* make-up artist. Simple. Almost as simple as faking the broken gates, to make sure you couldn't miss them.'

'Are you a Girton girl, Amanda?'

She chuckled. 'I'm no more upper-class than you, Patricia Lightowler, though I hide it a good deal better. Your father was a lens grinder, mine a London cabbie. Never went to no university, me darlin',' she said, in a rough *EastEnders* accent.

I'd had enough of her and her stories. I stood. 'I can't stay here any longer listening to you, I'm going.'

'Don't think so,' she said, the warmth draining from her voice. 'Sit down.'

'You can't make me.'

'Can't I?'

The knife wasn't very big but it was very, very pointy and, I imagined, in the hands of someone who had made a study of murder methods, probably deadly.

'I. Said. Sit. Down,' she repeated.

I sat.

'Now your phone.'

I handed it over.

'That's better,' she said, zipping it into the side pocket of her backpack.

'What happens now?' I asked, clasping my hands tight round my knees so she wouldn't see them shaking.

'What happens now is, you wait like a good little *hausfrau* while I brew us up two disgusting cups of horrible campfire tea. And while we drink them, I shall enthral you with the stupendous finale to my riveting story.'

Overuse of adjectives, Amanda. Not like you, I thought, but didn't say. *Could it be you're nervous?*

Fumbling with the knife, she filled a tiny kettle from the water bottle. 'Shit!' She looked up, troubled. 'No milk. You all right with black?'

Fifty-Eight

At some point during the night Amanda decided she wanted to show off the ochre pit. Given the situation, I wasn't fussed either way but, encouraged by a wave of that knife, I agreed. She struggled to light the lantern and, when it was lit, held it above her head, turning in a slow circle.

Under the hissing lamp, the pit wall seemed to come to life. As the light flickered, the colours danced from yellow and orange, through to red and dark brown.

'This is nothing,' Amanda said breezily. 'You should see it in daylight with the full power of the sun on it. It's as if the whole pit is ablaze. Old JMW did his best but even he couldn't capture its drama. You know, on my own these last days, I've grown to love it up here. I could just sit and stare. In awe.'

Yeah, right, I thought, finding it impossible to imagine Amanda being in awe of anything other than her own genius.

We sat, the only sounds the rustling of leaves and the scurrying of tiny animals going about their nightly business. In normal circumstances, it would have been a time for peaceful reflection. These weren't normal circumstances.

'Why did you take me on?' I asked, breaking the silence. 'Did you ever think I had any talent?'

'I can't tell you how happy I was to see you lolloping into the library that day,' she said, smiling at the memory, 'in your too-tight leggings and sweat-ringed top, all scratches, scabs, and inappropriate giggles. I was so bored before you pitched up, I could have chewed my own fingers off. The bald truth is, Trish, you amused me.'

Out of the string of barbs, I chose to home in on one. 'Lolloping?'

'Lovely word, isn't it? So onomatopoeic. Yes, your posture was terrible. You shuffled along as if heaving a sack of bricks. You've de-hunched yourself since, I'm pleased to say. Unfurling like a sweet little rosebud.' She made even that sound like an insult.

'I looked at you and realised fate had brought me this wonderful gift: the perfect patsy. I needed a second dupe, a counterpart to Pavel, and there you were, hanging on my every word like an enraptured child, simply begging to fill that role. Oh, but those lessons! What a challenge you presented! How could I transform this bland caterpillar into a multi-coloured literary butterfly?

'Not that it mattered, though the cash came in handy. No, my main motivation for persisting was to make you – or rather, your journal – my unwitting witness. And your name, of course. That still cracks me up. Pa-tree-ceeahh Light-owwwl-ahh,' she said, drawing out the syllables, making them sound even more ridiculous than they already did.

'If you needed money so desperately,' I said, clenching teeth and buttocks, 'why not sell the house? The Country Park is a sought-after location.'

'Gives me the creeps, that house. And it's a total

wreck.' Amanda gazed in the direction of Woodview. 'Besides, it's not mine to sell. Belonged to an old lady – classics professor at one of the colleges, I believe. Popped her crocs last winter, sitting in that Windsor chair at the kitchen table. Or so the teenage letting agent informed me with, I may say, an unnecessary degree of relish. She was found with that itchy old blanket wrapped round her knees. Funny that.'

She broke off, smiling as if recalling a fond memory. I shuddered, remembering the unhealthy embrace of that same blanket. 'The giant bottle of perfume, that was the old bat's too. About fifty years past its use by. Fine fragrances, unlike fine wine, don't improve with age. They rot.'

'Woodview isn't a family home then, left to you by a beloved aunt? Where you spent many a happy school holiday?'

Amanda looked puzzled. 'What makes you think that? No. Rented. The agents let me have it, fully furnished, quite cheap, while probate was being sorted. No, I don't have any living relatives. I'm poor Orphan Mandy, all alone in the world.' She put her fists to her eyes in a mockery of grief. 'Boohoo.'

Once more, the existence of son Louis seemed to have slipped her memory. If he even existed. Not that I was bothered. I no longer cared what was true and what wasn't. She'd told so many lies, I doubt Amanda knew herself.

'What about your books? You must get royalties.'

'Oh yes, my books. Can't remember the last time I had a decent seller. My agent and my publisher both dropped me years ago. I self-pub these days but it's a hell of a lot of hassle for very little return. No, truth be told, I've given up on the novel writing.'

'Yet you were happy enough to castigate me for not

persisting.'

'If hypocrisy were a crime, Trish,' she laughed, 'we'd all be in the clink. Like the use of 'castigate' by the way. Your vocabulary is improving.'

'You said *Love You to Bits* was a bestseller.'

'So it was. Number one bestselling romslasher for one whole day…' She paused for effect. 'In Tasmania. It's called marketing, Trish. Another thing you don't have a clue about.'

'That's what's behind this crazy scheme of yours, is it? You're skint?'

'And Pavel helpfully provided me with a way out. Hey, this'll crack you up,' she gurgled. 'He *luuurved* me, he told me many times. Even when I was being an absolute shrew, even when I smacked him one, even when I was fleecing the boy, he told me he loved me. Isn't that a hoot? Wept real tears the last time I saw him.'

'When was that, Amanda?'

She pulled at the wrist of the plastic gloves. 'God, but these things make your hands sweat! What? Oh Pavel. He didn't love me quite so much, it transpired, after he got the threatening phone calls. Not enough to stick around. I did enjoy making those. Quite took me back to my am dram days.'

'You made those calls?'

'Now she's impressed! Yes. Me. I used a microphone thing. The Voice Disguiser it's called. The Blackmailer's Friend, I call it. Can you believe they sell such devious devices to children? Even my own mother wouldn't have recognised me. Put the fear of God into Pavel. *Prepare to die, foolish boy,*' she said in a heavy accent. '*The Kandinskis never forget.* Did you see his face?

'And what did you think of my *pièce de résistance*, courtesy of a nice young man in a hairnet at the Waitrose fish counter? Don't look so disapproving. I may have gone over the top a little but, you have to admit, it gave my subplot the flamboyant climax it needed. Pavel sodded off not long after. So terrified, he was even willing to risk the wrath of Daddy, King of the Balkans. Didn't even stay to check his bank account.'

'You'd emptied it by then, I assume?'

'That engagement ring was the key. Once I had that on my finger, I got anything I asked for, including access to his account. Not bad for a twenty-nine ninety-nine ring, don't you think? Chucked it in the bin as soon as he left. Nasty, cheap thing turned my finger green.'

'Wow,' I said, hoping I wasn't overplaying my hand. 'That's quite a story.'

'Brilliant, isn't it?' she purred. 'People say I've lost my touch but I think, with this, even my worst enemy would have to admit I'm back on form. I can see the cover blurb now.' She looked up into the dark sky and sketched the shape of an imaginary banner in the air. '"Sinned against or sinner? Villain or victim? You decide." What do you think?'

What did I think? I thought she could no longer tell the difference between real life and fiction.

'And no-one will ever suspect me,' she said, hugging herself in delight, 'because they'll think I'm dead. A conceit worthy of the master, Lee Child, wouldn't you agree?'

'Nope,' I said, stirring myself to go on the attack. 'I have some serious issues with it, as a matter of fact.'

Her face fell. 'You do? Pray tell. I'm interested,' she said, as if we were critiquing a bestseller.

'Hold that thought,' I said. 'I need to be excused.'

'Go on, but be quick. And don't get any ideas. I've still got my little pointy friend. You really do need to see someone about that,' she called over, as I lowered myself gingerly – why ginger? – into the nettles. 'Or before you know it, you'll be into nappies.'

I took my time. I did need a pee but I also needed a few minutes away from Amanda's overpowering presence to gather my thoughts. Could I out-think her? When we'd first met it would have been out of the question but now I believed I had the measure of her. She thought she was invincible and that was her weak spot: her unshakeable self-belief.

'Hellfire and damnation!' I felt a wet warmth soak my trouser leg.

'The perils of a wee in the woods,' Amanda smirked, as I limped back, pulling at the damp patch in my jeans. She'd been busy stoking the fire while I was away, humming to herself, a familiar tune I couldn't quite place.

'I've spotted some holes,' I said, inching my stool closer to the merry blaze. The night was growing cool and my hands welcomed the heat, 'in your so-called brilliant plot.'

'I think you'll find I've thought of everything but don't let that inhibit you.' Amanda folded her arms. 'Fire away.'

'For a start, what about this?' I said, indicating our surroundings. 'When the police discover your camp, it won't take forensics long to work out who's been hiding here and, after that, why.'

'As you know, I hate loose ends,' Amanda said. 'A plot has to be neat and tidy or it won't convince. Hence these.' She waved her blue hands at me. 'No fingerprints, see. The tent and the other stuff did concern me for a while but I believe I've got it covered.

'I took the precaution of gathering some empty cans and dog ends from the litter bin in the car park the other day. I'd hoped to find a few used condoms and some silver noz canisters to add extra authenticity.' She gave a sigh of disappointment. 'But the young people of

Oxfordshire are less adventurous than you and I were at their age, it seems. Hey ho! One has to improvise.

'I've scattered the litter about and I'll leave the tent and the rest of the paraphernalia half hidden where the lazy coppers will find them. They'll take one look and dismiss this as a den where teenagers hung about in the summer hols, smoking, chugging cheap cider, and groping each other. The gloves, I'll dispose of at the airport.' She tapped her forehead with the point of the knife. 'Details, Trish. As I've told you many times, it's all in the details.'

'OK. What about the money? Won't Interpol, or whoever, be able to track you down through the money you stole?'

'Oh, Trish, Trish,' she said, giving me a pitying look. 'Even you must be aware there are countries tucked away in corners of the globe, where they are more concerned with how much you've got than how you came by it. Your slippery accountant ex-husband must have told you about anonymous, *no questions asked* bank accounts.'

'Like in Switzerland?'

'Switzerland is so last season!' she scoffed. 'No-one has a Zurich bank account any more. Not when there are other jurisdictions willing to offer the most discreet of services, and where there's no danger of being extradited back to the UK. Some have endless silver beaches and year-round sunshine. I prefer that, myself, to snow and mountains.'

'What bolthole did you have in mind, Amanda? You can tell me. It's not as if you're going to be able to go there now. Face it, you're rumbled. Your twisted house of cards is about to collapse.'

She cocked her head. 'Can a house of cards be twisted? It wouldn't stand up in the first place. Shame on you, Trish. You know how I abhor a messy metaphor.

Anyhow, my plan hasn't fallen apart, not entirely, because – guess what? – you, Patricia Lightowler, are about to let me go.'

She glanced at her watch and gave a little pout of irritation. 'Damn! Thanks to your meddling I've missed the two-fifty coach.' She yawned. 'Not to worry. We'll sit here by the fire a little while longer and I'll catch the three-fifty instead. So handy having that shortcut through the woods to the ring road.'

'How do you plan on getting all the way from there to the coach station? On foot?' Or will you call a taxi?'

'I'm not a total idiot. I'll cycle in on the old bone-shaker I lifted a couple of weeks ago, and stashed near the path. Shouldn't take long at this time of night. I'll dump it afterwards in the city centre, alongside the other abandoned bikes. Neat, huh?'

I let a silence settle, before saying, 'What makes you think, Amanda, that I'm going to let you walk away Scot free? Or even cycle away. I reckon, if it came to it, I could wrestle that knife off you.'

She met my gaze. 'Remember what I told you about false endings?'

'The story that appears to be over, then Pow! it's 'game on' all over again? Yes, I remember.'

'Bravo. You *were* paying attention, some of the time,' she said. 'And the importance of having a Plan B? Remember that?'

'Be adept at adapting.'

'Spot on. And, let me tell you, my Plan B is a corker. Stand by for an Amanda Turner *Fatal Attraction* finale to end all finales.'

Then, in the lamplight, with the moths performing daredevil aerobatics over our heads and the trembling leaves whispering secrets into the air, Amanda revealed her Plan B.

Fifty-Nine

I got Amanda to go over her back-up plan twice, to be sure. The first time I couldn't believe it. The second time, I still couldn't.

As plans go, Amanda's was clever. Clever but insane. Whatever I imagined – and my brain was shooting off in all directions by this point in the night – Amanda's idea was a hundred times more insane.

This is the gist. Anticipating something might go wrong with Plan A – the *make it look like Pavel has killed me* scenario – Amanda had set up an alternative reality for use in case of an emergency.

'And you, my dear Trish, are that emergency. Curse you!' she said, without a trace of resentment.

What was this new scenario? You must be dying to know. As it happens, dying was very much at the heart of it. Put simply, Amanda's Plan B was the *make it look like Trish has killed me* variation.

See what I mean? Insane. My jaw was in danger of dislocating.

'If you are to convince your audience, you have to think

of every little thing,' Amanda lectured, for all the world as if we were back in the airless summerhouse. 'One misjudged reaction, one illogical step, one badly researched fact and your credibility is shot to pieces. Once that's gone, you've lost everything.'

She'd planted clues, she told me, to back up her story. These clues of hers would tell of a warm-hearted novelist who, out of the kindness of her heart, had taken under her wing a needy but utterly talentless wannabe writer. She repeated the description several times to make sure I got the point. In return, the ungrateful, talentless woman had betrayed the warm-hearted writer by stealing her lover and plotting with him to rob her blind. But double-crossing them both, lover boy had high-tailed it back to his home country with the money, never to be seen again. Distraught and penniless, the talentless woman sought revenge on the kindly author, who she blamed for her woes.

'Took revenge? How?' I asked.

'She kills her.'

A long silence followed.

'Have I got this right?' I said at last. 'Your plan is to frame *me* for *your* murder?'

Amanda nodded enthusiastically. 'Genius, isn't it?'

'Why would the police suspect me, of all people?' I said. 'Where's your evidence?'

'Ah, you're neglecting to take into account my journal.' Amanda caught my look of surprise. 'Didn't I mention that? Remiss of me. You're not the only one who's been keeping a daily record, Trish. This is mine.'

She dug a silver memory stick out of her pocket. 'It paints quite a different picture from your carelessly scribbled, peanut butter-stained notebook.'

I'd taken a lot from Amanda. Insult after insult. Dig after dig. Putdown after putdown. That was as nothing compared with the stab of betrayal I felt at that moment.

'Peanut butter-stained?' I said quietly. 'Amanda, have you been reading my journal?'

'How else could I have manipulated you, you dolt! Besides, I couldn't resist, with you nipping to the loo every few minutes, leaving those rose-coloured covers peeking tantalisingly out from your mum's old handbag.'

The mention of my mother really got the blood pumping. How dare she!

'You read that stuff about my mother?'

'Very touching. I liked the sound of Grace. And the row with the twins, that was entertaining. And the battle with your sneaky ex-husband. What a dispiriting tale that is. Though your Mr. Bungle sounds like a real find. You should hang onto him. He might be useful on your defence team. And congratulations on the granny thing. Flo, is it, the daughter expecting the mistake sprog?'

'To think I was impressed! To think I credited you with amazing psychological insight, when you are nothing but a cheap charlatan.'

'Not so much of the cheap,' Amanda laughed good-naturedly.

'What's to stop me grabbing that memory stick and stamping it underfoot. Where's your evidence then?'

'You don't really think this is the only copy, do you? That would be a schoolgirl error. There's a duplicate locked in my desk.'

'But why would the police believe you? It would be your journal against mine?'

Amanda smirked, loving every second. 'Your journal, Trish?' She leant forward to poke the fire with the point of her knife. 'What journal is that?'

'This one,' I said, reaching for my handbag, reassured by its weight. But when I undid the zip, and dug about in the ripped lining, I found, not my journal, but a book.

Amanda was triumphant. 'Couldn't have two journals in circulation, could we, Trish? That would muddy the waters. This,' she held the memory stick in the air, 'is my insurance. I'm afraid your precious journal – if you'll pardon the expression – is toast.' She flicked a glance towards the flames. 'Makes a nice blaze, don't you think?'

Grabbing a stick, I fell to my knees, trying to rescue the blackened remains. It was no good. The book was well alight. As soon as I poked them, the pages disintegrated and embers, glowing red, broke off and soared into the darkness.

'All that work,' I groaned, sitting back on my heels. 'All them words.'

'You know what they say? Kill your darlings.'

***

'Want to know the difference between you and me, Trish?' Amanda declared, a while later. 'I am an artist, prepared to go to whatever lengths are necessary for my art. Prepared, indeed, to climb up to that high point.' She pointed the knife towards the ridge above, where a ragged hawthorn bush was starkly silhouetted against the night sky.

'What do you think? About thirty metres high, more or less straight down, give or take a few protruding saplings and sharp rocks? I'm prepared to climb up there and throw myself off the top, popping another handful of pills as I go. I've been sucking them down like jellybeans all night, in case you hadn't noticed. Not caring that, as I fall, my bones will shatter and my flesh will be torn. Not caring if, when I land in a broken heap, I am dead or dying. And I will do all of that because it's what I have to do to make this ending come right. To make this story work.'

It was as if she was describing a scene from one of her novels. As if she didn't realise what she was talking about was real life. And real death. Hers. I screwed my eyes tight shut but when I opened them, Amanda was still there, still informing me in excited detail how she planned to kill herself and pin the blame on me.

'There's a flaw in your plotting,' I said, as calmly as I could. 'For Plan B to succeed, you have to die, Amanda, or be badly injured. Where's the sense in that? You wouldn't win. You'd be dead. Or as good as.'

'Bit of a downside, I grant you. But what's the alternative if you shop me to the police? Poverty, shame, and imprisonment. Besides, think of the satisfaction of fooling everyone from beyond the grave. The ultimate creative triumph. Books would be written about the mystery of my death. Not by you, obviously, someone talented. There could be films. A Netflix series. Posthumously, I would be famous and it would all have been worth it.'

She lapsed into silence.

'Why would the police assume murder?' I said after a moment or two. 'Surely suicide is more likely.'

Amanda was delighted. 'I like it. You're beginning to think like a writer, at last. Because of this.' She patted her breast pocket. 'My suicide note.'

'Now you've really got me confused.'

'I am proud of this little twist,' she said, taking out a folded sheet of paper. 'Aha! No. Not so fast,' she said, as I tried to snatch it. 'If you could read it, you might note three things: it's clumsily worded, the signature is typed, and my name is misspelled. Amander with an 'er' – I ask you! Even the thickest copper should spot it for a phony. And when they discover it was written on *your* laptop,

Trish, I anticipate a *you do not have to say anything but it may harm your defence etc.* conversation with the local constabulary.'

'On my laptop? How?' Then I remembered. Amanda had offered to charge it up for me during our last lesson. She'd taken it through to the study and would have had plenty of time to type a few lines and print them out.

'And the pills. Mustn't forget the pills. *Had another dizzy spell today,*' Amanda said, putting on a frail, old lady voice. '*I don't understand why I feel so weak. Could someone be drugging me? Could it be* – dramatic pause – *Trish?*' She straightened up. 'Or words to that effect. It's all in the journal. You see, I've thought of everything.'

'I take my hat off to you,' I said. 'No wonder they called you the Queen of the Double Bluff.'

'Thank you.' Amanda bowed in mock appreciation. 'Now, if there are no more questions …'

Before I had time to react, she was running across the sand and powering up the slope.

It was the chance I'd been waiting for. I unzipped her backpack and, retrieving my phone, followed her.

'Amanda! Stop!' I called out. 'Don't do anything stupid! Anything even more stupid!'

Chapter Sixty

Too many ready meals took their toll as I panted after Amanda. It was hard going. The ground was thick with bushes and brambles, and between them, alongside the usual nettles, dozens of scratchy saplings, forcing me to jink from side to side. I reached the summit.

'Over here,' Amanda called, not even out of breath.

She was close to the edge, looking down on the half-circle of the ochre pit, arms outstretched, Christ the Redeemer dressed in camo, the knife still in her hand. Below her were the ochre walls and, below them, the sandy bottom we'd just left. I stepped back, feeling suddenly seasick. Amanda lifted her chin, eyes glittering.

'My, my. Someone's out of condition,' she said, taking a step nearer the edge. I heard the skitter of crumbling earth. 'Well, here we are, Trish. You and me. At the end of the line. No more chit-chat. Tautonyms, by the way, words like that are called. Like wishy-washy, dilly-dally or silly-billy. All words one could employ to describe a timid and indecisive person,' she said, not missing the chance to take another little pop.

'So. Decision time.' Amanda turned her back to stare over the abyss. 'What are you going to do?'

'This is absurd,' I said, playing for time as I fumbled with my phone. 'My nerves won't take much more.'

'Then decide. Are you going to stand by and watch me top myself, knowing there's a very good chance of being accused of my murder – or attempted murder? Because, in the unlikely event that I do survive, that is the tale I will tell, weakly but repeatedly, from my hospital bed.

'*She pushed me, officer,*' Amanda whimpered, back to the little old lady act. '*And I thought she was my friend.*'

'Or,' Amanda went on in her normal voice, 'will you do the sensible thing and let me go. Then we can both get on with our lives, no harm done, except to the bank account of a billionaire, who deserves everything that's coming to him. What's it to be, Trish? My life is in your hands. Ooooh, what's happening?' She swayed, hand to her head. 'Must be the sleeping pills.'

I made to move towards her.

'Stay where you are. Just pulling your leg. I'm solid as a rock. You always were easy to tease, Trish. So, make up your mind. Which is it to be? Let me go or watch me jump.'

'You're not serious.'

'Deadly. I'm starting the countdown. Ten, nine, eight…'

'You're bluffing.'

'Seven, six, five …'

'I don't believe you.'

'Four, three, two …'

'Amanda, please!'

She stretched her arms over her head like a diver and rose on tiptoe. I did a quick calculation. She was three, maybe four metres away. Could I get to her in time? She flexed her knees. Her body tilted. She was going to do it. I'd never make it.

'Hello-o!' A gruff voice rang out. A torch beam cut through the darkness, bouncing off the scrubby bushes and tufts of grass, and coming to rest on Amanda, poised on the edge.

It happened in a split second. Her head jerked round and, at the same moment, a figure dived for her legs. She lost her footing and, with a scream, overbalanced.

Sixty-One

'I'll take that,' Bernard said, disentangling himself from Amanda's limbs and grabbing the knife. Amanda rolled over and lay on her back, winded. He got to his feet. 'Mind telling me what's going on here?'

'Long story,' I said. 'Nice tackle, by the way.'

'Instinct. I was a useful number eight, back in the day.' We stood over Amanda, side by side, looking down. 'Would she really have jumped, do you think?'

'Hard to say. Still and all, I'm glad she didn't. And glad you got here. Eventually.'

'Your message right put the willies up me. What were you thinking, heading off into the woods on your own chasing, not to put too fine a point on it, a crazy woman?'

'Excuse me,' Amanda butted in from her undignified position on the grass. 'I am here, you know. Not that I want to interrupt your cosy little chat but, may I remind you, I have a plane to catch.'

'I think not,' Bernard said. 'You're staying right where you are until the emergency services get here, and we sort this out.' He got out his phone. 'Or have you already called them, Trish?'

'Leave it, Bernard,' I said, pushing his phone away. 'Let her up.'

Commanding is not how I used to think of myself but this was the new me, remember? There must have been something in my voice for, without another word, Bernard put away his phone and held out a hand to help Amanda.

'Thank you, Trish,' she said. 'Whatever else you were, you were always well-mannered.'

'Turn around,' I said. 'What time is it, Bernard?'

'Coming up to three.'

'There you are, Amanda,' I said, brushing grass and twigs from her shoulders. 'If you get your skates on, you should make the three-fifty coach easy.'

'You're going to let her go?' Bernard said.

Amanda raised her eyebrows. 'Glad you've seen sense.'

'You had me sussed from the start. I'm far too much of a wuss to risk you killing yourself, and I sure as heck don't fancy a stretch in prison.'

'But Trish!' Bernard protested.

'Trust me, Bernard. Let her go.'

We climbed back down into the bowl of the pit, Amanda sandwiched between Bernard and me. We waited, while she – Bernard standing guard – dragged the holdall and the rest of the gear to a clump of bushes and shoved them out of sight. Then she stuffed her remaining few belongings into the backpack.

That done, she stood before us, strangely formal. It was an odd moment. I thought she was going to shake my hand or, worse still, offer a farewell hug. She didn't.

'Can't say it's been a pleasure,' she said, 'but it has been memorable. I won't forget you in a hurry, Patricia Lightowler.'

'Likewise,' I said. 'And Amanda?'

'Yes?' she said, shouldering the backpack.

'May the best woman win.'

'She has, Trish. She has.'

With a quick glance around the campsite and a casual wave, Amanda climbed up the earth ramp and was gone, striding through the nettles towards the path that led to the ring road, the stolen bike, and eventually the airport. Bernard and I watched in silence, before wearily clambering up the ramp ourselves, and following the path to Woodview.

Sixty-Two

'You took your time, I must say,' I said, as we walked towards our cars. 'Typical copper, never there when you need them.'

'Sorry to have kept you waiting, ma'am,' he said. 'Didn't realise I was on twenty-four-hour watch. If I hadn't woken for a jimmy and seen them missed calls, you could've been waiting still.'

'See it doesn't happen again.' I gave him a nudge in the ribs. 'Next time I'm stuck in the woods with an unstable, knife-waving author.'

'Yes, ma'am,' he said, saluting.

It was cover, the bantz. I knew it and I sensed Bernard did too. As an ex-copper he was used to finding himself in sticky situations. This was new to me. The nearest I'd come to high drama in the past was being on the top deck of the late bus from Oxford in the small hours of a Sunday.

I was shaken, I don't mind admitting. Any hint of a hug or suspicion of a kiss from him at that time and I would have deliquesced – take that for a word, Amanda Turner! – into quivering blubber. No, a round of gentle teasing and fake indignation with a kindly man suited me fine.

It was still dark when we got back to mine. Quietly, so as not to disturb Flo, I poured us both a stiff drink, dusting off Gregory's twelve-year-old Macallan and best whisky tumblers. Then we had another. We dozed off after the third. I woke, as dawn was breaking, my head resting romantically on Bernard's shoulder, my drool soaking unromantically into his shirt. If Bernard minded, he didn't show it.

We tiptoed through to the kitchen to make ourselves an early breakfast. When I raised the blind, I discovered an unexpected sight: someone had fitted a dimmer switch to the sky. The eye-piercing blue we'd been used to seeing most of the summer, had gone. The sky was streaked with grey skid marks.

I stepped outside, watching as the sun climbed and the clouds built, creating a layer cake of pinks and greys. A movement high up caught my eye: a hot air balloon taking advantage of the still morning air. I watched until it floated out of sight, flaring and hissing like a tiny, bad-tempered dragon, wondering if the occupants felt short changed at paying top dollar to witness sunrise over an executive housing estate.

The air was chill. I shivered and pulled my cardy round me, sensing a freshness on the breeze. Rain was on its way, sure as eggs is eggs. First since May. As I went inside, I felt a drop fall on my bare neck.

***

Don't know about you, but I find there's nothing like almost being framed for murder for giving me an appetite. I was so ravenous, I was attempting my nemesis: poached eggs.

Bernard had made such quick work of the first stringy effort, I was wondering whether to have another go, when he said, 'Why phone me? Not that I'm not flattered. But why me, not the police? I've been retired from the Force more than eighteen months.'

'The honest answer is, I didn't want to make a tit of myself with the proper police,' I explained. 'Not while there was a chance it was all in my head. You were a safer option.'

Bernard looked unconvinced. 'I doubt the proper police, as you call them, would approve of you letting Amanda go. Not with what she was up to.' He spelled it out. 'Conning money out of that Pavel bloke, fitting you up for murder, not to mention waving a knife in your face. Off the top of my head, that's embezzlement, perverting the course of justice, and threatening with a bladed weapon, for starters. Remind me again why I let you talk me out of taking her in?'

'Because you trust me?'

'Could still call a mate at the Met and see if he can't get a block put on the airport, you know. It might not be too late.'

'You won't. Not when you hear what I have to say.'

'This'd better be good,' Bernard said, taking the saucepan from me. 'Meanwhile, I'll take over the eggs. It's a knack.'

Bernard didn't even have time to get the water simmering before we were interrupted by a cry from upstairs.

'Mum!' Flo called. 'Come here. Quick.'

I raced up the stairs, all other thoughts forgotten.

'Is it the baby?' I got out my phone. 'Keep calm. I'm calling an ambulance.'

'No need.' Flo was lying on top of the duvet, fair hair spread across the pillows, T-shirt pulled up to expose an ever so slightly rounded pink belly. She looked radiant. Like a pregnant angel. 'Look,' she said, gesturing me closer. 'Jemima's having a right old kick-about.'

The skin of Flo's belly bulged slightly on one side, fluttered, subsided and bulged again on the other.

'Have a feel if you like.' Flo took my hand and directed it. I caught her eye and we both beamed. There was nothing at first and then I felt butterfly wings brush against my palm. Delicate but strong. In an instant, I time-travelled back more than twenty years. 'Oh, Flo,' I said, tears threatening. 'There really is a little person in there.'

'I know,' she grinned. 'Fuckin' fierce, innit?'

This was one of those significant family occasions when a little speech would have been nice. Nothing fancy. A few heartfelt words that could be repeated down the generations. The sort of speech a grandchild might one day talk about: 'Tell me again, Mummy, what Granny said the first time she felt me wriggle in your tummy.'

If only I'd had the composure to come up with one! Of all the things I could have said, what I came out with was, 'Jemima, Flo? You are kidding! Please tell me you're not going to saddle the poor mite with Jemima.'

I never found out whether Flo was serious or not. At that moment we heard a key in the door.

'Nell!' Flo screamed. 'You came!'

'Of course I came, you wally,' Nell shouted up the stairs. 'I wasn't going to let you steal all the attention, was I?'

Flo clambered off the bed, showing more athleticism than a four-month pregnant mother has any right to, and thundered down the stairs. The sisters hugged and kissed and joshed each other in the hallway. Nell called her sister Fatso, and Flo told Nell she was only jealous because she hadn't got herself up the duff by the most arrogant prick in the whole of Southampton. I watched from halfway down the stairs. Business as usual in other words.

'I thought you were living it up in Paris with Jean-Pierre?' Flo said, holding her sister at arm's length.

Jean-Pierre? Paris? This was news to me. Last time I heard, Nell was somewhere in Spain with a boy called Miguel.

'Sadly, didn't work out,' Nell said, sounding anything but sad. 'JP opened my eyes to so much, then suddenly I'd had enough of art galleries and poetry. All I wanted was to be at home in my own crappy town with my own crappy family.' She sighed, with all the worldly wisdom of a nineteen-year-old. 'I hopped on the ferry. I was already at the train station, Flo, when you phoned. And here I am. Nice surprise, eh? So, can I have a feel of the little bastard?'

They headed for the sitting room, still laughing and jostling each other, then froze. Bernard was standing in the kitchen doorway. To be honest, I'd forgotten all about him.

'Hello,' he said, sticking out a hand in greeting. 'Bernard. Friend of your mum's. Good to meet you.'

'Mum!' As one, the girls swung round to stare at me, eyebrows somewhere near their hairlines. Just occasionally, they are more twin-like than they know.

'Bernard and I have been out in the woods all night,' I explained. 'Least I could do was invite him back for my famous poached eggs. You girls want some?'

Epilogue

The next voice you hear will be that of Trish Lightowler.

Three weeks. Has it only been three weeks? Seems longer. I was right. The raindrop that fell on my neck was just the starter. It's been raining almost non-stop since. Fair stair-rodding today. It would though, wouldn't it, it being August Bank Holiday weekend and stuff. The beginning of the end of summer; the beginning of the start of autumn; the beginning of the start of a lot of things.

With any luck, the beginning of the end of Amanda. Yes, I let her leave the country. Did nothing to stop her catching that coach and boarding that plane. Why? I did it to make sure she's caught red-handed. I did it so she wouldn't be able to talk her way out of this one.

Let her try! The video evidence on my phone – wobbly though it is – of her confession should be more than enough to condemn her. *Spoken words fly away, recorded words remain*, to misquote WHSmith.

I did it to … OK, the truth and nothing but the truth. I did it to show I was cleverer than her.

I'll never know if she would have gone through with her plan; if the pills were sleeping tablets; if she would have jumped from the top of the pit. I wouldn't put it past her. Then again, it could all have been one big, monstrous bluff, like most of what she said.

I think of her sometimes. I like to picture her landing at the grandly named, but ramshackle – judging from Google Images – St Mark and All Saints International Airport on the island of Kweqiao – pronounced Kweck-kway. I see her emerging from the little six-seater, stretching her arms and squinting into the sunlight. I watch her striding across the tarmac – don't suppose they run to airport buses – already looking forward to her first self-satisfied vape.

I pulled it off, she's thinking. *Got away with it. Fooled the lot of you.*

I picture her, barefoot on the beach, paddling in the surf, loose dress flattened against her trim body in the warm offshore breeze, the strap of her bikini peeking out at the shoulder. Not the horrid lime green leopard print, of course. That's still in a drawer at Woodview, far as I know. This is the new designer bikini I imagine her buying from the hotel shop. Ludicrously expensive but why count the pennies when you've got millions? The straw hat I see her wearing, headband streaming behind her, comes from the local market. Amanda knows it's not a real market, more a money trap for foreigners, but it amuses her to haggle.

I see her leaving her suite in the five-star hotel. She gives the uniformed doorman a haughty nod, before being driven by an eager young real estate agent, inappropriately dressed in dark suit and tie, to a white-washed villa set in secluded gardens, high in the hills, with views over the bay, and a curved infinity pool. I see him smiling and handing over the keys. I paint her into a Caribbean paradise.

I'd fitted the pieces together, you see, as I sat round the campfire, listening to Amanda's baloney. Figured it out. The meeting with Sergei at the White Hart wasn't to pick up a passport for Pavel, to give him another identity to escape the clutches of the Kandinskis. They exist, by the way, the Kandinskis. I Googled them. Nasty pieces of work. No, the counterfeit passport – made, by the way, in a backstreet printshop in Bristol from a blank stolen from the Bolton factory where British passports are made – was not for Pavel. It was for Amanda. For her getaway.

It was easy to trick Pavel, with his poor grasp of English, into giving her an introduction to Sergei and his contacts. How Pavel got out of the country, I don't know and I don't care. As any threat was entirely invented by Amanda, I don't expect he had any trouble. Probably only had to mention the name Kandinski for Daddy Dobransky to whisk him home in a private jet.

And Kweqiao? What? Name ring a bell? Allow me to bring you up to snuff. The Republic of Kweqiao is an archipelago of islands – the largest also called Kweqiao – *with sugar-sand beaches and exactly the right amount of cotton-wool clouds flitting across perfect azure skies. Not only a haven for the discerning. A real home.* Like it said in the brochure.

It was the brochure that gave it away. And the song Amanda had hummed as she stoked the campfire. *Island in the Sun.* A gentle Caribbean calypso. You were always such a tease, Amanda!

Kweqiao was a good choice. With its own independent jurisdiction and *very* discreet banking system, for many years it provided a safe hideaway in the sun for the world's despots, gangsters, and thieves, along with their dirty money. Note, I said *was*.

The name, with its eccentric spelling, had stuck in my

mind, you see. So when, some weeks later, it popped up on my laptop in a long-read BBC News feature, I paid close attention. A new Kweqiaon government had been elected, I read, on a climate change mandate. The incoming regime had decided all-inclusive eco resorts were more ethical – not to say secure – than money laundering. In short, the article said, the islands had cleaned up their act. The Fugitive Offenders and Mutual Legal Assistance Treaty was signed, as luck would have it, in early May, coming into immediate effect, and including a new agreement between the islands and the UK.

Despite priding herself on her thoroughness, Amanda had failed to keep herself abreast of Kweqiaon extradition arrangements. Sloppy research, Amanda. Stale intel. You're good, but you're not infallible.

I've come to realise nothing about that woman was as it seemed, even her endless collection of expensive clothes.

Flo explained it to me. 'Wardrobing, it's called, Mum. You'd buy stuff, wear it once or twice, then take it back. As long as you kept the labels on, most places would give you a refund, no questions asked. Used to see it all the time at work, and loads of girls at uni did it.'

'Not you, I hope.'

'No. Not me.' Flo gave me a look that told me all I needed to know. Not Flo. Of course not her. Though I'll need to have a firm word with her sister.

That explained why Amanda had such an impressive collection of outfits but less-than-impressive undies. Shops don't hand out refunds, you see, on pants and bras. As for the makeup, I doubt very much Amanda paid a penny for most of it. Lipsticks, mascaras and eye pencils are, after all, a handy size for slipping into your pocket or handbag, out of sight of the CCTV cameras.

Now I come to think of it, it's a good metaphor for

the woman herself. Classy on the outside, cheap and tacky underneath. What my bonkers mother would have called *all fur coat and no knickers*. If only I'd had the perspicacity to read the signs.

I'm so enjoying these fancy words!

***

I phoned the Kweqiaon embassy. After being transferred round the building, I got put through to a well-spoken official who listened intently as I suggested it would be of interest to check the papers of one Miss Leigh Bakker. 'It's Leigh. Spelt L E I G H. And Bakker with two k's,' I said, adding under my breath, 'Assuming Sergei got the spelling right.' She'd recently arrived on the main island, I told him, and I had good reason to believe her documentation was false and her wealth stolen.

Keen to distance themselves from their old image and promote their new, ethical ways of doing business, he promised they would look into it and keep in touch.

I daydream of the moment when a couple of solemn-faced police officers with razor-sharp creases in their dazzling white shorts wake Amanda from her poolside siesta. I picture the expressions passing across her tanned features: puzzlement, surprise, confusion, anger and finally, realisation. It is over. She has lost. The best woman has won. How I love to picture that!

Peter and Bernard, meanwhile, have put their heads together and made the authorities at this end aware of Amanda's activities, in the process bonding over legal chitchat and becoming unlikely friends. So if – I mean, when – Amanda gets shipped back, there'll be a welcoming committee waiting on the tarmac.

I anticipate with great pleasure the moment when the Queen of the Double Bluff gets her just desserts. It doesn't do to underestimate me, Patricia Lightowler, Princess of the Triple Bluff.

Not that I dwell that much on Amanda Turner. I have too much else on my plate. Two daughters to introduce to the new *takes no shit* version of their mum, a nursery to paint, a baby travel system to buy, and a ton of soft toys to get down from the loft and put through a delicate wash. What a Christmas it's going to be!

Did I update you on the divorce? With so much going on, it slips my mind for days on end. Peter visited The Garden Boutique Hotel in person and, over a cream tea, informed its owner, Joseph Gardener, of the severe penalties for aiding and abetting a person to commit perjury.

'How did he react?' I asked.

'Dropped his jammy scone and his affidavit forthwith.'

Peter invited me to sit in, out of sight, on the video call that spelled the endgame for Gregory. Peter impresses me more and more. He was terrifyingly stern! Like Felicity, he has the split personality that often seems to be doled out, along with the blazers and the funny hats, at public schools: low personal self-esteem combined with copious amounts of public confidence.

'May I once again remind you,' Peter said, Rumpole factor cranked up to eleven, 'in this country we take a dim view of people who fail to divulge financial information during divorce proceedings. A maximum penalty of …'

Gregory's little box lit up as he interrupted, blocking out both voices.

'Repeat please,' Peter said.

'I have instructed my people,' Gregory said slowly and in evident pain, 'to offer a very generous settlement, to include assets from MRH Holdings. Satisfied?'

'Thank you. We'll take a look at the details,' Peter said coolly, 'And get back to you.'

Meanwhile, out of sight, I was punching the air and literally jumping for joy, mouthing 'We won! We won!' I was so happy I could have cried. After the call ended, I did. Cry, that is. Big, ugly sobs.

Peter hovered over his seat, frantically pushing his specs up his nose, uncertain if he should comfort me or if that would be crossing a professional line. I solved his dilemma by, cheeks still wet, grabbing him and giving him probably the biggest, longest, tightest hug he's ever had in his repressed, ex-public schoolboy life.

Next step is the Final Order. Six weeks and one day after that, I'll be free of Gregory. Haven't forgiven him but have agreed to do the mature thing and talk to him by video call once a week. With some effort, I'm keeping the conversations this side of civil. I take care to look smart. Top half, at least. Got two cotton blouses from Seasalt, one red, one blue, bought specially for the occasion. I keep them at the ready, clean and pressed, on a hanger.

There is a snag to all this civility. It means every seven days I have to gaze upon the ongoing manifestation on Gregory's face. He's growing a beard. Not a designer six-o'clock shadow or a topiaried goatee. A full-on fluffy thing. Week by week he's transforming into Bluto from the old Popeye cartoons, and not the on-trend hipster I suspect he thinks he looks like. With my new maturity, I make no comment.

And Madison-Rose is pregnant. He threw that one in at the end of our last chat. 'If Flo hangs on till January, I could be a dad and a granddad all in the same year. Ain't that dope?'

Didn't lower myself to point out everything is not about him. Wouldn't waste my breath. And *dope*! That's not Gregory. Not the Gregory I knew.

They are postponing the wedding until Madison-Rose has got her figure back. 'Though she's already engaged the most expensive wedding planner in New York,' Gregory said, and laughed. There was something in his laughter that made me think, even the biggest society wedding won't give him whatever it is he's searching for. Almost feel sorry for him. Almost.

And I'm writing. Yes, really! A crime novel, or maybe a mystery, I'm not sure, based on a real-life case, thank you for asking. Felicity is helping. I quickly came to the conclusion I wasn't ever going to be able to do a book on my own. Not a whole one. Amanda was right. I don't have the grit. I need a co-author to keep my nose to the grindstone. Plus, Felicity says, me and good grammar ain't always on the best of terms.

I said we should call ourselves Felicity Lightowler. It has a ring. Too many syllables, Felicity says. Hope she's not going to be awkward. We're already halfway through chapter five. I'm doing my best with the plotty bits. I have the inside track, after all. Felicity is doing the descriptive stuff. You know, sunrise and sunset, gentle pattering of rain, innermost thoughts and deepest feelings, etc. etc.

Felicity is Tigger-ishly keen and we have one huge advantage: excellent source material. Stand by for the big reveal. We have my journal. Yes! I know! How about that? Amanda hadn't burnt it. One of her cruel bluffs. I had another of my hunches, you see, and went back to the pits. Bernard and I dug around in the undergrowth near the black scar of her campfire, and there it was, a little damp round the edges and smudged, but otherwise unharmed. I never found out what book Amanda had barbecued that night but I'm willing to bet it was a Charles Dickens.

I'll change the names and mess about with the details but I have the main story. Thank you, Amanda. No, I don't feel sorry for her. Why should I? She can get back to her old trade. Banged up twenty-three hours a day, she'll have all the time in the world for writing.

Wish they'd hurry up with the extradition though. Waiting makes me nervous. Peter's done his best to find out what's going on but we've heard nothing definite. I'd like to see Amanda in the dock, though Peter has warned me not to get my hopes up. He worries if Pavel can't be traced or refuses to give evidence, she could wriggle out of the embezzlement charge. I don't like to think about that. Let's hope they make the other charges stick.

***

I went again to the Country Park. Without Bernard this time. Had ghosts to lay. Took the side path over the fields to the main pit. The bullocks have gone. Poor things. Climbed to the high point at the top and stood where Amanda had posed, then scrambled down the ramp and looked up.

At that moment, the clouds parted and a sunbeam cut through the trees, catching the ochre walls. For the first time, I saw the half-circle in its full sunlit glory. The walls were on fire, rippling and heaving, alive with glorious shades of lemon and tangerine, pumpkin and carrot, mustard and dark strawberry red. It was, to use a messy metaphor that would have driven Amanda round the bend, a fiery fruit and veg bowl of colour.

'Fuckin' fierce!' I shouted at the walls.

Then the clouds closed in and the pit was once again

just an orangey-red hole in the ground.

I thought about what had happened that night, about what could have happened. My thoughts drifted to Flo and how it won't be long before she gives up work and we can spend all day, every day together, preparing for the little one's arrival. I voiced this thought the other day and she gave me a look which made me wonder if she's looking forward to that time quite as much as me. I'll have to watch I don't overstep the mark.

Bernard and I have been out several times. Once for a French meal, very fancy! I think he was trying to impress. He succeeded. And once to a pub quiz night. We came last because we talked so much we didn't hear the questions. Turns out he's a Jack Reacher fan like you-know-who. Lee Child and his brother Andrew are being interviewed at some literary festival up north. Harrogate, I think. Bernard has invited me to go with him as my birthday treat. Might help with the writing, he said. And take my mind off turning fifty, he probably thought, but was too kind to mention.

I'm tempted to say yes but that would mean negotiating the ticklish subject of rooms. Two separate singles or one double? I'm not sure I'm ready for a double-room relationship yet but how to broach the subject without dying of embarrassment? Preposterous, isn't it? I might be a braver and bolder Trish but, fifty in a few weeks, and I still can't talk to a man about S E X without wanting to hide my face in my hands.

What else? After I finish writing this, I've got an appointment at the Furry Friends Animal Shelter to see if they have a little black kitty with golden eyes. If he hasn't been claimed, I'm having him.

Oh yes, and this would please Amanda Turner. Got a letter this morning. An appointment at the urology clinic.

Not till Easter. But still.

I've been through some rocky times, but I think you could tell from the smile I'm smiling now that I'm well on the way to finding my bliss. Hope you're satisfied, Grace. Still and all, I'm happy with the way new, improved Trish has panned out. Happy with the way the year's panned out, come to that. What do you reckon, Ivy?

Oh, I'm allowed a voice again, am I? What do I think?
I think the year ain't over yet, Trish. Not by a long
chalk, me ducks.

Acknowledgements

For the most part, we authors type and scribble alone. But it's safe to say, hardly a book would make it to publication without the support, practical and emotional, of a host of other people.

So, thank you to my friends – I'm surprised I still have any – for not allowing their eyes to glaze over when I banged on about ochre pits and rom-conning. I must especially mention those kind souls who read early versions of *A Novel Solution* – and, even so, encouraged me: Lesley Bootiman Byrne, Alice McVeigh, Steve Sheppard, and Carol Watts, and most particularly my sister, Jude Fowler.

My thanks to the writers in my Oxford writing group, who have become long-standing friends and trusted beta readers: Louise Ludlow, Imogen Matthews, and Anna Pitt.

More recently, I've made writer friends as a member of the Breakthrough Book Collective. Thank you in particular to Stephanie Bretherton (Cheers for the title by the way.) Stevyn Colgan and Ivy Ngeow, and the many others, talented authors all, who give their time and expertise for the benefit of fellow writers. Look out for our short story anthologies!

Thanks to Elizabeth Haylett Clark of the Society of Authors for helping me negotiate the (to me anyway!) boring, but important, legal stuff.

And an extra-special thanks to Stuart Debar of SRL Publishing for being brave enough to take me on and for holding my hand throughout editing and publishing.

Any errors or omissions, of course, are entirely due to my own incompetence and butterfly mind.

Almost lastly, I have to thank Shotover Country Park. Not only has it provided our family with wonderful walks, but it also gave me the gift of a setting for *A Novel Solution*, appearing as Oaker Wood Country Park. Oxford ochre was indeed a thing and there are still scant traces left of the pits from which it was dug. I may have made the location a little more dramatic – some might say, melodramatic – than it really is today but, hey, poetic licence, folks! I didn't, however, exaggerate the beautifully atmospheric, bosky nature of the country park.

And lastly, lastly, I have to thank my family. Writers' families must be among the most patient and long-suffering in the world. To Michael, Matthew, Naomi, Ian, and Bethany, not forgetting Ben who provided valuable first-hand knowledge of Shotover, and Chase the dog, thank you. I love you all.

SRL Publishing don't just publish books, we also do our best in keeping this world sustainable. In the UK alone, over 77 million books are destroyed each year, unsold and unread, due to overproduction and bigger profit margins.

Our business model is inherently sustainable by only printing what we sell. While this means our cost price is much higher, it means we have minimum waste and zero returns. We made a public promise in 2020 to never overprint our books for the sake of profit.

We give back to our planet by calculating the number of trees used for our products so we can then replace them. We also calculate our carbon emissions and support projects which reduce CO2. These same projects also support the United Nations Sustainable Development Goals.

The way we operate means we knowingly waive our profit margins for the sake of the environment. Every book sold via the SRL website plants at least one tree.

To find out more, please visit
www.srlpublishing.co.uk/responsibility

Milton Keynes UK
Ingram Content Group UK Ltd.
UKHW040748040124
435437UK00001B/30

9 781915 073280